CW01337363

BLOOD RED FORD

A Detective Loxley Nottinghamshire Crime Thriller

By
A L Fraine

Book List

www.alfraineauthor.co.uk/books

Acknowledgements

Thank you to Emmy Ellis for your amazing editing and support.
Thanks to Kath Middleton for her incredible work.
A big thank you to the admins and members of the UK Crime Book Club for their support, both to me and the wider author community. They're awesome.

Thank you also to the authors I've been lucky enough to call friends. You know who you are, and you're all wonderful people.

Thank you to my family, especially my parents, children, and lovely wife, Louise, for their unending love and support.

Table of Contents

1

Today had just been one of those days. From the moment Roxy had walked in, the shit had started hitting the fan. But then, weren't all office days like that? The flexible shift pattern she'd taken advantage of had been amazing. Working from home had made life so much easier, and she'd actually been getting more done as a result.

It was a win-win as far as she was concerned.

And yet, the company seemed reluctant to let them keep their new freedom. They were constantly pushing for them to spend more time in the office in spite of the increased productivity.

The company was rooted in the past, when the only way for people to work was for them to be in the building, day in, day out.

For now, the faceless bosses, further up the chain of command, were satisfied with her coming in once a week on average to show her face and act like a good little employee.

But, as usual, those days were filled with far more crap than any other day. Because she was there and available, she'd end up bogged down in pointless requests, comments and complaints that kept her from doing what she needed to do so that tomorrow, she'd need to spend the day catching up.

That was just Roxy's routine these days, and today had been no different. She'd ended the day with a splitting headache and the need for a stiff drink. Luckily for her, she'd had an evening out with the girls planned for a while now, and tonight was the night, the perfect night, for it to take place.

The drive into Newark was easy enough, and as darkness fell, she drove past others out on the town. Friends and lovers enjoying their evenings with drinks and good food.

She was looking forward to this and pushed on, driving deeper into Newark, heading for the St Marks Place multi-storey car park, which was not too far from where she'd arranged to meet her friends.

She navigated her way through the streets, past glowing traffic lights and looming buildings, watching the people around her, wondering what was going on in their lives and drawing conclusions from the brief glimpses she caught of them.

An old man, hunched and frail, hurried home. A gaggle of young women in their party best, accessorized with sashes and fluffy headbands, celebrated their friend's hen night. A homeless man was sitting on the side of the pavement, wrapped in layers of clothing with all hope absent from his eyes, and a group of young men and women were posing for a selfie as one held out their phone.

Roxy frowned, remembering an odd incident from the morning. She'd walked into the office, and noticed a man with his phone out, apparently filming or taking photos of her. She wasn't sure which.

The man had seemed oblivious as she'd glared and continued on regardless until she'd moved out of sight. It had freaked her out at the time, but she'd soon forgotten it as she'd got into the routine of the day.

It was only now, after seeing the group taking a selfie, that she'd remembered. She'd not seen the man again and had come to the conclusion it was just one of those odd things that she'd never have an explanation for and moved on.

But not before possibly linking it back to her old boss and the debacle that her dalliance with him had conjured from nothing.

But that was four years ago now.

Realising she was closing in on her destination, she guided her car up the entry ramp and into the car park. Finding a space she felt confident driving into, she flicked the indicator on. A swift manoeuvre later, she turned the engine off, satisfied with her parking.

She checked herself quickly in the mirror before grabbing her bag and climbing out into the chill evening air. Glancing around the multi-storey that surrounded her, Roxy peered into the shadows attempting to orientate herself and figure out the quietest and safest route to the street.

This level of the car park seemed quiet, and when she locked her car, the *cha-thunk* of the locks slamming home echoed around her.

Tyres squealed, and an engine roared.

She turned. A large Transit van careened round the corner onto her level. It raced towards where she'd parked.

Roxy hung back to let it pass and busied herself with her car door, making sure it was locked. She didn't want anyone nicking it. With her phone in her other hand, she opened WhatsApp to check on the group chat with her friends and let them know where she was.

The van skidded to a stop right next to her, its side door sliding open. Three men jumped out before it even came to a rest and rushed towards her.

"Get her."

Roxy screamed. The lead man grabbed her head and slammed it into her car. Light flashed behind her eyes, cutting her scream short. Intense pain bloomed as the hit rattled her brain. All strength left her legs, and she started to crumple.

"Roon, a little help?" the lead man snapped. He ripped the phone from Roxy's hand and threw it to the floor.

"I'm here."

"Blood? Do your job."

"I am. I'm doing it."

The men crowded around, catching her before she hit the floor. Realising what they were doing, she tore herself out of the daze, doing her best to ignore the intense pain that rang through her head, and yelled.

"No. Aaargh, no," she cried. "Let me go. Help. Help me."

"Shut up."

A gloved hand clamped over her mouth as two of the three men hauled her towards the van. The third held his phone aloft, filming the whole thing while grinning like a hyena.

"Get her in."

"Relax, I'm on it."

In a moment of horror, she realised she'd seen the man filming before. It was the same one she'd seen out in the street this morning.

"You bastard." But her shout was muffled by the thug's gloved hand.

"I think she recognises you," one of the men remarked as they threw her into the van.

She landed with a thud. One of them still had hold of her legs, so she kicked and fought, trying desperately to get loose.

The man who'd initially grabbed her stepped in and backhanded her across the face, snapping her head to the side. She tasted blood.

"Wait, I missed that. I need to get it all on camera."

"Get in. We need to go."

"All right, I'm coming." The door slid shut with a rumble.

"Ruddy, go."

"I'm going."

The engine roared, and the van started to move. Roxy tried to wrench her hands free from the man's grip, but he was too strong.

"Aaaargh, help," she cried at the top of her lungs.

The man swung for her again and caught her on the cheek. "Shut the fuck up, will you? Gag this bitch before she blows the whole thing."

He clamped his hand over her mouth. Moments later, they taped her mouth shut. She had a horrible gritty taste in her mouth as they tied her wrists and ankles, yanking and pulling on her arms and legs, adding to the list of aches and pains.

The whole time that the two men worked to restrain and silence her, the third man stood over them, his phone in hand, filming her. He roved the phone around, trying all kinds of angles. He seemed to be getting a perverse kind of satisfaction out of it.

Then the two men backed off, leaving her on the metal floor, feeling every bump and jolt as they drove through the night.

"All right, that's it till we get back," the lead thug said and pointed to something she couldn't see. "Bag her."

Through tearstained eyes, Roxy watched the man the first had referred to as Roon, pull out a black fabric bag and slip it over her head. The material was soft and blocked out most of the light, but she could make out light and shadows between the threads and still hear their crude banter.

Unable to move or defend herself, she concentrated on her breathing and tried to bring it under control. Her pounding heart thundered so hard she thought it might explode out of her at any moment, like that gross film about that alien thing.

She needed to regain control of herself if she wanted to escape. Being in a state of blind panic wouldn't help at all.

"Did you get what we needed?" the main guy asked.

"Yeah," the man who'd been filming answered. Had one of them referred to him as Blood? "Check this out."

The tiny sound of the phone filled the van as they played back the video of her being kidnapped.

One of them laughed. "Hey, look at that. Hahaha. She's a mess."

"Quite the difference from this morning, hey?" Blood replied as he played another video.

It sounded like a busy street. He was playing them the video of her walk into work, and she came to a sudden and scary realisation. That this was planned. This hadn't been a random attack, they wanted to kidnap her. She'd been chosen. But, how did they know she'd be here, tonight... Unless... She remembered being on a call with her mates as she'd walked into work, making some final arrangements. She'd told them where she'd planned on parking, meaning it was entirely possible these goons had overheard her and made their plans.

She cringed at their laughter and tried flexing her wrists and legs, attempting to free herself from the bonds until one of them kicked her side.

"Oi! Fuck about and find out, bitch. Got that?"

She lay still and kept her breaths shallow. It didn't hurt quite so much that way.

The drive seemed to go on forever, but it was probably not much more than half an hour. The lights of passing cars shone in through the windows, visible through the hood.

Cars filled with people were going about their evenings, with no idea that the van they passed concealed a kidnapped, brutalised woman. It made her wonder how close she'd come to crimes like this? Had she walked or driven past people in similar circumstances?

Eventually, the van slowed, turned, and came to a stop. And then the engine shut off.

"We're here," one of the thugs called out.

There was movement all around her, making the van judder. The side door opened, and they pulled her from the van. She yelped, her voice muffled by the gag. As soon as she sensed their closeness, she lashed out, swinging her fists at them, but they grabbed her, and someone punched her in the gut.

She nearly threw up but managed to keep it down. With the gag still in place, she might have drowned had she actually vomited.

"What did I tell you? Huh? I can make this far more bloody painful for you, missy, if that's what you want."

Roxy clenched her teeth at the unseen thug and stopped fighting. If she was going to get out of this, she needed to conserve her energy and avoid doing anything stupid. They'd not killed her yet, and they'd had plenty of opportunity, so she doubted they'd kill her now. They wanted her for something. A ransom, maybe?

Someone lifted her from the ground, carried her a short way before entering a building. From the sound of the footsteps, they were walking over a stone floor in a smallish room. They seemed to move down some steps and into a hallway or across a long room. She wasn't sure. All she had to go on was the sound of their footsteps and the occasional brush against a wall or doorframe. Metal clinked and scraped, and then they dropped her to the hard floor.

Roxy cursed as her bonds were released, her hood removed, and the gag ripped from her face. "Crap," she grunted. Her eyes adjusted to the dim lighting.

They'd thrown her into a dirty, grimy cell off a short corridor. Instead of a wall and door leading back into the hall, there were bars with a metal door set into them. The only light came from the bare humming bulbs in the corridor ceiling.

The thugs backed out of the cell and slammed the barred door shut before locking it with a key. The same thug as before filmed her again.

Roxy got up and scanned around in disgust. The room was about as bare as it could get, and it stank to high heaven. The only concession to comfort was a thin foam camping mattress that had seen better days, and the only other noticeable feature was a hole in the floor in one corner, which she guessed was supposed to be the toilet.

Her nostrils burned from the stench as she wrinkled her nose in disgust.

"There you go," the lead thug said. He'd been the one to attack her first back in the car park and was easily the biggest of the four men standing outside her cell. "You should get comfortable. The Cardinal will be along soon."

She heard his words, but she could only stare at the ugly excuse for a man with pure hatred in her eyes. As far as she was concerned, he was a pathetic waste of oxygen, and given half a chance, she'd claw his eyes out.

He smirked at her cold stare. "I know, you hate me. That's fine. But you should make the most of this because things are only going to get worse from here on in, girl."

"Don't you 'girl' me," she snapped. It was a stupid thing to say, but in her simmering rage, it was all she could think of.

"Ho-hooo, feisty."

The other guys mocked her, too. "Damn, girl, coming out with the zingers."

She felt about two feet tall.

"I tell yeh, it's a shame, it really is. You're a looker. Aaah well, can't be helped." The man turned and ushered the other men back up the corridor.

In sudden blind panic, Roxy rushed to the bars. "Wait." She reached for him, but he was just out of reach. Fear and desperation clawed at her mind. "Please. You can't leave me here. You can let me go. You don't have to do this. This

Cardinal doesn't need to know. I'll do anything. I'll do whatever you want. Just let me go."

The man paused and looked back at her, a hint of pity in his face. He smiled and shook his head. "If I had a hundred pounds for every time someone said that to me…" He sighed. "Babe. You're hot, and under normal circumstances, I might well take you up on that offer. We all might have." He took a step closer. "But honestly, it's just not worth it." He smiled again. "I'd try to get some rest if I were you."

With that, the man turned and followed his men back up the corridor and around the bend, laughing at her offer while making crude comments and suggestions.

Roxy cursed quietly to herself as she turned back to the cell and the dirty mattress. Frankly, the place looked riddled with disease, and the thought of sleeping here and using that poor excuse for a toilet sent a shiver up her spine.

How the hell had this happened? How had she ended up here, of all places?

Sleep? She scoffed at the thug's suggestion of getting some rest. Her body brimmed with nervous energy as she desperately hunted around for anything that might help her escape.

She couldn't stay here. She had to get out. She had to escape.

But how?

2

"Okay, thank you," Rob said to the sergeant on the other end of the phone line. "I'll keep you updated." He hung up and took a moment to think things through.

He'd only been at work for an hour, and already it looked like another busy day. Most of this first hour had been spent talking to that sergeant and going through the case being handed over to the East Midlands Special Operations Unit because it fit with their remit as a unit focused on more serious and organised crime.

Like all officers of the law, the members of Rob's unit were consistently overworked, and while new cases kept coming in, old ones had a way of taking up much of their time on a day-to-day basis.

Finding and arresting the suspect was really just the beginning. Once the exciting bit was over, there was always a mountain of work to do. From interviewing and reinterviewing suspects and witnesses to go over every part of their story, dealing with the exhibits and getting everything ready for the possible court case. They were always on the phone to, or meeting with, the CPS or prosecution barristers as they repeatedly read through every scrap of evidence, looking for any holes they needed to plug. It was non-stop, and while doing all that, they'd have new cases coming in that needed their attention, too, such as this one.

Getting up from his desk, Rob walked over to DCI Nailer's office. He knocked and leaned in. "Guv?"

"Are we taking it?" Nailer asked as he looked up from his monitor. He was aware of the talks that Rob had been having.

"Yeah, we are. I'd like a team meeting to bring everyone up to speed. We need to get cracking on it. Time is of the essence on this one."

"Isn't it always?" Nailer asked, standing. "Go on then, muster the troops. I'm on my way."

"Guv," Rob confirmed and turned back to the room. "Team meeting, guys," he said as he crossed the room, making for the incident room via his desk. He grabbed his laptop and the printed file he'd started creating for the case and walked into the side room.

Scarlett was first in.

"What's been dumped on our doorstep today?" she asked light-heartedly as Rob connected his laptop to the TV.

"You'll find out in a moment," Rob remarked with a smile as Nick, Ellen, Tucker, and Guy joined them, with Nailer bringing up the rear.

The DCI stopped in the doorway and leaned his shoulder against the frame, crossing his arms as the smell of fresh coffee wafted across the table from the various half-drunk cups several team members had brought in. "There's no rest for the wicked," he added.

Scarlett grunted. "Makes me wonder what we did in a past life to deserve this." She took her seat.

"As long as they're not eating people, I'm sure we'll be fine," Tucker remarked, referring to their previous large case. "That was not nice."

"Still having nightmares?" Nick asked.

"Made me sick to my stomach."

"Me, too. I'm never eating beef casserole again," Scarlett added and made a gagging motion.

"All right, settle down," Rob called out, bringing the room to order. "We've had a new case referred to us, and we need to jump on it quick. We have a young woman who's gone missing." He pulled a printout from his file and stuck it to the whiteboard with a magnet. The sheet of paper had the smiling face of a young woman with dark hair and a pretty face. "This is Roxanna Wells, better known as Roxy. She disappeared last night in Newark while on her way to visit her friends. The local plod took it on and started looking into it. They spoke to her friends and family, and they say she set off into Newark to meet her friends but never made it. Luckily, Roxy's friends got suspicious and started searching for her. They'd already found Roxy's car parked in a multi-storey car park in Newark, and discovered her phone discarded on the

22

floor beside it. As well as talking to her friends and sending officers around to her family, they also checked the security cameras of the car park. What they found points to this being much more organised and serious than they had initially thought, and it's why this case has been referred to us."

Rob paused for dramatic effect before continuing his narrative. The team listened intently and made notes as he spoke.

"They discovered that almost all the cameras in the car park complex had been vandalised earlier that day, leaving them with just one obscure camera angle that caught the kidnapping. Rob leaned over his laptop and hit the space-bar. The video he'd queued up started to play on the TV beside him.

It showed Roxy getting out of her car as a white van pulled up. Three men jumped out, grabbed her, and threw her into the vehicle. It was then driven off at speed.

Rob hit pause. "This was not random. This was planned and carefully executed, and it's only by pure chance that we have this footage at all."

"Has anyone run the plates on that van?" Nick asked.

"Yep. They're fake, so that's a dead end."

"Anything from the family?" Scarlett asked.

"Actually, yes. We do have one piece of information given to us from both Roxy's family and her friends that might prove key. Just over four years ago, while she was working down in London, Roxy embarked on a brief affair with her boss at work, who was a very rich, but very married businessman. It didn't last long, and she quickly called it off when this man apparently tried to strangle her and then hit her. After ending the affair, Roxy reported it to HR and then the police, accusing him of sexual harassment and rape."

"Do we have a name for this boss?" Ellen asked.

"Truman Collins," Rob said, checking his notes to ensure he'd got it right.

"And what happened to him?"

"The case went nowhere, and he was never convicted. But it did result in Truman's wife divorcing him and restricted access to his kids, which he wasn't happy with by all accounts."

"But that was in London?" Guy asked.

"That's right. Roxy was living in London at the time but moved north to be closer to her family after this happened. As far as we know, Truman still lives down south. All the case files have been transferred to us. You can find them on the system, but I think we need to go and talk to Roxy's family and friends ourselves and see what we can dredge up. Do bear in mind, though, that this affair happened four years ago, so this disappearance might have nothing to do with Mr Collins at all. For all we know, there's a new spurned

24

boyfriend we don't know about, or a local stalker or something…"

"Or a gang she pissed off," Tucker added, pointing to the TV playing the kidnap on a loop, showing the three people grabbing her off the street. "There were at least four people involved in that abduction. Three to grab her and one to drive."

"What's that guy doing?" Scarlett got up and pointed to one of the three men who jumped out of the van. He seemed to hang back and had his arm raised.

"I'm not sure," Rob muttered. He squinted at the screen.

"It looks like he's filming it." Ellen leaned forward in her seat to get a better view.

"Yeah, it does," Scarlett agreed. "Why would he be filming it? That's evidence against them, surely, and they're not wearing masks or anything to hide their identity."

"I don't know," Rob admitted as he watched the film loop around once more. "All right, Ellen, Tucker, I want you to go and speak to Roxy's friends to go over their story. Guy, Nick, I need you two to go through the case file so far with a fine-tooth comb and do some digging into this rape case. See what you can find out."

"Aye," Nick agreed.

"Scarlett, you and I will pay Roxy's parents a visit."

"Perfect," Scarlett said.

"Excellent. Okay, you all have your jobs to get on with. Let's see what shakes loose."

3

Roxy sat on the dirty, disgusting mattress with her back to the brick wall, utterly defeated as she stared at nothing. She'd barely slept and had refused to lie down on the foul, stained mattress that was no more than a couple of inches thick with a foam core that was worn out and overused.

It barely did anything to soften the stone floor, and there was no way she was going to lie down on it. Especially after the night she'd had.

She remembered waking up to the soft patter of tiny feet on stone and found a rat sniffing the air and staring at her. She'd screamed and jumped to her feet, trying to make enough noise to keep the vermin out in the corridor and dissuade it from coming through the bars and into the cell.

The second time she'd seen one, she wasn't quite so hysterical, but that same fear and revulsion spiked her adrenaline, and she'd yelped and made a fuss until the thing skittered off.

A little while ago, perhaps a few hours, she'd become so desperate to relieve herself that she was forced to use the hole in the floor. It felt like the most demeaning, disgusting thing to go in full view of the corridor, knowing that at any moment someone might walk by and see her.

She'd shed a few tears over that, as it felt like all hope of release was fading away, and she was actually stuck here.

Her stomach rumbled.

She'd not made it to the meal with her friends the previous night, and so far, no one had brought her any food. Her belly ached, desperate for sustenance, and her mouth felt like some distant part of the Sahara Desert.

Why was she here? What was this all about, and who was doing it to her?

The only explanation to it she could think of was that Truman Collins was behind this somehow. He hated her for what she'd done to him, he'd made that perfectly clear to her back during the trial, so maybe this was some kind of revenge?

He certainly had the motive and the means, but there were parts of that idea that didn't make sense. Truman was down south somewhere, working in London, not up here. Then there were the thugs and this underground cell block, none of which seemed like something Truman would do. It just didn't make much sense.

The more she thought about it, the less sense it made. She'd had no contact with him for years. Would he really wait this long?

Angry and frustrated with herself, she squeezed her eyes shut, slapped herself in the face, and roared at the uncaring world around her.

"Aaaagh! Why? Why me? What the hell is this all about?"

It wasn't the first time she'd shouted and screamed since being locked in here. But no one came.

It was useless.

As she sobbed into her hands, she suddenly had a funny feeling she was being watched and snapped her head up, looking through glassy tears. A man standing outside the cell bars, staring at her. With her vision swimming because of her crying, she thought the man had been sunburnt or something.

But after wiping her eyes to clear her vision, she saw the truth. He wore a bright-red full-face mask, and only his eyes were visible. His hood was up, hiding his hair, too, and he continued to stare at her.

For a moment, Roxy just glared right back, unsure what was going on. She frowned and narrowed her eyes. How long had he been there? She glanced around her cell and then back at the impassive figure. He hadn't moved.

Roxy got up from the mattress and rose to her full height, keeping her eyes locked on the man. He held his hands behind his back, out of sight. What was he planning?

29

"Who are you?" she asked, keen to find out where this was going.

He didn't answer.

"What is this? Are you trying to freak me out? Who are you?"

The man shifted his weight and then took a few steps across the front of her cell, turning away from her. She could see his hands. He wasn't carrying anything. After a moment, he stopped and turned, looking back at her.

After another pregnant pause, he finally spoke, his gruff voice muffled slightly by the mask. "I hope you're worth it."

Roxy raised an eyebrow. "Worth it? What do you mean? What are you talking about?"

The man sighed. "Eat and get some rest. You've got a big day tomorrow."

"What? What food? What do you mean? What's happening tomorrow?"

"Food will be brought down," he said before turning and walking away, up the corridor, the opposite way the men had gone the previous night.

Roxy darted to the bars and pressed her head up against them to watch him.

"Hey. Don't leave me here. I'll do anything you want, just let me go. Please."

The man sauntered up to the door she could only just make out, past the two cells opposite and presumably another beside hers, and opened the door. He glanced back and shook his head before moving through the doorway.

"No, please. Let me go. Please. They'll be looking for me. I won't..." The door slammed shut against her yells. "...I won't say anything..." she muttered quietly, finishing her sentence.

She cursed and kicked the bars in frustration, making them ring out.

"Fuck. Goddamn it. Aaaaagh. Let me out, you bastards. Let me out. Please." Her anger dissolved into sobs as she dropped down to the mattress and let the emotion overtake her.

4

"Any thoughts on the case so far?" Rob asked as they approached Newark and the home of Roxy's parents. "I know there's not much to go on yet, but we have a strong lead."

"It seems quite open-and-shut at first blush," Scarlett commented. "The victim ruined a man's life just a few years ago. I know that it's four years since that happened, but that pain is not going to fade much during that time."

Rob nodded in agreement. "No, it's not. Four years isn't a long time. Not really. We can't get complacent, though. We've thought something was obvious before and been proven wrong later on."

"After these first few cases, there's no way I will ever think that any of them will be easy."

Rob smiled. "Yeah, now you're getting it."

The Wells' household was modest and located deep in a suburban estate, filled with nice gardens, regularly trimmed lawns, and well-maintained flowerbeds. Nothing terrible should ever happen in such an idyllic place. And yet, here they were, the bearers of bad news, about to talk with the parents of the kidnapped woman.

"At least we don't need to break the news to them," Scarlett remarked. "I always hate that part."

Rob agreed. "Be grateful for small mercies."

They exited the car and approached the home. An invisible air of despair lingered over the house, and it felt like the neighbours were watching. The news would be out by now. Gossip like this spread like wildfire, especially in small, close-knit communities. He could only imagine the conversations that were going on behind closed doors as the residents expressed their privately held opinions of the girl who'd accused a millionaire of rape.

Rob led the way, glancing at the windows of the neighbouring houses. He wondered if he might see someone watching them from the darkness of their living room while feeling terrible for the Wells family but also secretly grateful that it hadn't happened to them.

The front door opened after a single ring of the bell, revealing the two parents, the wife standing behind her husband as they stared out with expectant expressions.

"Michael and Sandra Wells?" Rob asked.

"That's right," Michael answered.

"Morning. I'm Detective Loxley, and this is Detective Stutely. We'd like to talk to you about Roxy if that's okay?"

"Have you found her?" Sandra asked.

"What?" Michael scoffed. He turned back to his wife.

"No, sorry," Rob cut in, sensing tension.

33

"Why would you ask that?" Michael snapped. "We knew they were coming. They're taking over the case."

"I... I know. I just... I don't know." Her voice rose in pitch as her emotions threatened to bubble over.

Michael sighed, appearing to notice the pain he'd caused. "I'm sorry," he muttered and pulled her in for a hug. He looked up at Rob and Scarlett. "I'm sorry, this has been... difficult."

"You don't need to explain yourselves to us," Scarlett said. "We understand."

"May we come in?" Rob pressed.

"Of course, of course," Sandra said. "Please." She led them inside and through into the kitchen. "Would you like a tea? I've been brewing up a pot."

"If it's no trouble," Rob confirmed.

"Um, yes please," Scarlett said.

Sandra went to work, grabbing a couple more cups and deftly pouring the steaming beverage before checking if they needed milk and sugar.

In short order, the cup was on a coaster on the table. "Thank you." Rob waited for her to join them at the table.

"Biscuit?" Michael placed a sizable Tupperware container on the table before them, filled with an enviable selection of crumbly treats.

When Rob spotted some chocolate-covered Hobnobs, he simply couldn't resist. "Thank you, you're too kind. You don't need to do this."

"With everything you're doing to help us, this is the least we can do for you," Sandra replied.

"Is there anything new to report?" Michael added. "The other officers said they were handing the case to you because of some new evidence."

"That's right. Now, we have been briefed, but I'd like to hear from you, exactly what you know about Roxy's disappearance so far. If you don't mind?"

"No, of course, that's fine," Michael agreed and glanced at Sandra who nodded along.

"We don't know much," Sandra admitted. "We know she went out to meet some friends but didn't show up. So they eventually went looking for her and found her car and phone. That's when they called the police and us. We've been interviewed along with Roxy's friends and told them what we know about Roxy's life, but that's it really."

"Thank you," Rob replied, impressed with Sandra's composure under very stressful circumstances.

"So, what is this new evidence?" Michael asked.

"I'll get to that," Rob answered. "But to give you a little more context, we're part of the East Midlands Special Operations Unit, a multi-county organisation of officers working together to tackle violent and organised crime across the East Midlands. Normally, we wouldn't deal with disappearances like this, but there's a few elements to this case that meant we were asked to step in. The main reason is that we now know that this was an organised abduction perpetrated by a group of individuals. We have CCTV of Roxanna being accosted by at least three men in the multi-storey car park where her car was found. Not only that, but it seems like this was planned rather than random because their CCTV was vandalised earlier that day, with only a few cameras escaping and remaining operational."

"So, this was a gang?" Michael asked, incredulous.

"Well," Rob answered. "That depends on your definition of a gang, I suppose. But if you're asking if this was done by more than one person, then yes, it was."

Michael looked over at Sandra who met his gaze. "Do you still think...?"

"It has to be." Sandra's face was resolute, before she turned back to Rob and Scarlett. "You need to investigate Truman Collins. He's the only person I can think of who'd do this to her. He hated her for going public. I can't think of anyone else who'd want to hurt her or us."

"Because of her rape allegation," Scarlett clarified.

"He raped her. He definitely did it. But as usual, the justice system in this country failed yet another woman. It's criminal how people like him can get away with that kind of behaviour. According to Roxy, he was well known for it around the office, although she didn't know just how much until after things got out of hand. He flirted with all the girls and paid them to keep their mouths shut. But when you're a multimillionaire, you can do that. The rules don't apply to people like him."

"So, she wasn't the first?" Rob asked.

"She's probably not the last either," Sandra answered.

"How did it all happen? Do you know?"

"He flirted with her, took her to dinner, and bought her expensive jewellery. You know, the usual. Roxy admitted flirting with him. She said she found it exciting and was flattered by the attention he gave her. But then, one night, he chose to take it to the next level. Roxy wasn't so sure and said no. But Truman didn't want to hear no." She pulled a face and sniffed. "I can only imagine that he's surrounded by yes men, agreeing to everything he says. So he didn't like her refusal. According to Roxy, he grabbed her by the throat and forced her, but..." She took a breath to control her rising emotions. "She eventually threw him off, and he lashed out."

"He hit her," Rob stated.

"He did," Sandra confirmed. "He hit her hard."

"But Roxy is no pushover," Michael added. "Apparently, she forced him away and ran out of the apartment. Within moments he was flooding her phone with text messages, apologising to her, saying he didn't know what came over him, and offering her money to say nothing."

"What did she do?" Scarlett asked.

"She decided to make a formal complaint to the company HR team. She also spoke to some of her friends working for the company, who put her in touch with others who all said that this is what he's like. This is who he is and to take the money and move on. But Roxy wasn't having that, and when HR didn't do much, she went to the police and accused him of rape. That's when things got out of hand. The case went to court, but nothing happened. He wasn't convicted of anything. However, it did seem to ruin his family life once his wife found out who he really was."

"His wife divorced him and managed to get custody of his kids," Michael added. "That really pissed him off."

"That's why it has to be him," Sandra stated. "He hates her."

"It *was* four years ago," Rob replied. He didn't believe that would make much difference to someone like Truman, who would probably bide his time before making a move, but he wanted to challenge their story, just as a lawyer would at court.

"Four years is nothing," Sandra replied.

"It's less than that," Michael added.

Rob was about to jump in to refute that before Michael explained.

"It's true that the assault happened just over four years ago, but the court case wasn't heard until much later and dragged on for a while, so it's probably not much over two since things went quiet."

"This happened in London, right?" Rob asked.

"Yeah," Michael confirmed. "She moved down for work but moved back following the incident. She couldn't be close to him anymore."

"Do you remember the names of the officers you dealt with?"

"Not really," Michael answered.

"Only the one who kept us informed throughout," Sandra added. "Detective Kristal Powers. She was great. If you need to talk to anyone about the case, she's the one."

"Thank you." Rob made a note and raising an eyebrow at the curious name. Not that he had much room to talk. "You said in your initial statements that you didn't know anyone who'd want to do this to her."

"Yes, that's right," Sandra agreed.

"So, there are no other jilted boyfriends, no one she's annoyed or anything?"

"No, not at all. She wasn't like that. She didn't hurt anyone, and she wasn't seeing anyone either."

"No boyfriend or anything?"

"Not as far as we knew, and she wasn't shy about telling us about these things."

"I understand." Rob moved on to more mundane questions about her life and routine, trying to get a better understanding of who Roxy was and what her day-to-day life was like. It sounded to him like she enjoyed a quiet life, without drama or trouble, which after everything that had happened, made perfect sense.

It wasn't long before Rob and Scarlett finished up and bid the Wells family goodbye and returned to their car.

"They're convinced Truman Collins is behind all this," Rob stated.

"Understandable," Scarlett commented. "He has every reason to want to ruin Roxy's life."

"He does," Rob agreed as he started the engine and made their way back to Sherwood Lodge, the Nottinghamshire Police Headquarters.

"They're convinced it's him," Rob said, after detailing his conversation with Roxy's parents to DCI Nailer. "They can't think of anyone else who'd bear such a grudge."

"It's the obvious choice," Nailer confirmed.

"Have you tracked him down yet?"

"We have, actually," Nailer confirmed. "He works mainly in London, as we expected, but lives in Surrey and commutes to work. We have an address for him, too."

"Surrey?" Rob asked. "Scarlett's home turf."

"Indeed. It's also Jon Pilgrim's stomping ground, so I thought you might want to call your former DCI and see if he can help us. We could do with sending someone round to talk to Mr Collins."

"Absolutely," Rob answered with a smile. It had been a while since he'd spoken to his old boss, so it would be good to catch up and see if he could help. "I'll get right on it."

Turning away from Nailer's office, Rob pulled out his phone, found the entry on his contacts list, and hit call. It took a few rings before it connected.

"Rob!" Jon exclaimed on the other end of the line. "As I live and breathe. How are you? It's good to hear from you."

"And you," Rob replied. "How are you?"

"Oh, you know. Busy saving the world."

Rob smiled. "I know the feeling."

"Is this a social call or work-related?" Jon asked.

"Business, I'm afraid," Rob stated. "We've got a missing woman up here, and the only lead we have so far is a man called Truman Collins. She used to work for him, but that ended when he allegedly attempted to rape her. That was four years ago. It happened in London, but Truman himself lives in Surrey."

"I see. And I take it you'd like us to knock on his door, right? See if he's taken any trips up north recently?"

"I would, yes. I can send you the relevant details. I'd just like to know where he was last night and what his state of mind is right now. You know, the usual stuff."

"Gotcha. Leave it with me, and I'll see what I can do."

5

Sitting at her desk, Scarlett continued to read through the details of Roxy's case against this wealthy businessman, Truman Collins, and found herself making links between Roxy's experience and the experience of her university friend, Ninette, who'd recently become one of the victims of the Mason gang's vendetta against Rob.

Like Roxy, Ninette had been attacked and reported the sexual assault to the police, only to be failed by the justice system that let the man go free and be a potential risk to other women. The situation annoyed Scarlett, and she ground her teeth in frustration at the so-called justice system because what both of these women had been through was anything but justice.

They'd done the right thing, followed the rules and been brave enough to speak their truth and demand something be done, only to be let down by that same system.

It was at times like these that she wondered if there was any point in doing her job. They spent days, weeks, and often months hunting for evidence and clues, taking statements and getting everything ready for the court, only for a rich man to come along with the best legal representation that money can buy and wriggle out of it on some technicality.

It wasn't right.

With a sigh, Scarlett leaned back in her seat. It creaked under her weight. She stretched as Nick crossed the room behind her, whistling.

"Did I wake you up, Stutely?"

"Yeah, be quiet next time," she answered with a smile.

Nick wandered over to the sectioned-off break area with its small sink, kettle, and microwave. He checked the water level and flicked the kettle on before leaning against the counter with his hip.

Scarlett turned back to her screen, only for a thought to spring to the forefront of her mind.

Ever since the drugs raid on the Mason gang, she'd been playing with the idea of contacting Calico Black, Nick's friend from the army. She'd helped out on that operation and impressed Scarlett with her skill set, something that Scarlett felt more than a little envious of. And with her desire to take down the Mason gang, she couldn't help thinking that she could learn something from Calico.

But she'd need to go through Nick to get to Calico.

Scarlett glanced back at Nick, who was still alone in kitchenette and briefly considered her pitch. She was basically asking for his friend's number. Would he mind? Would Calico mind if Nick asked her? She hoped not.

For a few seconds, she hesitated, self-conscious, and wondered if this was a stupid thing to ask. But the inhibition didn't last, and she quickly threw caution to the wind and got up from her desk.

Rob and Guy both looked up.

She caught their eyes. "I'm gonna get a drink. Anyone want a brew?"

"Sure," Rob answered.

"Yeah, why not," Guy added before they both refocused on their screens.

Scarlett nodded, turned, and wandered over to the corner where Nick still waited for the water to boil.

"Couldn't stay away?"

Scarlett smirked. "Keep dreaming."

Nick raised an eyebrow and pointed to the kettle. "I meant from the coffee." But then he grinned, amused.

"Oh, yeah. Well, I guess." She felt nervous for some reason she didn't fully understand but busied herself with gathering three mugs and throwing a teabag into each one. With that done, she joined Nick in the long wait for the steadily boiling water. "So, um. How you doing?"

"Fine," Nick replied, eyeing her curiously. "Everything alright?"

"Yeah," she answered. "Why?"

"You're acting weird."

She sighed, frustrated that he'd noticed her nervousness. "Sorry. I just... Can I ask you a question?"

He shrugged. "Of course."

"And look, you don't need to say yes. You can think about it, or say no, it's cool. I don't mind."

He just stared at her for a long moment. "...Okaaaay. This sounds serious."

"Honestly, I don't mind if you say no."

"What's your question?"

"I was wondering if you had Calico's number?"

Nick frowned, seeming confused. "Calico? Why?"

"I don't know. Well, that's not true. So we chatted while we were on that drugs raid. I was impressed with her, and I said I'd love to hang out sometime, and she said sure." She remembered the brief back and forth she'd had with Calico after her help subduing several of the guards. Even just the thought of that night and watching Calico go through those gang members and taking them out thrilled her. Her heart beat that little bit faster at the idea of being able to defend herself like that.

"She said that?"

"Yeah," she answered honestly. "She seemed open to the idea of meeting up sometime."

"Okay," Nick replied as the kettle finished boiling. He poured the teas while Scarlett waited for his answer. He finished and placed the kettle back on its base.

"So, what do you say?" Scarlett pressed, eager for some kind of answer.

"I'll talk to her." Nick turned to face Scarlett. "I'm not being funny, but Calico and people like her prefer that I do not give out their number to anyone who asks, no matter who it is. Their past and their job is sensitive."

"I understand," Scarlett replied, understanding Calico's need for privacy.

"Good. I'll let her know that you asked after her and that you'd like to meet up, but then it's up to her. That's the best I can do, okay?"

"That's perfect," Scarlett confirmed with a smile. "Thank you."

6

"So yeah, that's it, really," Ellen said with a shrug. They'd returned from visiting Roxy's friends and taking separate statements from each. "They all agreed that Roxy was a kind, friendly woman who, apart from Truman Collins, didn't have any other enemies. Every single one of them seemed to have genuine affection towards Roxy, and they all blamed Truman for it without any doubt at all."

"So, basically, they just confirmed what we already know?" Rob asked, leaning back in his chair as he listened.

"Pretty fuckin' much," Tucker agreed.

"Leaving us with just the one lead," Rob sighed. "Well, Truman better have a cast-iron alibi, that's all I can say."

Nearby, Scarlett got up from her desk carrying her bag. "It's late. I'd better get going."

Rob turned to look out the window and then glanced at his watch. She was right. They were well past the end of their shift.

"All right," Rob answered and said goodbye just as his phone vibrated. He picked it up off of his desk and noted the single name on the screen. Pilgrim.

"Aaah, this might be interesting." He answered while Ellen and Tucker made for their desks. "Jon. Good to hear from you. I was wondering when you'd call."

"Yeah, sorry for the delay," Jon said. "Mr Collins was a tough man to track down. But we did it, and I have some news for you. But it's not good."

"Oh, really, because so far, everything our end points to Truman Collins."

"Well, you might need to rethink that because he wasn't even in the country."

"Excuse me?"

"He was in Spain on a business trip, and we've already got photographic proof because it was a public event, and there's coverage of it online. I'll send you some links. But this means he was nowhere near Newark at the time of the abduction. He's due to return home tomorrow, so we'll see if we can catch up with him then, but otherwise there's not a lot to say really. Do you still think he did it?"

"Shit. Well, right now, I honestly have no idea. What I can say is that all of Roxy's friends and family have pointed to Truman, saying he's the only one who would have any desire to hurt her. They don't know anyone else who might want to do this. One thing to note, however, is that Truman himself, wasn't there. It was a group of three or four men. We have footage of a van pulling up in the car park and three men jumping out to grab her. We've run the plates, but they're fake and a dead end, so we're now looking to trace the van using traffic cams and ANPR. But Christ knows how long that will take."

"So, what's your working hypothesis? Are you thinking that he paid for these guys to kidnap her?"

"I don't know, but it's certainly possible," Rob replied. "He's got the money."

"Oh, yeah. Most certainly. Anyway, that's all I have for you right now."

"Great, thanks. Keep me updated on your progress," Rob stated.

"We will," Jon confirmed. "As soon as we know something, you'll be the first people we call."

"Excellent," Rob said, relieved. "So, how's things? How's Kate?"

"Yeah, good. Kate's well. You should come and visit sometime. It would be good to catch up."

"Yeah, I know," Rob replied. "I really should. I've just got so much going on that finding time is difficult. Anyway, thanks for your help."

"Any time," Pilgrim answered and ended the call after they'd swapped brief farewells.

A short time later, once Guy, Ellen, and Tucker had all left, Rob finished up and got to his feet. He turned to see Nailer still in his office and walked over.

"I'm off home. There's not much more we can do until we speak to Truman or get more CCTV footage."

"Fair enough," Nailer said. "I take it Ellen and Tucker didn't discover anything new either?"

"Nope, nothing. Just more fingers pointing at Truman. I have also been in touch with the MET and requested that the detective the Wells family mentioned gets in touch. So hopefully, she'll call tomorrow as well."

"Excellent, good work. Now get out of here and get some rest. With any luck, we'll bring this home in the next twenty-four hours."

Rob raised his hand to show Nailer his crossed fingers. "Here's hoping."

Gathering his stuff, Rob checked around one last time to make sure he wasn't leaving anything behind or out on display before he left the office behind with a brief wave to Nailer. The man frequently worked late, but then he was similar to Rob, with no ties at home, meaning he could dedicate his life to the job.

As Rob approached the exit, making for the car park, a figure joined him from a side corridor. It was Matilda, looking tired and ready for an early night. She met his gaze, and smiled.

"Oh, hi, Rob."

"Pulling another late one?" he asked, offering her a conciliatory smile.

"You know as well as I do that our clients don't keep regular office hours." She smiled over at him.

"Don't I know it," he exclaimed, sensing an element of awkwardness in her that was a fairly recent phenomenon. It had appeared following the confrontation with Rainault at his apartment when she'd discovered his link to the Mason gang.

Since then, she'd backed off, and any interaction between them had been stilted and not quite so smooth. She needed time to process what had happened and what she now knew about him.

But that had been a few weeks ago, and it felt to him like this was dragging on.

Or was he being insensitive?

The revelation that his father was the leader of the Mason crime family, which counted his three older brothers as its ringleaders, was not a small one. And while plenty of people within the force already knew about it and that he'd been estranged from them for over twenty years, there were still plenty who didn't know. Matilda, it seemed, was one such person.

She was taking it hard.

They walked silently through the Lodge, the weight of the expectation to make conversation bearing down on him the whole time. He despised these pregnant silences and wanted desperately to fill them with small talk but didn't know where to begin.

He opened the security door with his badge as they made their way out, swapping just a couple of words before finally making it outside.

Away from the oppressive corridors of the station, Rob felt suddenly free to raise the subject of his family without being overheard but struggled to find a way to open that conversation. She smiled as he flailed around, desperate to talk to her.

"I'm over there," she said, pointing in the opposite direction to where Rob needed to go.

Had she parked so far away on purpose? His car was quite distinctive, after all, he reasoned, while stealing a glance over at Belle, his beautiful Ford Capri.

"Look, Matilda. I'm sorry about... you know, the whole thing with my family."

She stopped and stared at the ground.

He spoke before slowly looking up. "I wanted to tell you before but..."

"But, you didn't."

He sighed. "No, I didn't, and I'm sorry about that."

"I know. You've already said that… several times."

He flinched at the sting in her words, and she appeared to notice his reaction.

"Sorry," she muttered. "I didn't…" She seemed to struggle to find the words. "I know it's been weeks, but I'm busy and, well, I just need time to process all this. I like you, Rob, you know that, but this whole thing with your family, it's massive. You're a police officer. I'm a solicitor. It could ruin us."

"I know."

She sighed. "Sorry, of course you know. You've lived with it for years. But I suppose that's the point, isn't it. I haven't. So you're just going to have to be patient with me, okay?"

"I understand. I'll be around when you need me," he said, waving to the Lodge.

"Thank you, I appreciate it." She smiled and reached out with her hand. She squeezed his arm affectionately. "I'll see you around."

"You will."

She turned and walked towards her car, running her hand through her hair. Dejected and adrift, he turned away and approached his own vehicle. The 2.8 Injection, 1985 black Ford Capri, Mark 3, waited patiently for him, like an ever-present protector and friend. He placed his hand on its roof, inserted his key, and unlocked the door. He took his time, his mind filled with thoughts and worries about where all this left him and Matilda. It wasn't the best reaction he'd ever had, but he'd had worse, and time was a great healer.

He was about to step into the car when Matilda drove by. She glanced over and waved at him as he passed. He waved back, but then she was gone, leaving him alone with his thoughts.

7

Standing to one side, Guy watched the proceedings with interest and some suspicion. The room was filled with a who's who of the Mason gang, all there to discuss recent events, of which he was a key part.

He'd worked secretly within the police for years, feeding intel back to Isaac and the gang, which they'd used to great effect. But one of the things under scrutiny today was his more recent attempt to incriminate Rob, mainly because it hadn't worked.

He'd entered into a partnership with Bill Rainault, and despite his best efforts to entrap Rob with some dirty money planted in his apartment, he'd somehow found the package and escaped the consequences. One benefit of the operation's failure was the revelation of the support he had from several key figures within the EMSOU leadership. These people would make any attempt to entrap him that much harder, not least because the EMSOU was now aware of the gang's attempts to do this. Despite this positive, the gambit had still failed, much to Guy's annoyance.

He'd been aware of the glares of distrust and concern that had been shot his way since arriving. He couldn't blame them really. Failure was not tolerated for long within the firm, but luckily for him, he had a track record of successes and valuable intelligence that he'd passed on to them behind him, which would stand him in good stead.

"So, where are we with the Columbians now?" Isaac asked. He stood at the head of the room, near the fireplace, his figure a little stooped but no less imposing at the age of sixty-five. Isaac Mason, the godfather of the Mason gang, turned slowly to the room and let his gaze pass over the assembled men and women.

Guy knew many of them, but not all. The most obvious were Isaac's sons, Sean, Oliver, and Owen, who sat closest to their father.

"I'm trying to talk to them, but they're being difficult," Sean answered. "They're not happy that their couriers and product were captured in a single raid when they bent over backwards to accommodate us."

"Trying?" Isaac asked.

"I don't think they know how to handle us, and I get the distinct impression they're looking for a partner elsewhere, someone who won't leak to the feds."

"Have we nailed down that leak yet?"

"Not yet," Sean answered. "We have our suspicions, but..." He glanced up at Guy. "We need intel."

"Guy?" Isaac asked.

"I'm looking into it. But I'm not in that particular circle of trust, so it's not that easy. Informants typically only trust one or two officers and are reluctant to switch to new ones. I'll see what I can do, but I can't make promises."

"Look harder," Isaac barked.

Guy chewed on the inside of his cheek in frustration, annoyed at the shift in mood towards him. He needed to do something to change things and regain their trust.

"Should we be worried about the cartel?" Isaac asked, addressing Sean again. "Can we expect any pushback?"

"I'm not sure," Sean stated. "If they side with one of our rivals, that could be a risk, depending on the terms of the deal. I wish I could give you a better answer, but there are too many unknowns."

"What about our supply of product?" Isaac asked, using coded language for drugs. It was always worth being careful, just in case of any bugs that might be planted and listening in.

"We're back to capacity." The man who answered was Carter Bird, one of the men who worked directly for the Mason brothers and took on much of the dirty work that the gang indulged in by delegating it to their subordinates. "We took a hit after that raid, but we've made up the shortfall since then."

"But we haven't expanded," Isaac asked, with an edge to his voice. He wasn't happy.

A guilty expression appeared on Carter's face, but he didn't sugar-coat the answer. "No."

"I'm talking to one of the Mexican groups," Oliver said, only for Isaac to curl his lip in undisguised revulsion.

"And I'm making inroads with another Columbian group," Carter added.

Isaac grunted. It seemed he didn't like getting the drugs from the Mexicans. "Wonderful." He looked away, clearly frustrated by recent events, and kicked the base of the fireplace. "Speaking of setbacks," he said and turned to Guy. "What about you? Do you have anything to add? Anything to brighten my mood after your fuck-up with that messed-up anticorruption officer?"

Guy narrowed his eyes as he stared back at the old man. So far, he'd not told anyone about his most recent discovery, that Erika was the daughter of DCI John Nailer, Loxley's boss. The whole situation with her was bizarre, and he was determined to get to the bottom of it. She called him Dad, and he didn't seem to object, but only when they were in private. No one in the EMSOU seemed to know about his daughter, least of all Rob, who Erika lived next door to.

But why? What interest did Erika have in Rob? Why would she choose to live there and for Erika and Nailer to hide their relationship?

Something was going on, that was for sure, and Guy was determined to get to uncover this little mystery. But he'd do it away from the prying eyes of the Masons, because if the truth was as juicy as he suspected it might be, it could just be the bargaining chip he needed to get back into Isaac's good graces. So he wasn't about to spill the beans here. No, he'd keep this quiet and decide for himself when to reveal the truth.

However, he wasn't an idiot, and it wouldn't go unnoticed by the Masons, who were always watching their most valuable assets, that he was starting to go on a few dates with Erika.

He needed to lay the groundwork without giving it all away.

"I'm looking into something," Guy said, picking his words carefully.

"Something?" Isaac asked, thoroughly unimpressed. "What?"

"I'm wondering if we can use some kind of leverage against Rob at some point, so I've been investigating the people he's closest to, including his neighbour, who he seems quite friendly with."

The eyes of the Mason brothers and their father were locked on to him, and their expressions ranged from interested to bored.

Isaac seemed the least interested of the lot and sighed to himself. "Fine, you do that. At least you'll be keeping out of trouble that way."

Guy smiled to himself as Isaac, Sean, and Oliver looked away. Owen held his gaze for a little longer, a curious frown on his ugly face. As the most violent and unpredictable of the brothers, he was probably wondering when his dad would give him the order to kill.

Not today, bucko!

Guy mouthed the word 'what' at him without making a sound.

Owen rolled his eyes and turned away, leaving Guy to fade into the background as the conversation moved on. He'd been dismissed by Isaac, and that suited him just fine.

8

Sitting in the passenger seat of the Incident Response Vehicle, PC David Morton held on as Russ threw the marked police car around the corner and raced up Spital Hill, in Retford, as the night drew in.

"By heck, steady on. It's only kids messing about." The night was young, and he didn't fancy being in a collision already.

"I don't think you'd be saying that if it was your house," Russ answered, skidding around onto Wellington Street. "I think you'd want us there, sharpish, like."

"Aye, all right," David answered.

Russ took the right-hander onto Holmes Road, their blue lights flashing and siren wailing.

Up ahead, a small crowd gathered in the street, shouting and jeering. They raced towards the group. People turned and backed away.

Beyond the sparse crowd, a group of four young teenagers between the ages of eleven and fifteen, stood in the front garden of a house on the right. Its windows were smashed, and they sprayed graffiti all over it.

"Shit, here we go," David said as Russ brought the car to a screeching halt.

They jumped out.

"Oi, that's enough of that. Come away."

He rushed through the low gate hanging off its hinges and made a snap evaluation. Making an educated guess as to which one might be the ringleader, he grabbed the most enthusiastic vandal.

He pulled the teen's arm into a lock and relieved him of his spray can, forcing the kid down. The onlooking crowd shouted, jeered, or clapped, depending on whose side they were on. David reached for his cuffs and slapped them into place with a satisfying click while the kid continued to shout and protest. He attached the second cuff to a metal railing leading down from the front door and reached for another of the little shits. But the kid ran, slipping out of his coat before racing into the road between the watching neighbours.

For a moment, David considered running after him but then thought better of it. Russ had a third one cuffed and laid on his front, and the fourth one seemed to have already disappeared.

"Two out of four ain't bad," David remarked.

Russ grunted. "Could have been better."

He couldn't argue with that and turned to the kid he'd nicked. The first thing he noticed was red smears of blood under his nose. For a moment, David thought he might have hurt him but then quickly discounted it. The crusty stain looked old. That had happened before they had arrived. "Right then, who are you, and what's this house ever done to you?"

"He fuckin' had it coming," the kid bellowed. "He deserved it, the bastard."

"Who did?"

"The shit who lives here, of course. Idiot."

"Watch your mouth. Do you know the owner's name? Is he here?"

"Nah, mate. He fucked off, didn't he, after he did this to me." The kid pointed to his nose. "The bastard. I can't wait to see his face when he comes home to this."

David sighed and looked up at the house, getting his first clear view at the damage the kids had done. The downstairs windows were smashed, including the one in the front door. And they'd scrawled tags, insults, and just general rubbish on the walls. David noticed at least two mentions of the Red Man in amongst the four-letter words.

He rolled his eyes at the urban myth.

"Right then, you little shit, you've had your fun."

David turned to see a man leaning over the fence from next door. He was talking to the kid.

"Sir?" David said.

"Come on, shit for brains, get in," the man continued.

"Can't, can I?" the kid grumbled and rattled the cuffs against the metal bar.

"Bloody hell." The man frowned.

"Sir." David stepped closer. "Sir. Are you responsible for this child?"

The man's eyes were filled with disdain for David and the uniform he wore. "What of it?"

Sensing that this man might not be the most cooperative in the world, he decided to be just as awkward. "Well, let me spell it out for you, shall I? He's vandalised your neighbour's house. So..."

"And? He's a dick. He had it coming."

David pulled a face at the interruption.

"He broke my bastard nose," the kid said, gingerly touching it.

"Stop whining," his dad suggested, his tone devoid of any concern.

"What's your name, sir?" David pressed, getting in the man's face.

"Why should I tell you?"

David shrugged. "It's just easier that way. I mean, if you want to be difficult, be my guest, but I can ruin your night, too, if you'd like? Your choice."

The man stuck out his lower lip. "Otto. Otto Frank. My kid's name is Bobby."

65

David smiled, pleased they were now getting somewhere.

"I'll call an ambulance," Russ said behind him. "I think he should get his nose looked at."

"Sure," David confirmed before focusing to Otto and Bobby. "Let's start at the beginning, shall we?"

9

With a roar from the V6 engine, Rob swung his Ford Capri into the reserved parking spot at his apartment block and gave the handbrake a yank. It clicked into place, bringing the vehicle to rest while the beast beneath the bonnet rumbled contentedly after another brief workout on the drive home.

But Rob's mind was far from any thoughts about his car or how much he enjoyed driving it. His mind was set on his brief interaction with Matilda and what this might mean for them.

Before she'd found out about his family, they'd been getting quite close, and he'd started to harbour thoughts of them getting together and making a go of things, but that all felt so far away now.

He'd cursed himself many times over the last few weeks for not telling Matilda sooner. He should have been more honest with her from the start.

But, if he had told her, she might never have been interested in him. The cold hard truth of his family history might have scared her away.

He grumbled to himself. Recriminations never got anyone anywhere. He'd made choices, felt the consequences, and things were the way the were. Rob had to learn to deal with it and move on.

It might be that Matilda would never feel okay with him being a Mason, estranged or not, and this was the end of his relationship with her. His stomach twisted itself into a knot at the thought. He dismissed that idea, preferring to live in the hope that she would eventually come round and everything would be okay.

Frustrated, Rob climbed out of his car, locked it, and made his way inside with the weight of the day's events heavy on his shoulders. Right now, all he could think about was getting inside, eating comfort food, showering, and collapsing into bed. He might even throw in a little TV if he felt the desire, but he wasn't sure.

The stairs up to his floor felt like Everest, and he slowed as he neared the first floor until he finally set foot on the landing and turned towards his front door.

A sudden clatter and several thuds of movement from the door to his right snagged his attention. Erika's apartment.

Confused, he turned to look, until the door opened a moment later, and Erika appeared.

She beamed at him. "Aaah, you're back."

Rob blinked, bemused by the flurry of movement he'd picked up on the other side of her door. She must have been waiting and rushed to get the door when she heard him.

"Err, yeah. I'm back," he agreed. "Are you okay?"

"Yeah, fine. I, um, I was waiting for you," she said with a self-conscious smile. "Sorry, I didn't mean to surprise you."

"That's okay. How can I help?"

"I wondered if you had a moment?"

Rob raised an eyebrow. Where was this going? "Um, yeah. I can spare a moment." He made to approach her door. "Your place?"

"Yeah, my place is fine," she confirmed, running her hand through her dark hair. She was about twenty years his junior with a pretty face and coffee-coloured skin. Her bright, wide green eyes sparkled in the light.

She waved him through and followed him in. Her apartment was much like his own in basic layout, but that was about as far as the similarities went. She seemed to like clutter, and although the place wasn't dirty, there was just lots of stuff everywhere, on the sideboards and hanging on the walls.

She waved towards the island in her kitchen, much like his own, and the stools to either side of it.

"So what was it you needed me for?" he asked as he took his seat. "Have you got a jam jar you need opening?"

It was her turn to raise an eyebrow. "I can do that myself, thank you very much, Mr Big-strong-man."

He smiled, and so did she.

"No, actually, I wanted your opinion on something."

"Okay. If you say so. Although, I'm not sure my opinion is all that valuable."

"On Guy Gibson."

"Aaah, Casanova."

Guy had taken an interest in Erika a few weeks ago, got her number, and then several days ago, announced he'd been on a date with her. Nick, who also admired Erika, had not been very amused. So, if she'd been on a date with Guy, why was she interested in his opinion?

Rob narrowed his eyes. "You've been on a date with him, right?"

"Yeah. I was just wondering what you thought of him? He seemed nice enough, and I enjoyed that first date, so I just wanted a second opinion from someone who knows him. You know? What's he like? Do you know of any red flags I should be aware of?"

"Red flags? Honestly, no, not really," Rob admitted as he considered her questions and what he knew about Guy. He didn't hang out with him and didn't really know him outside of work, but he seemed friendly. "I don't know what to tell you really. He seems like a nice guy. You probably know him better than I do, which should give you an idea of how much time I've spent with him."

"So, he's all right, then, yeah?"

Rob shrugged. "I mean, as a work colleague, yeah. But you shouldn't judge him based on what I'm telling you. I think you need to make your own mind up."

"Yeah, I guess," she said, thinking things through.

"You're a bright young woman. I'm sure you'll figure it out."

She smiled at his compliment. "Here's hoping. How's your day been?"

"Exhausting," he replied and got up off the stool. "Sorry I couldn't be more help."

"Don't be silly. This was useful, thanks."

"I mean, I've never dated the guy, so I've got no idea if he's good boyfriend material, you know?"

"Well, I'm glad of that, because that alone could be a red flag. I mean, anyone who settles for you…"

"Oi, you." He pointed at her.

She grinned like a Cheshire Cat. "I'm kidding."

"Good thing, too," he remarked. "Anyway, I'd better be getting back. Otherwise, Muffin will be wondering where I am. I'm sure he'd be jealous if he knew I was round here."

"Aww. It's been a few weeks since I've seen that cutie pie. Give him a stroke from me, will you?"

"Sure thing," Rob agreed. "I'm willing to bet I'll be asking you to feed him before too long."

71

"And I'll be ready and waiting for him with treats." Her winning smile spread over her pretty face.

"No wonder he likes you so much," he muttered. "Good luck on your next date with Guy. I'm guessing it's not tonight?"

"No," she confirmed. "Tomorrow."

"Okay. I hope it goes well."

"Me, too," she answered with a smile. "See you later."

Rob said his goodbyes and finally returned to his home. Pleased to be back, he grabbed the letters that were scattered on the mat and walked through into the main living space, where Muffin sat on the arm of the nearby sofa, looking regal. He cocked his head to one side as he watched.

"Evenin'," Rob said to his pet. "Hope you didn't miss me."

Muffin meowed loudly.

"It's good to see you, too." Rob glanced at the cat's empty bowl. "Christ, you licked *that* clean. Shall I get you some dinner?"

Muffin was quick to jump down and weave through Rob's legs while he opened a packet of chicken for him and served up his evening meal. Muffin tucked in greedily.

Rob stroked him. "That's from Erika. She says hi."

Muffin didn't seem to care, so Rob left him to his food and returned to the side where he'd dumped the letters and quickly rifled through them.

A handwritten letter with an expensive-looking envelope stood out like a sore thumb. Rob frowned at its distinctive appearance and felt sure he recognised the handwriting, but he couldn't place it right away.

Taking his time, he opened the envelope and removed the folded piece of paper, which was also thick and well-made.

Unfolding it revealed it to be an invitation to the wedding of Scarlett Stutely and Chris Williams, and it was only a few weeks away now.

Rob smiled at the invite with its flowery writing as he read it through again, pleased that she'd chosen to invite him.

After a moment, he grabbed his phone, took a photo of it, and sent it to Scarlett with a caption: *You kept this quiet*. She'd not mentioned it all day, although she must have sent it a few days ago.

She was quick to see the message. *You're welcome*, she answered.

Rob grinned at her text and composed a reply. *I'll see you on the big day. I'll need to go suit shopping now.*

You're damn right. I'm not having you show up in a work suit.

Rob grinned at the text. It was good to have something to look forward to.

10

It was late as Lois stepped out of the bar. They'd closed nearly an hour ago, and she'd been busy helping clean up before the manager said she could head home.

Pleased to be done for the night, she walked into Cannon Square and turned right, heading towards Retford's town centre. Home was on the other side of Kings Park, and with any luck, she'd make it there in maybe ten or fifteen minutes, all being well.

Predictably, plenty of revellers were still in town, drinking and staggering around. As she made towards the Market Square, she glanced down Market Place towards the pedestrianised Carolgate, and then right, along Bridgegate.

She usually preferred going through town, but recently she'd avoided it if it looked a little busy. She'd had a few encounters with drunks, and twice now, she'd had a man follow her partway home.

Tonight was another busy one, and the idea of walking through the streets alone filled her with dread, so she turned right and started up Bridgegate.

She passed several closed shops, their windows whitewashed and covered in newspaper on the inside and graffiti on the outside. She wondered if there was anyone

74

inside these disused stores. They could be doing anything in there, hidden from prying eyes.

Maybe someone was being held hostage, gagged and tied to chair, metres away from freedom but unable to reach it. She shook her head, banishing the dark thoughts, and wondered if she needed to stop reading crime fiction.

Scrawled across the shopfront, someone had taken a dark-red spray paint and written: *The Red Man Watches.*

Lois pulled a face at the words. She'd heard about the urban legend that had been floating around town for a while. People talked about it in dark corners, over drinks or around a glowing firepit, debating who the Red Man was or what the myth was really about.

She'd heard several versions of the tale, from him being a local serial killer to some kind of bogeyman who people used to scare each other. No one knew for real, but the stories continued anyway, perpetuated by the delinquent youth who revered him as some kind of rebellious leader hidden in the shadows.

They kept the tale alive through their imaginative portrayals of him in graffiti around town or scratched on the inside of public toilet stalls.

She'd had her own debates about him with friends but didn't have much of an opinion about him beyond the conclusion that they were just silly stories designed to scare people.

Having tried a couple of different routes going this way around, she preferred to stick to the streets rather than cut through the park, but honestly, even that wasn't too bad. It was often better than the centre of town and was quite relaxing, even though it was darker and away from the roads.

Walking up Bridgegate, she ducked around the queues outside Lucky Days Chinese Takeaway and pressed on. She salivated at the smells of rice and chicken, even though she wasn't hungry. After a few drinks in town, a trip to Lucky Days was often the best way to round out a night with friends.

Further up, she approached the bridge over the River Idle and spotted a small knot of lads heading her way. She immediately recognised one as someone who'd followed her home and the rest as a group who seemed to enjoy tormenting young women walking alone.

Hell, even if she hadn't recognised them, their boisterous behaviour and disregard for passing cars would have worried her anyway. They shouted at a driver who got too close, banging on their car as they passed, yelling insults at the top of their lungs.

She wanted nothing to do with them.

So far, they'd not seen her or weren't taking much notice of her, so she ducked left into the car park beside Swannack

House and strode towards Sports Direct and the entrance to Kings Park at the far end. She made it about halfway in and slowed, wondering if the group might walk past the entrance, allowing her to return to the road and continue along the street, but her luck had run out.

The group walked into the car park and made their way towards her. Her heart thumped as her breath caught in her throat.

Had they seen her?

She didn't want to risk finding out and turned towards the small gate at the back.

The gate was one of several side entrances into Retford's largest park and led onto a gravel path that ran alongside the River Idle. From there, you could take several routes through the large rural oasis and enjoy the park's scenery before leaving through one of the many other exits.

Lois wasn't thinking that far ahead, though. She only wanted to keep as far away from these troublemakers as possible. Ducking through the gate onto the gravel path, she stared into the gloom, hoping there would be no more unwelcome encounters. Home wasn't far now. She just needed to get through the park and out the other side.

She'd done it before, so tonight should be no different.

Taking a deep breath to steel her nerves, she strode on through the night, keeping her head down but her eyes up and alert. She stuffed her right hand in her pocket and grabbed her keys, manipulating them so she gripped several between her fingers. They protruded like lethal metal claws from her fist and would mess up any attacker's face should she be forced to defend herself.

The gravel crunched beneath her feet while the river flowed beside her, soothing her nerves. Ahead, through the trees, the main bridge arced over the river, and so far, she'd seen no one.

It looked like she'd chosen wisely after all.

Seconds later, a cry of pain sounded over the river followed by shouts and the sounds of movement in the undergrowth. She froze and scanned around. Spotting activity on the other side of the river, she squinted into the darkness. Then she saw it. A group of men—big, burly men—crowded around another smaller, slimmer man, beating the shit out of him.

"Help. Help me. Please. You're killing me. Stop, please," the man cried in desperate wails, interspersed with grunts of pain. "Oh God, please. Help. Someone help me."

"Holy shit," Lois hissed under her breath as she stared in horror.

The group moved closer to the river, closer to her, and a man wearing a red mask seemed to be directing the thugs.

What the hell?

She wasn't sure why she quickly ducked behind the nearest tree and hid from the group, but it felt like the right thing to do. Peeking through the leaves, she watched the men kick the man on the ground, their boots slamming into his body and face with unrelenting force. Even in the darkness, she could see the blood flowing from his nose, mouth, and the countless cuts covering his head and body.

They were killing him, while the man in the red mask looked up and scanned around, searching for witnesses. Lois hid, ducking down behind the tree, wondering what she should do.

Who was this red-masked man…? A link materialised in her mind. Could it be the Red Man from the graffiti?

"Help me, please."

He wouldn't last much longer, he needed help, but what could she do?

Remembering her phone, she stuffed her hand into her pocket. She should call the police and get them to come down and sort this out, if there was a patrol nearby. Pulling out her mobile, she tapped her screen before suddenly stopping and turning it off. They'd hear her if she started talking, even over the river. She glanced behind her, towards where they were beating the man. There might be a river separating them, but she had a distinct feeling that if they saw her, they'd be on her like a shot.

Turning away, she looked ahead, away from the river at a wide area of grass with patches of thick bushes and trees. Perfect hiding spots for her to make a call.

Taking a deep breath, she made a run for it, sprinting across the path into the field. Running as straight as she could to avoid being seen, she waited until the last possible moment before ducking left behind a large bush.

After a quick check that she was out of sight, she made the call, asking to be put through to the police. Seconds later, they answered and asked her the nature of her call.

"I'm in Retford, in Kings Park, and a group of men is attacking another man. They're kicking and hitting him. They're killing him. You need to send someone."

"Don't worry, we will. Someone will be with you shortly. But you need to tell me exactly where you are and what you saw. Where are you?"

Lois described her location, telling the operator where she'd entered the park and how far in she was before going into as much detail about the men as she could.

"Can you see these men now?"

Lois took a long, shaky breath. "I'm hiding. One moment, I'll have a look."

"Don't put yourself in any danger," the operator said.

"I won't." Removing the phone from her ear, she pressed the illuminated screen to her chest to hide the glow. She took a few steps around the bush and leaned out.

The men were gone. All of them. Including the man who was being beaten up.

"What the...?"

11

The crisp morning air filled Phoebe's lungs as she jogged towards town. She was on the first leg of her usual morning jog that took her through the town centre, into the park, and back home into Hallcroft on the northwest side of Retford.

As always, she relished these short breaks from the usual chaos of home first thing in the morning. Getting up and out of the house before the calls of "Mum!" rang out was one of those small but significant pleasures in life.

She loved her kids, but she did sometimes wonder if they had an ounce of common sense between them when they either spilt toothpaste down their freshly washed t-shirt, couldn't find their underwear even though it was right there on the bed, or had found—usually by stepping in it—a warm pile of sick kindly left by their elderly cat.

And all the while, her husband, Pete, walked around the house, getting ready for work, oblivious to the hundred-and-one jobs that needed doing each day.

She loved him dearly, but sometimes she wondered if he lived in a dream world half the time. It was probably his mother's fault.

To be fair, he did occasionally take his used mug and place it *near* the dishwasher.

He'd probably want a gold star for that or something?

Today was her day off, although that in itself was something of a joke. Her 'days off' were generally busier than her days *in* the office because she'd either be cleaning, running to the shops, or working her way through the countless other things that needed doing because her adorable but useless husband failed to see them.

Jogging along Bridgegate, towards town, she passed other early risers jogging or walking their dogs before the work day began. What were their days like, she wondered? Just as chaotic as hers? Probably. That was just life in general, wasn't it?

A tight pain formed in her side. She cursed the developing stitch and her irregular breathing that had caused it but took it as an opportunity for a break that would also delay her getting home for a bit. Bonus!

Slowing to a walk as she reached the bridge over the River Idle, she took a sip from the water bottle she held and caught her breath. As befitted its name, the sound of the river flowing lazily beneath her was lovely to hear.

Leaning on the railing, she clasped her side where the stitch gripped her and scolded herself for not regulating her breathing. She concentrated on a more regular in-and-out rhythm with her eyes closed, and after a few moments, the pain faded.

She focused on the railing next to where she gripped it and noted the tags that had been daubed on it with black marker pen. *The Red Man lives*, one of them said. Who on earth was the Red Man?

"Mornin'," said a passing man on his morning jog in short shorts that showed off his toned legs.

Phoebe admired them for a moment before pulling her eyes away and taking one last glance along the river.

She was about to turn away when a shape caught her eye. Something that felt out of place bobbed in the water below. It looked like a jacket, maybe, but it was oddly filled out as if someone was wearing...

Phoebe's eyes widened in shock. She suddenly realised what she was staring at. She gasped, her hand clamping over her mouth as she took a step back. "Holy crap." She nearly stumbled into the road in front of a passing car. It honked as it drove by. "Aaah, bugger." She steadied herself and returned to the railing. Surely she was wrong. It couldn't be.

Could it? She leaned closer, squinting to get a better look.

The river flowed, and the shape wobbled as the water tried to carry it further long, but it was caught on a branch. The movement showed more of the shape and left her in no doubt.

It was a body.

A man, by the looks of it. Was he dead? He had to be. He was facedown and wasn't making any attempt to catch his breath.

For a long moment, she didn't have any idea what to do and briefly considered shouting for help before she suddenly remembered her phone in the side pocket of her leggings.

She slipped it out and quickly dialled 999.

12

A loud and disconcerting noise yanked Rob out of the rather lovely dream he'd been having, bringing him to bleary wakefulness in moments. He pushed himself up on to his elbows as he tried to remember where he was, before realising he was in bed at home. The noise was his phone, ringing loudly.

At the end of the bed, Muffin stirred and lifted his head. He sent a judgemental glare towards Rob.

"Don't you start," Rob remarked. He snatched up his phone and noted the call was from work. He answered it. "Hello?"

"Inspector Loxley?"

"Speaking."

"This is control. Your presence had been requested at a crime scene in Retford, sir."

"Right now?" Rob asked as he tried to focus on the clock and read the time. It was a stupid question, of course they meant now. They wouldn't mean next week, would they?

"I'm afraid so, sir. I'll send the details over to you."

"Great, thanks," he replied in a droll tone before the girl thanked him and hung up. Rob did the same and swung his legs out of bed and held his head in his hands. He groaned.

Retford.

He'd managed to keep his visits to that small market town in the north of Nottinghamshire to a minimum for twenty years, but it was inevitable that there would be cases that would take him there, especially now he was part of the EMSOU. In fact, he was surprised he'd dodged it for this long, but all good things must come to an end, eventually.

Leading any kind of investigation in Retford, his home town, would greatly increase the risk of encountering his former family, and naturally so. The idea of spending more time close to them did not sit well with him, not after their recent activities around him and his team. Scarlett had lost a friend to them, and Rob had experienced several meetings with his brothers and father, none of which he wanted to repeat anytime soon.

But it wasn't as if he had much choice in the matter. His siblings seemed to have taken a greater interest in him since his promotion and transfer into the EMSOU, and he doubted they'd give up trying to either recruit, discredit, or hurt him just yet.

Rob sighed as his mind circled through these well-trodden thoughts about his family and where he stood with them. It was nothing new, but they still had the ability to keep him awake at night as he wondered what might happen next.

He shook his head and pushed those dark thoughts to one side; he couldn't let himself get sidetracked right now. He had a job to do, but it wasn't a job he would do alone. Igniting the screen on his phone, he pulled up his contacts list and tapped the image of the smiling blonde to call Scarlett.

The phone rang several times before she answered it, her voice just as slurred as his was.

"Hello?"

"Morning, partner," Rob announced. "It's another lovely day on the force for us."

There was a long silence on the end of the line. "What on earth are you going on about?" She yawned.

Chris muttered something in the background, but Rob couldn't quite make out what it was.

"We've been called out. Seems there's a crime scene in Retford they want us to check out."

"Retford? What time is it?"

"Early."

"I could uninvite you to the wedding for this," she muttered.

Rob ignored her comment. "I'll pick you up in half an hour."

"Err, yeah, sure," she grunted. "Whatever." She hung up.

Rob smiled to himself. At least he wouldn't have to suffer the early morning alone. Getting up, he threw his phone onto the bed and stretched, making several of his joints pop as he did so, before he walked over to the window and opened the curtains. With his hands on his hips, he gazed out over the river.

Retford.

There was nothing for it, it seemed, he'd be heading home for the first time in several years, and the first time with the EMSOU and as a DI. His family were bound to show up at some point, it was inevitable, and that could be half the battle. There was no need to fight it, he'd let them come to him and he'd deal with them as and when he needed to. In the meantime, he had a job to do.

He smiled at his faint reflection in the window.

"Let the games commence."

13

Teri jerked awake. Her body briefly spasmed as she awoke with a shock from the restless slumber she'd been drifting in and out of all night. For a few seconds, she wondered where she was while vague memories of fitful dreams tugged at the corners of her mind. Images of looming shadows and masked men covered in blood played across her mind's eye, making her shiver with revulsion.

Still curled up on her sofa, her phone still in her hand, she suddenly remembered what she'd been doing all night and lifted her phone.

She pulled down on the screen and hunted through the notifications, desperate to see his name, but there was nothing. No texts, no calls, nothing. She opened up WhatsApp and doubled-checked her messages, just in case, but the two lonely ticks at the bottom of her frantic messages remained steadfastly grey. He hadn't replied.

The lack of contact sent a wave of nausea through her chest, which settled deep in her belly. She felt hungry, but there was no way she could eat anything. She wouldn't be able to keep it down.

Swinging her legs off the sofa, she hung her head, running her fingers through her hair.

What had happened to him? Why was he not answering his phone? He should be back by now, surely. There was no way it could take this long.

But if she was right, then that could only mean one thing. Something had gone desperately wrong. But how could it? They'd been so careful to make sure no one knew. They'd followed the directions of her contact to the letter, knowing full well what the consequences would be should there be a leak.

Teri shook her head. She didn't want to think about that.

For a moment, she considered calling her contact to see if they knew anything. But that would be going against their instructions, and if it had started going to shit, now wasn't the time to jeopardise things further.

Besides, the one thing she knew for certain was that she didn't know anything. She didn't know what had happened and was just second-guessing herself. She was making assumptions based on dark thoughts and nightmares.

That was no basis for anything other than fantasy. But this was reality. Cold, stark reality, and she needed to know what the hell had happened.

Morning light filtered through the half-closed blinds. A new day had dawned, but she wasn't looking forward to it.

She needed to be smart about this. She needed to think things through rationally and make smart choices if she was going to get through this. She snorted to herself.

"Well, I'm fucked then," she muttered.

Or maybe not. She wasn't an idiot. She'd come this far, and it was entirely possible that her fears were irrational and that everything was fine.

Was he just being cautious and not giving any reason to suspect him? Was that why she'd not heard from him?

He was doing exactly what their contact had told them to do by refusing to answer messages. But wouldn't he have seen them? Wouldn't the ticks have turned blue?

The dark thoughts returned, and she wondered if the meeting he'd gone to had gone horribly wrong? Had it not happened? Had the meeting taken place but had been interrupted? Or... or something else, maybe?

The waiting was killing her, and yet, that was her only option.

Teri threw her head back and yelled in agonised frustration before pulling her legs up, wrapping her arms around her knees, and wishing for all this to disappear.

14

Rob pulled up outside Scarlett's house on the Park Estate in Nottingham to find her waiting at the end of her drive. She held an insulated coffee and wore a glum expression on her pale face.

As he came to a stop, she approached, opened the car door, and dropped heavily into the passenger seat of his Ford Capri, slamming the door shut behind her.

Rob raised an eyebrow. "Not a morning person?" he asked, making an assumption.

"Not today."

He silently resolved to leave her to her coffee and wait for its effects to kick in. There was no rush to discuss anything just yet, not if she didn't want to.

Dropping the clutch, Rob sped off through Nottingham, navigating the city streets easily and enjoying the feel of his car and what it told him about the road beneath them. You didn't get that feedback today with these modern cars. Everything was cushioned, with rounded edges, and the cars almost drove themselves. He didn't know for sure, but he wouldn't be surprised if there was more computing power in your average modern car than there'd been inside the moon rockets. He knew that was true of phones, so it made sense for it to also be true of cars.

As Rob made it out into the countryside and pushed north towards Retford, he realised he'd not mentioned the wedding invite and felt bad for not thanking her in person the moment she'd got into the car.

Was that why she was in a bad mood? He didn't think so. Besides, she'd had some of her coffee by now.

"By the way, thanks for the wedding invite. I really appreciate it. It was a bit of a surprise, to be honest. I mean, we're only your work colleagues, and you've not been up here very long."

She smiled, and it was nice to see her mood lighten. "That's okay. You're more than just my boss, Rob. You're a friend, too, and it's not as if I have many of those up here."

"Well, I appreciate it," he replied, allowing the car to fall into silence again until Scarlett broke it a few moments later.

"Look, I'm sorry. I just woke up on the wrong side of the bed today. I didn't mean to take it out on you. It's not your fault."

"The coffee's kicking in, is it?"

"A bit, yeah. I'll be right as rain by the time we get there. What kind of delight are we dealing with today, by the way? What's happened?"

"I don't have much to go on, but the brief I was sent says a body's been found in the river in Retford. I don't know much more than that really. I guess we'll find out when we get there."

"A body in the river? Lovely. What a treat. Sounds like a great way to start the day to me."

"Doesn't it just," Rob agreed. "Hopefully, no one will want to eat this one," he muttered, referring to their last big case.

They raced north, passing Mansfield and Clumber Park, until they finally made it into the modest market town in the north of the county. Rob drove along Babworth Road into town, over the railway bridge, past the Roman Catholic church and Lawn Tennis club, until he reached the Hallcroft Roundabout and turned right along Bridgegate. A police car had parked sideways across the street just past Rectory Road and an officer directing the oncoming traffic away from the crime scene. Rob pulled up and showed the officer his ID.

"Morning, Officer," Rob said.

"Aaah, good morning, sir," he replied after checking the badge and waved him through.

Further up, they came to the outer cordon and were similarly allowed to drive through and park a short distance from the inner cordon, along with the other emergency vehicles in attendance.

As he climbed out of the car, Rob's phone vibrated in his pocket. He fished it out and checked the caller ID, but it was a mobile number he didn't recognise.

"Hold on a moment," Rob said, waving his phone at Scarlett as she exited the other side of the vehicle. He tapped accept and put the phone to his ear. "Hello?"

"Aaah, morning," a female voice answered on the other end of the line. "Is that Detective Loxley?"

"Speaking," Rob replied. He didn't recognise the woman right away.

He glanced up at Scarlett, who watched him with a frown. She gave him a look that asked, who is it?

He shrugged. "Who is this?"

"DI Powers, from the Met. I believe you wanted to speak to me about the Wells case."

"Aaah, yes. I did. Thanks for calling me back." He smiled over at Scarlett and gave her a thumbs-up. "You were involved in the Roxy Wells rape case against Truman Collins, I believe?"

"I was, yes. That's a few years ago, though."

"Four years," Rob clarified. "Since it happened, that is."

"That's about right."

"Well, the reason for the call is because Roxy has been kidnapped. A group of men attacked her the night before last in a Newark car park and threw her into the back of a van.

96

We've been talking to her friends and family about it, and they all say it must be Truman Collins because of her case against him. So I was curious what your thoughts on this were and if you had any insight. Do you think Truman would be capable of hiring some thugs to abduct Roxy?"

"Capable? Well, he certainly has the resources to pay for it, that's for sure. He's a very wealthy man. But as for whether he'd actually do such a thing, I'm less sure."

"I've been led to believe that Roxy's case against him ended up causing him some problems that he might well bear a grudge for."

"You're talking about his wife, right? Well, it's true that after Ellen Collins found out what he'd allegedly been up to with Roxy and others around his office, she left him and put him through a painful divorce. That much is certainly true. She took him for everything she could and got a massive payout, plus a bunch of his assets. She also got full custody of their kids, and he sees them maybe once or twice a week now."

"So, he's pissed about that, right?"

"He wasn't happy, that is true. But was he upset enough to take his revenge on Roxy? That is a lot harder to answer, although in my experience, it pays never to underestimate the depths someone will go to when they have no other choice."

97

"So you think he could do this?"

"Maybe. But I think most parents who love their kids would go the great lengths to protect and be around them. Wouldn't you?"

"I'm single and don't have kids," Rob replied. "But I am quite aware of the lengths family will go to for something they care about."

"Well, there you go then. Have you spoken to Mr Collins yet?"

"No. He was out of the country yesterday, but I believe he's back sometime today."

"He lives in Surrey these days."

"I know. I've got a friend down there who will pay him a visit for me," Rob explained.

"Oh? And who's that?"

"DCI Pilgrim?"

"Of course. I know him," she replied. "Okay. Well, if you need anything further from me, let me know. I'm happy to help."

"Thank you, DI Powers."

"Call me Kristal, and good luck with your investigation."

"Thanks, Kristal." He ended the call and turned to Scarlett, who'd perched herself on the car's front wing. "All done."

"Was that useful?" she asked.

"Potentially. I'd certainly consider her a much more neutral outside observer than the Wells family, plus she'll have investigated Truman and maybe even have spoken to him. So I think she could be valuable."

"And what was her opinion then? Does she think Truman did it?"

Rob pulled a face. "She was more diplomatic than that. She thinks he might well be capable of paying for this but stopped short of saying that he will have done it, for obvious reasons."

"So nothing groundbreaking, then."

"No. But I'm glad I spoke to her. Anyway, we'll deal with the Roxy thing later. Let's see what's going on here."

Scarlett nodded in agreement as they walked towards the inner cordon, where a waiting officer signed them in and directed them towards a nearby woman wearing a white forensic suit pulled down to her waist. Aged approximately in her thirties, she had long dark hair that she'd tied up and looked up as they approached.

"Hi, how can I help you?" She glanced at their IDs.

Rob offered his hand. "Detective Inspector Loxley, and this is DC Scarlett Stutely, EMSOU."

She took his hand and shook it, but her face betrayed her as a look of annoyance flashed over her features. "Oh, you made it then. Better late than never, I suppose."

"Yeah, sorry. It's a trek from the city. We got here as soon as we could."

"Mmm," she grunted. "Right, well, I'm Sergeant Susanna Parsons. Nice to meet you, I guess. I suppose you'd like to see the body?"

"That would be nice," he answered, getting an odd feeling about her. She didn't seem too pleased to see them.

"Grab a forensic suit over there and come and find me." She pointed to a nearby van before wandering off up the road, untying her barrier suit and slipping it back on.

He watched her go and then led the way to the nearby van and removing one of the overalls sealed in plastic. "She's a grumpy one," Rob remarked as he pulled the oversuit on.

"Well, you can be a disagreeable bugger at the best of times," Scarlett groused while slipping a leg into her own suit.

"I suppose I walked right into that one."

"Give her a chance. She probably doesn't like us slick city folk coming here and taking over."

"Well, she'll have to lump it because that's our job."

"You tell her that. See how well it goes down." She smiled, amused.

"Err, no. I'll just put on my most winning smile and be super nice to her."

"That'll work," Scarlett said, deadpan, her words dripping with sarcasm. "Right, come on then, Mr Agreeable, let's see what these provincial country folk have for us."

"Oi. I grew up here, you know."

"Oh yeah, I forgot. Are your family here, too?"

"Probably. Not that I'm about to go looking for them." Rob glanced up the road towards the outer cordon and the knots of people and reporters standing just outside it. He didn't recognise anyone, but that didn't mean they weren't already here, watching. "Just keep an eye out."

"I will, don't worry."

"Right then, missy. Are you ready?"

"I'm waiting on you, slow coach."

They walked up the road in the direction Susanna had gone and soon found her waiting for them.

As they neared the bridge, Rob made out the other side of the cordon further along the road leading into the town centre. It had been years since he'd been here, but he knew it well, and the feeling of being back in Mason territory chilled him.

Susanna waited for them beside a gate on this side of the bridge that led onto a narrow gravel path along this side of the river. Walking through, they kept to the designated route that had been marked out for them to use. Susanna approached the low wooden railing on the riverbank and pointed out into the river where several police divers worked, scanning the riverbed for clues.

"The body was found over there, snagged on that branch which kept it from sinking. We've since removed the body from the river and have it over there, in the car park." Susanna pointed to a white tent visible through the trees that lined the far bank.

"All right. Let's take a gander, shall we?" Rob turned back to the gate but did a double-take on seeing some elaborate graffiti on this side of the wall. It showed a huge red man looming over several miniature buildings, including a crude representation of the Retford Town Hall. Beneath it, the words *Red Man Rules* were artfully drawn in spray paint. It was skilfully done. "Wow."

Susanna grunted. "Less said about that, the better."

Rob gave her a look. "What? I mean, I'm not the biggest fan of graffiti, but you have to admit, that's impressive."

"Oh, right. Erm, yeah. I guess."

Narrowing his eyes, Rob wondered what he'd missed. "Why? What were you thinking I meant?"

She pointed to it. "The Red Man? Have you not heard...? It's a thing... Don't worry about it. It's not important. Come on." She led them back out onto the street and over the bridge.

He followed her into the car park on the other side where a small, boxy tent, guarded by police, waited for them. On the side facing the river, so as few people as possible could see in, the entrance flap was pulled to one side, revealing a lifeless and pale body laid out on a sheet. Around him, forensics officers worked, taking photos and checking him over.

Rob estimated he was in his early twenties, in jeans, trainers and a hoody, and it looked like he'd been subjected to a sustained assault. He was covered in cuts and bruises, although the blood had long since been washed away by the river.

"Jesus," Scarlett hissed.

"Wow. He suffered," Rob remarked.

"It seems that way," Susanna agreed. "He was badly beaten before being dumped into the river. We don't yet know if it was the attack that killed him or if he drowned."

"I'm sure the pathologist will be able to clear that up," Rob muttered. "What about ID? Do we know who this guy is?"

"There's no ID on him, no phone, nothing. That's what we have the divers searching for."

"What about the dumping site? Where did our victim enter the river?"

"We're looking into that now," Susanna explained. "We'll search both sides of the river up into the park, but we think it was somewhere between here and the park bridge, because just past it is a small weir that a body would probably have got caught on had he been thrown in on the other side of it."

"So that gives us a limited area to work with."

"It does. We're organising search teams to see what they can find."

"Excellent. Although, his attackers probably stole his wallet and phone to prevent easy identification."

"Yeah, we know," Susanna said. "Right. Is there anything else?"

Rob grimaced at her gruff attitude but let it slide. "No, I don't think so."

"Will you be running this investigation from Retford or back at HQ?"

"I think we need a local base of operations," Rob answered. "Is there somewhere we can use?"

The cloud over Susanna's mood seemed to darken, but there was little she could do. "Right. Okay, why don't you come back to the station so we can discuss it," she replied, clearly frustrated by his request.

"Sounds good," Rob agreed, determined to remain friendly and calm in the face of her hostility.

He shot her a winning smile, but she didn't seem to notice and turned away.

She took two steps before turning back to him. "Do you know where you're going?"

"To the station?" Rob clarified. "Yeah. I used to live here. Don't worry."

Her eyebrows climbed up her forehead. "You used to live in Retford?"

"I was raised here. It's my home town."

"Oh." A brief look of approval washed over her features before she turned and walked away. "Okay. See you shortly."

"You're in there," Scarlett remarked, leaning in to stage whisper to him.

"You think?"

"Oh yeah, she wants you. She wants you bad."

Rob smirked. "I doubt that. Come on, Stutely, let's go ruffle some more feathers."

15

In Nottingham, Bill sat in the window of the small café just south of Arnold on the Mansfield Road and quietly seethed. The coffee before him slowly cooled as steam rose from the untouched cup. He'd bought it because there was little chance of him sitting here unquestioned without it, but he'd forgotten about the drink ages ago.

Instead, he focused on the napkin he held in both hands and slowly tore it to shreds. He ripped it into tiny pieces until he was left with nothing but a pile of shredded tissue paper.

Then he got another and did the same while imagining it was Rob Loxley, and he was tearing the smug son of a bitch limb from limb, making him suffer like a child might torture a mayfly by pulling its legs off.

One day, he'd get his revenge on Loxley for what he'd done. He'd enjoy humiliating Rob and causing him pain as he poured out his hate on that little bastard. One day, at some point in the future, he'd get his chance. Rob couldn't dodge him forever.

But thoughts of Rob only angered him further, his rage boiling up inside and threatening to bubble over. Pulling the napkin into his fists, Bill clenched them, squeezing them tight as he gritted his teeth and screwed his eyes shut.

Rob would get what was coming to him one day. Images of him punching Rob in the face, sending teeth and blood flying, played in his mind's eye. But he couldn't allow himself to get too upset over what had happened. He needed his wits about him. He needed to relax.

Sucking in several deep breaths, Bill calmed his heart rate and allowed the rage to cool and return to a near-constant simmer. It was always there, just below the surface, hot and ready to boil over at a moment's notice, and he'd been like that since the day he'd been dismissed from the police.

That was Rob's fault.

His career had been everything to him, and he'd relished his job, even in the face of certain hatred. The police needed to be free of corruption, otherwise, the public trust would falter. That could never happen, which meant there was a need for the police to monitor their own and root out the bad apples early.

The wider police force might distrust the units who watched their own, but it was essential. Bill had found his calling in the Police Standards Unit, especially after Loxley had told him about his links to the Mason crime family.

After that, Rob became his pet project, but it seemed that no matter how much he tried to make others see him for what he was, he was either ignored or told to drop it.

And after his latest failure, his logical conclusion was that the police could be beyond saving. They were corrupt to the core, and without systemic reform, nothing would change.

He'd hoped to be a part of that change, but it seemed the police were done with him, and there was no going back.

The café door opened, and Guy Gibson stepped into the small shop. He paused at the door and locked eyes with Bill as if reconsidering their meeting before he sighed to himself and walked in, sliding into the seat opposite.

"About bloody time," Bill sneered.

"Piss off," Guy replied. "I'm here, aren't I? It's what you wanted. That's what your hundreds of phone calls were about, right?"

Bill curled his lip in disgust. "Don't act like you weren't part of this. You don't get to walk away and forget about what I did. I was the one who took the risks, and I was the one to suffer the consequences. You're as guilty as I am."

"I took risks," Guy hissed. "I'm taking one now, being here with you in public. I'm sure there would be a few questions if we were seen talking."

Bill waved his words away. "You hate Rob just as much as I do."

"So what?" Guy asked. "What do you want from me, Bill? And no, I can't get your job back."

"What do I want? I thought that would be obvious. I want Rob out of the police. I want his career in tatters and his true allegiances revealed. That's always been what I wanted. Or did you forget? The job's not done, Guy. Rob is still a serving officer of the law."

"And what do you want me to do about it?"

"I want you to stop ignoring my calls, stop blanking me and work with me."

"Or what?"

"Or I'll reveal your part in what we did."

"My part?" Guy asked, putting on an innocent expression. "I'm quite sure I don't know what you mean."

"Don't play coy with me. We both know what you did, and it wouldn't take much to prove it. Or do you not think I've taken precautions?"

"Is that a threat? It's not a good way to get what you want."

Bill scoffed at Guy's bravado. "It got you here, didn't it? And you're not storming off either, so I beg to differ. I can ruin you, just like Rob ruined me."

"Expose me, then. See what happens?" Guy pushed. "You're not the only one to take precautions, you know. I have a backup plan if things go pear-shaped."

"What are you going to do? Go crying to Mummy?"

"Fuck off."

"Oh, I forgot, your dad's a former officer, right?" Guy smiled and chuckled to himself. "I bet he was pissed... or have you not told him?"

Bill shrugged as he thought back to his first visit to his parents following his dismissal and the almost deranged rant his dad had subjected him to. He'd been furious and made Bill feel like a disobedient schoolboy. "He knew. He's still got friends in the police, so he knew before I got home. He probably knew before I was thrown out."

Guy shrugged. "That sucks."

"He heard about everything I did when I was on the force. I couldn't put a foot out of line without him ranting to me about it. He thinks I'm tainting the family name if you can believe that. He hated me for joining anticorruption, and now he hates me for getting sacked. But I'll show him. I show him *and* Rob. You wait."

"You think you can still bring Rob down now you're not on the force?" Guy asked, sounding curious.

"Why not? Why should that stop me? It might make it easier."

Guy looked away and frowned for a moment. "Actually, it might."

"You agree?"

"Yeah?" He seemed a little taken with this new idea. "You're not bound by the limitations of the police anymore.

110

You can do whatever's needed to make this happen now. You could even work outside the law."

Bill frowned at the man opposite. He seemed thrilled with the idea, judging by his sudden enthusiasm and tone of voice. But Bill wasn't sure. "I don't think..."

"No, this is perfect. Now you're not an officer, Rob doesn't stand a chance. You can play dirty, but Rob can't."

"We already tried that, or did you forget? Planting that money in Rob's apartment was hardly what I would call working within the bounds of the law, and I was the one who took the heat for you."

"And I never thanked you for that, did I?" Guy replied with a smug smile.

"No, you didn't. But next time, we'll do it the other way around. I'll plant the evidence, and you can take the heat."

"Fair enough." Guy answered. He smiled, seeming almost giddy with excitement. "Now that you're no longer an officer, you can finally get your sweet revenge."

Bill shook his head at Guy's remark. "I might not be an officer any longer, but I can still go the prison. So don't expect me to put a gun to Rob's head."

Guy smiled. "I wouldn't complain if you did, and besides, you have an officer on the inside who might be able to help you out a bit if you do get into any trouble with the police."

Bill wasn't sure he could take Guy at his word, but he'd love to be proved wrong. "You can get me off a murder charge?"

Guy raised an eyebrow. "Well, maybe not..."

Bill sneered at him. "Yeah, thought as much. It's a nice idea, but I want to enjoy my freedom *after* Rob is locked up. I don't fancy joining him in there."

Guy shrugged. "Whatever."

A phone buzzed.

Bill checked his pocket, but it wasn't him. One second later, Guy pulled out his phone. Bill caught a glimpse of the text notification and recognised the name of the person who'd sent it.

"That's not the Erika who lives next door to Rob, is it?"

Guy's head snapped up. He fixed Bill with a glare before glancing down at his phone. "You know her?"

"In passing," Bill said. "She acted weird once when I paid Rob a visit. It was as if she was protecting him and stopping me seeing something in Rob's apartment."

"Like what?"

"I don't know, she never said and just made up some bullshit excuse for why she dragged me into her apartment." He made a dismissive wave with his hand. "She seems a little crazy for my tastes."

"We could all do with a little crazy in our lives from time to time," Guy replied, putting his phone away. He looked up and gave Bill an appraising glare. "Especially you."

"What I *need* is a partner who's going to help me bring Rob down, and if you truly hate Rob as much as you said, then I think we need to stick together." He fixed Guy with an expectant expression, hoping he'd agree.

"Stick together?"

"Do you want Rob out of the police or not?" Bill snapped, staring at the other man.

"Of course." Guy stared back, his eyes cold and severe but also inscrutable.

Bill couldn't get a read off Guy at all and wondered what his real motivation around Rob was.

Maybe he'd find out one day.

16

Rob glanced up the road towards the knot of journalists and onlookers as he unzipped his white overall. "I can see the headline already," he muttered. "Blood Red Ford."

"Excuse me?" Scarlett looked confused.

"Hmm? Oh. Retford. Legends has it that the town was founded on a red clay ford over the river, and was originally named Red Ford. That changed over time to Retford."

"I see." She didn't sound too impressed. "How very poetic."

"I know right. I have a gift for words."

"If you say so. I don't think she liked us very much," Scarlett remarked as they finished removing their forensic suits and stuffed them in the bin bag at the van.

Susanna had walked away, leaving them alone, but Rob noticed how Scarlett kept her voice low and checked her surroundings before she spoke.

"We're outsiders interfering on her patch, so I get it." Rob gave Scarlett a cocky look. "But I think she liked me just fine. She clearly hates you, though."

Scarlett blew a raspberry at him. "You think that's all it is? She doesn't like us interfering?"

Rob grunted, adjusted his jacket and pulled on his coat. "Now who's paranoid? I know we've dealt with a lot of police corruption, but not everyone's on the take, Stutely."

"I know. I'm just keeping my mind open, as all good detectives should."

Rob smirked. "Should I write that one down? That's a good tip."

She gave him the finger. "What's up with you today? You're full of jokes."

He sighed as they walked up the road towards his car. "I don't know. Maybe it's just being back in Retford. It's put me on edge."

Before he got in, he checked to see if they could get through the crime scene, but there was no way they were doing that. He'd have to go right around the town to get to the police station.

"Everything okay?" Scarlett asked when he finally joined her in the car.

"Yeah, there's just no fast way to get where we need to go. We've got to go right around the town."

Scarlett shrugged. "That's okay. You can give me the guided tour."

Rob gave her side-eye. "There's not much to see, honestly. Retford isn't exactly London. It's a small market town with not a lot going on."

Scarlet pointed at the crime scene before them. "I beg to differ."

"Usually," Rob clarified and started to turn the car around.

"Don't talk it down. It looks like a lovely little town. You're making it out to be some backwater in the arse end of nowhere."

Rob sighed, aware of his own prejudices. "I know. I just have history here, that's all."

"I understand that. But it doesn't have to taint everything."

"No, I guess not."

"But, seeing as we're here and the subject has just come up, do you know where your family are?"

"Where they are?" Rob glanced at Scarlett as they left the cordon and headed back up Bridgegate towards the Hallcroft Roundabout.

"Where do they live?"

"It's been over twenty years since I last had meaningful contact with them, and it's not as if I've been keeping tabs on them. I want nothing to do with my dad or his... firm."

"So, where did he live?"

Rob sighed as he recalled his childhood and the house he'd called home so long ago. Those memories were filled with images of his mother, with whom he spent much of his time growing up. He knew now that his mother had been trying to protect him from his father's influence and keep Rob out of the firm, but back then, he hadn't understood it, not as fully as he did now.

He missed his mother.

"The family home was a big house out on London Road, in the White Houses area, as it's known. But he owns property all over Retford and the county. I spent most of my childhood there. It was the house that had the least connection to the firm, too. That's probably why my mum liked it."

"Okay, and where is that?"

"South," Rob answered as they approached Hallcroft Roundabout and made their way around it. "A few minutes' drive from here."

"Cool." She turned to look out the window. "It's nice."

"It's a roundabout," Rob said, deadpan.

"It's a nice roundabout."

"Hmm."

"So, have you never returned since you left twenty years ago?"

Rob shrugged. "Not for any meaningful length of time, no. I've passed through, but I usually try to avoid it. It can be interesting coming back, though, and seeing what's changed."

"See," Scarlett replied, smiling. "It is nice coming home. You shouldn't let your family taint this for you. This is your home town, too, you know. You must have some fond memories of it."

"Yeah, I do. Mainly of my mother."

"Good. Oooh, look, you've got a Morrisons here. Nice."

Rob chuckled and shook his head. "Yeah, lovely. It's a real draw for the tourists."

Rob Drove along Amcott Way to the traffic lights.

"Home Bargains!" Scarlett exclaimed. "Quality shop."

"Jesus," Rob sighed as the lights changed and he turned right up Arlington Way.

"Huh. There's more of it there."

"Hmm? More of what?" Rob tried to follow where Scarlett pointed and only saw a small triangle of grass beside the road, surrounded by vandalised red-brick walls.

"That Red Man graffiti. Over there, too."

She gestured out of Rob's side of the car, and now he saw it.

Redman's Retford, it read, scrawled over the wall with back spray paint. This wasn't like the work of art he'd seen at the crime scene. This was just an eyesore.

"Ugh," Rob grunted in disgust.

"What's all that about then?" Scarlett asked, curious.

"I have no idea," Rob replied, baffled.

"So, it wasn't a thing when you lived here?"

"Not that I remember," he confirmed, frowning. He tried to think back, but nothing presented itself from the depths of his memory. "It's probably some gang leader or something trying to muscle in on the Masons' patch."

"Yeah, maybe," Scarlett muttered, but she didn't sound convinced.

"Good luck to 'em, I say. They'll have a hell of a job dealing with the Masons. They're about as entrenched as it gets."

"Maybe I'll ask the guys at the station. Maybe one of them will know."

"Go for it. I'll be interested to see what they say after seeing Susanna's reaction to the art at the crime scene."

Rob drove through several more sets of lights before turning right after the bus station and cutting down New Street, past a car park on their right that used to serve the old Co-op that was no longer there, and a building supplier opposite.

Turning left onto Carolgate, Scarlett cooed while looking behind them at the pedestrianised high street. "See. There's some nice shops up there. It's quite cute really."

"That is not a word I'd use to describe Retford," Rob remarked. They bore right at the T-junction and set off down Wharf Road, passing the fire station and the Little Theatre before they arced back on themselves. The road changed into

Chancery Lane as they finally headed north again towards the crime scene.

Kings Park, the town's main park, was on their left, and again it triggered memories. Rob recalled spending hours here with his mother, playing on the swings and slides, having picnics, enjoying the crappy crazy golf course it once had and a thousand other things that they'd done together.

Although he'd not realised it then, she was most likely trying to keep him away from the lure of his father's business. When he was young, he remembered that his mother would include his older brothers in her trips out, but as they'd got older and harder to control, they'd peeled away from her until it was just him.

Somehow, over the years, she'd perfected her technique for keeping them away from his father's influence and applied everything she'd learnt to Rob, but even then, he'd only got away by the skin of his teeth.

After his mother had disappeared, it was only because John Nailer had found him that he'd escaped at all. He'd had a lucky escape and owed his current crime-free life to Nailer. That wasn't something that would be easy to repay.

Part way up Chancery Lane, opposite Exchange Street, Rob pulled in to a crescent-shaped parking area at the main entrance of Kings Park and stopped.

"Are we here?" Scarlett asked and opened her door.

"Yep," Rob confirmed and climbed out after her.

"Erm, I don't think this is right."

"Hmm?" Rob looked up at the building on the corner of Exchange Street and Chancery Lane and realised his mistake. "Aaah, shit."

The large red-brick building on the corner had an impressive tan archway entrance with the words *Police Station* carved into it, but it was deceptive. Once, years ago, this had been the town's police station, but it had long since closed and was now both a bar and hotel, called The Old Police Station and the Kings Park Hotel, respectively.

Having found out years ago, Rob had known, but he'd forgotten this little detail.

"Sorry, my mistake," Rob muttered. "Although, if you fancy a drink...?"

"Maybe later," Scarlett answered with a wry smile. "So, where do we go now?"

"I think..." Rob began as he fished his phone out and checked Google Maps. "Aaah, yes, we're close. It's just round here."

They returned to the car and set off again, around another car park and pulling in behind the Town Hall, to a small parking area with a scattering of police cars and other vehicles inside. They got through the barrier with little

121

difficulty and found Susanna standing waiting for them with her arms crossed and a scowl on her stern face.

"Another warm welcome," Scarlett remarked. She went for her seat belt.

Rob met Scarlett's gaze briefly but said nothing and climbed out.

"You took your time," Susanna said without any greeting.

"Stopped to take a look at the Old Police Station."

"Aaah. It's a nice bar, actually. You should try it. As a former Retfordian and current detective, I think you'd appreciate it."

"I'll take a gander."

She grunted and glanced at his car. "Into your classic cars, then?"

Rob shrugged. "I guess." He didn't see the need to get into the story of it being a present from his mother in the days before she'd disappeared. It wasn't any of her business.

She seemed slightly offended by his curt reply and rolled her eyes. "Let's get you set up then, shall we?"

17

Stepping out of the shower, Mary Day grabbed the nearby towel and buried her head in it. She tried to shake the anxious feeling that had taken root deep inside her and was so far refusing to budge. She'd slept terribly, tossing and turning all night while thoughts of what could have been rattled around her mind.

Worse still, she had no idea what had happened to her informant. He'd run the other way, and that had been the last she'd seen of him.

Was he okay? Had those men caught up to him?

Frankly, it felt like a miracle that she'd lost them and got out of the park without too much trouble. The drive back to Nottingham had been a nervous one, with her hands shaking the whole way home as she'd tried to process what had happened.

He'd not given her much before those thugs had turned up and chased them through the park, but what he had told her had been enough to churn her stomach. He'd confirmed something about a pet research project she'd been working on for years now, but it was only with last night's meeting that she felt she was getting any closer to the truth.

There were still so many questions she needed answers to, but at least now, if he was to be trusted, she knew one thing that she hadn't before.

The Red Man was real.

She'd written two articles on the phenomenon over the last few years as she'd looked into the urban myth that gripped the small north Notts town of Retford and had spoken to all kinds of people about it, trying to get to the bottom of a tale that seemed to thrive in the shadows. She'd chatted to the graffiti artists who daubed the Red Man's name all over the town and beyond, and to teenage gang members, house owners, local councillors, and police officers. But until now, no one had been able to give her anything concrete.

To some, he was just a bogeyman parents used to scare their kids into behaving. Others believed he was a serial killer or a local gang leader, but no one had ever met him or truly knew what he did or who he was.

It was always the same old story.

My mate's friend heard from someone that they'd been told... et cetera. No one ever had direct knowledge or experience of the mysterious man. And yet, his shadow seemed to loom large over the residents, not least because of the endless graffiti about him that was just everywhere.

But last night, the informant assured her that not only was the Red Man real, but that he'd met him several times and knew what he did because...

She shook her head, preferring not to think about it too much. Thoughts about her meeting and the chaos that had erupted when those thugs had turned up only served to make her feel worse.

No, she needed to put it out of her mind until she got to work, and then she could look into it more and see if she could reopen communication with the contact who had put her in touch with the informant.

She had a horrible feeling the informant would not want to talk to her anymore, though, not after what had happened. But she'd needed to try. She was on the brink of something huge, and she needed to know more.

With a sigh, she pushed those thoughts from her mind and finished up in the bathroom, drying and dressing herself before finally heading down to breakfast.

"Morning," Vanessa, her housemate, said brightly as she walked in.

She was sitting with her boyfriend, Ben, at the kitchen table, and they were both all smiles and happiness. A world away from Mary's clandestine meetings in the middle of the night.

"You were out late last night."

"I was working, chasing up a story."

"Aaah."

"Did you stay over last night?" Mary asked Ben and caught the look Vanessa gave her.

He smiled like the cat that got the cream. "Yeah. Is that okay?"

"I guess."

As Ben glanced away, she met Vanessa's gaze and wiggled her eyebrows.

Vanessa rolled her eyes.

"What's the story about? Anything juicy?" Ben asked, referring to her meeting. "Should I keep an eye on the papers in the next few weeks, or can you give me the inside scoop?"

Mary pulled a face. "I need more info before I write anything yet. The meeting didn't quite go to plan."

"Oh?" Vanessa asked, peering at her. "Are you okay?"

"Fine. I'm fine. Don't worry about me."

"Oh, sorry. That's tough," Ben remarked. "I'm not sure I could do your job."

"Likewise," Mary shot back. "I'm terrible with blood, so I wouldn't be any good as a paramedic."

Ben shrugged. "You learn to deal with it. I think Vanessa's got the rougher deal out of the two of us, though."

"I don't know about that," Vanessa answered. "I think both jobs are tough. How about we swap sometime to see?

I'll drive your ambulance, and you can have a day on the ward."

Ben laughed. "You'd like that, wouldn't you. No more wiping old men's arses for a living, hey."

She punched him in the arm. "I think there's a little more to it than that."

As their conversation moved on to more mundane affairs, Mary grabbed some toast and marmalade before they left the house. Ben went to the hospital with Vanessa in her car while Mary jumped into her little Mini Cooper.

The morning roads were the usual nightmare of snarled traffic and angry drivers.

Making her way into town and the office of the *Nottingham Echo* paper, Mary parked up in her usual place and walked the short distance through the throng of people also making their way to work.

Dodging through the crowds as the city came to life around her, she didn't have time to think about the events of the night before, and it wasn't until her building came into view and she spotted a couple of fellow journalists that she realised she needed to face up to the events of the previous night.

For a brief moment, the thought of going in rooted her to the spot as the bottom fell out of her stomach. Was it the knowledge that the Red Man was real, complete with hired goons who wanted to kill her, or was it that she would have to face up to her boss about the mostly failed scoop she was supposed to have had this morning?

She grimaced and swallowed nervously at the memory of telling her boss about the huge scoop she would get about her Red Man story. Apart from the word of a random stranger, she had no proof that the Red Man was real and no way to reach out to the informant directly. She'd need to get in touch with her contact and see if they could arrange a second meeting.

Annoyed, frustrated, and anxious, she resolved to enter the building with her head held high. She might not have everything she needed, but at least she had a story. It would be a fluff piece without any further contact from the informant, but it was better than nothing.

A passing pedestrian bumped into her. She stumbled.

"Hey," she called out.

"Move it," the man called back as he strode off with barely a backward glance.

She sighed and pressed on. Better to get it over with so she could crack on with work and try to make something of all this

The lift ride up to her floor passed all too quickly.

Once out of the lift, she wandered around to the open-plan office she called home during the working hours of the day and saw the usual familiar faces she shared it with. She nodded and smiled but kept her voice down and hoped to pass unnoticed to her desk.

"Day," an all-too-familiar voice called out.

It was both gruff and shrill at the same time, which was something of a feat in itself, and it cut right through to her soul. Coming to a sudden and almost involuntary halt with the shock of the shout, she turned as editor-in-chief Palmer Cobb leaned out of his side office. She smiled at the overweight man and the sight of his impressive belly, barely held in check by the stretched-tight shirt.

"Sir." She walked over to stop him from raising his voice further and making even more of a scene than he already was. "What's up?"

"Don't play coy with me, Day. You had your meeting last night, right? The big scoop on this Red Man obsession of yours. Did anything come of it?"

His condescending tone grated on her nerves, but there was little she could do about that. Well, she had to offer him something to try and keep him from telling her to drop it.

"We met," she confirmed.

"Aaah, so he was real then, was he? Not some figment of your imagination?"

"Of course he was real and knew what he was talking about. But the meeting was, um... interrupted, so I'm going to have to try and reschedule."

"That's a shame. So did the snitch have anything to tell you about this bogeyman you're *so* obsessed with? Or can you get back to some *actual* journalism for once? I think you've spent enough time on this, don't you?"

The knot in her belly that had twisted into place when he'd first called her name gripped tighter at his suggestion that she move on. "I'm not so sure, sir. There's something big here. I know it."

He sighed. "All *I* know is that you're wasting company hours on a wild goose chase, Day. I need results from you, all right? If this goes nowhere, then find another story."

"I understand. I will, sir. Don't worry."

He grunted. "You could be doing something useful, like covering the murder in Retford last night. You were there, after all."

"What?" Mary's heart skipped a beat. "Murder?"

"Yeah, in the park. Someone was found in the river. You're a little late to the party, though, Day. While you were getting your beauty sleep, some of us were working. Now go on, get out of here and come back to me when you have something concrete."

He walked away as the yawning hole beneath her threatened to swallow her hole. A murder? In Retford's park? Could it be?

She turned, raced to her PC, and logged in. It only took a few seconds to find the story that was developing in the small north Notts town, and for the suffocating fear to grip her even tighter than it already had.

Palmer was right. A body had been found in the River Idle towards the centre of Retford, at one edge of the park. Right now, the report continued, the body remained unidentified.

"I bet I know who you are..." she whispered.

Shit. She looked away from the horror story on her screen and tried to think straight. What should she do?

She closed her eyes and attempted to think about this logically without freaking out. First things first, she needed to confirm the identity of the victim. Was it the informant, or was it someone else? That was key. But how could she do that?

Her contact!

Yes. That was the easiest way. She just needed to get in touch with her contact, the one who'd put her in touch with the informant.

Pulling out her phone, she navigated to the curious name her contact had given her and stared at the single word.

Riddle.

Mary had been in touch with the hacker, Riddle, for a couple of years at this point, although they had never met or even spoken before. All their correspondence had been over emails and a messenger chat that Riddle had set up on a weird, encrypted app that Mary had never heard of before, and it was only recently that Riddle had agreed to share their phone number with her. Mary wanted a way to get in touch with Riddle quickly should something bad happen, and the Hacker had eventually agreed and given Mary a phone number on the proviso that she only used it in an emergency.

She paused for a moment and considered the situation that she found herself in, before finally hitting call. If this didn't qualify as an emergency, she wasn't sure what did.

The line connected after three rings.

"Mary," said a digitally distorted voice. It was impossible to decern gender.

"Riddle," Mary answered. "Have you seen the news?"

"About the murder? In Retford?"

"Yeah," Mary replied, disliking that this murder was already on Riddle's Radar. "Is it...?"

"I don't know. Maybe. The only contact I've had with either of you was your message last night, saying that you'd met but had been interrupted. I've not heard from him yet. I can try to get in touch, though. What happened?"

"A group of men appeared and chased us. I got away, but I don't know what happened to him."

"Fuck. That sounds like them. Shit. Where are you?"

"At work," Mary answered without thinking about it.

"You want my advice? Get out, now. Assume he knows where you live, where you work, and who your family and friends are. He's got eyes and ears everywhere. Do you understand?"

"Er, yeah, but where do I go?"

"I don't know, and you shouldn't tell me either. I don't want to know. Also, I'd advise you pay for anything with cash for the foreseeable."

"You're kidding."

"Look, you do what you want. But you've already told me that after your previous two Red Man articles, you noticed cars following you and the anonymous death threats you got. Imagine how the Red Man will feel when he knows his secret is out? Do you want to be there to find out how pissed he is?"

Mary thought back to the death threats and the times she'd ben followed and shivered.

"I understand," Mary replied. "Thanks."

"Good luck."

Grabbing her things, she stood and marched out of the office, wondering when she'd return.

18

Rob raised a hand to Susanna as she waved them towards the station.

"I'll be there in a moment. I just need to report back to my DCI."

"All right," Susanna muttered with a shrug. She crossed her arms and put her back to the wall beside the door while she waited.

He was expecting an eye roll, but she stopped short of that, much to his surprise.

Dismissing her bad attitude, he turned away and glanced up at Scarlett while he pulled his phone out. "I won't be a moment. You go ahead."

"I'll wait here, by the car, if it's all the same," Scarlett remarked in low tones. "She might bite."

Rob grunted and called Nailer.

"Rob, how's it going up in Retford? I know it's been a while."

It was reassuring to hear his friend and mentor's voice as he walked out of earshot of Susanna.

"Yeah, it has. Nothing I can't handle, though," he reassured his boss. "I was always going to end up back here at some point. Might as well get it over and done with."

"Yeah, true," Nailer agreed, sounding sympathetic.

"It's going all right so far, although the local sergeant is being less than friendly. I don't think she likes us muscling in on her patch."

"You two play nice up there," Nailer said in a mock warning tone. "I'm sure she'll come round."

"One can hope," Rob said and glanced back at Susanna.

She scowled across the car park at him. Rob waved cheerily at her, and she rolled her eyes in reply. Aaah, there it is, he thought, smiling to himself.

"And the case? What have you got up there?"

Rob turned away from Susanna and concentrated as he recalled the details so far. "We have an IC1 male, mid-twenties, found in the River Idle close to Retford Town centre on the edge of Kings Park early this morning by a runner. It looks like he was badly beaten, but we're not sure if he died of his injuries or drowned, but I guess we'll find out soon enough. Either way, we have a murder investigation up here."

"And an abduction in Newark," Nailer reminded him.

Rob grimaced at the mention of the other case they had going on. "I'll leave that to Nick. He can work with Ellen and Guy."

"No problem. So, what's your next move?"

"I'm about to head into Retford station and discuss it with their sergeant, so we'll see how that plays out, but I think we'll need some kind of base up here."

He thought back to the Clipstone investigation and how useful it was to be local. It was the obvious choice to make. He was less sure about where that base should be, though. The Retford station wasn't a twenty-four-hour building, so that might make things difficult.

"Do what you need to do, Rob," Nailer stated, his voice confident and supportive. "I'll back you all the way on whatever course of action you feel is best."

"Thanks. I'll be in touch."

"No problem. Talk soon."

Rob hung up.

"That sounded positive," Scarlett commented.

"It was. He'll support us however we choose to move this case forward."

"Perfect," Scarlett remarked. "And it sounds like you're leaving Nick in charge of the abduction?"

"Yeah," Rob agreed. He could have given Nick this case and stayed out of Retford, but he felt a need to be here and finally start to confront the demons of his past. He'd been away from Retford for a long time, and while he didn't plan on moving back anytime soon, or ever, he didn't want to have to avoid it his whole life. Besides, if he was going to take the fight to the Masons and bring them down, he'd need to come here one day.

"Will you be bringing Tucker up here then?"

"Maybe. Let's see how things go, shall we?" Rob answered.

They walked across the small courtyard and approached Susanna, who looked bored and exasperated by the whole affair.

"Ready now?" she asked as if she was talking to a particularly dumb child.

But Rob just smiled and allowed her venom to wash off him. "Absolutely. Lead the way."

He glanced at Scarlett, who seemed to be bristling beside him before he followed the sergeant in through the rear security door.

They made their way upstairs to a room with numerous desks inside, laden with monitors, keyboards, files, and empty coffee mugs. Several uniformed officers worked on the computers. In the middle of the room, talking to one of the seated officers, was a young woman who didn't look like she was out of her twenties. She had blonde hair tied back and an infectious smile below bright, engaging eyes. Her uniform told Rob she was an inspector, matching his rank, but in uniform. But despite what some thought, being a detective didn't give him any seniority over her.

"Oh, ma'am, I wasn't aware you were coming to visit," Susanna said, sounding surprised.

The blonde made a face that said, 'Really?' before shrugging and smiling. "I wasn't about to miss the biggest case Retford's seen in months, Sergeant. When something like this happens, my place is here to reassure the public while the CID do their job." She nodded to Scarlett and himself.

"Well, yes," Susanna remarked.

"Are you going to introduce me?" the inspector asked.

"Yes, of course," Susanna answered. "This is Detective Inspector Loxley and Detective Constable Stutely from the EMSOU."

"Special Operations," the blonde stated with a raised eyebrow. "Of course." She offered her hand. "Inspector Holly Clifford, I'm the Bassetlaw Neighbourhood Policing Inspector. Welcome."

"Thank you. Sorry we're visiting under such tragic circumstances," Rob began and shook her hand. "I've heard of you, haven't I?"

"Have you?" Holly asked.

"Holly has been very active in local policing," Susanna remarked, sounding proud. "She was behind one of the national initiatives to protect vulnerable women."

"Aaah, yes, that's right. I knew I'd heard of you. Good work."

"Thank you," Holly replied. "So, what do you have?"

Susanna ran through what they'd found, going over the description of the body and the circumstances in which it was found, before following that up with a brief overview of the investigation as it was progressing so far.

"Okay," Holly said once Susanna had been over everything. "So we're doing door to door, we're cordoning off the banks of the river, and we're mounting a search for clues. All good stuff. Rob, any thoughts about how you want to proceed from there? You're a long way from home."

"We are. For starters, I think we'll need a room to work out of. Some kind of office space with IT support, so we have a local base of operations. It doesn't have to be here, though. I know this building has a closing time and overnight services are run from Worksop, so we can set up elsewhere..."

"Nonsense, I won't hear of it," Holly cut in. "This station will be your base, and I'll ensure you have round-the-clock access. We'll adjust the shift patterns if need be so you have someone here at all times. With a case this big, I won't have you renting an office somewhere."

Rob inclined his head in deference. "That's very kind, thank you."

He stole a glance at Susanna, who was doing her best to hide her annoyance.

"My pleasure," Holly said and then nodded to Susanna. "Sergeant Parsons will look after you and give you whatever you need. You have a room they can have, right?"

"A whole room?" Susanna sounded shocked.

"They're going to need it," Holly pressed.

Susanna ground her teeth. "I'm... sure I can work something out... One of the meeting rooms, maybe."

"Excellent. That's settled then," Holly said brightly before addressing Rob. "Our resources are yours to use, whatever you need. If you have any questions, just ask."

"I have one," Scarlett spoke up. "What's the deal with all this Red Man graffiti? Who is he?"

"An urban myth," Holly replied easily. "Something the local youth have latched on to, that's all really."

"There have been some theories stoked by hearsay and some hack opinion pieces in the local press, but there's not much beyond that, I'm afraid," Susanna agreed with her superior.

"Yep," Holly confirmed. "Not something you should worry about. You've got enough on your plate without concerning yourself with tall tales."

"Oh, okay. Thanks. We were just wondering as we'd seen a lot of graffiti mentioning him."

"Yeah. It's a pain. We're trying to deal with it, but they keep popping up around town."

"We'll find them," Susanna added, sounding confident. A moment later, she sighed. "Right then, let's find you a room, shall we?"

19

Standing in the hallway of his parents' house, Bill listened to the dial tone of the landline, trying to make out the noise his mother was complaining about. It sounded normal to him, though. Just the typical drone that indicated the line was ready for use.

He tapped the cut-off switch a couple of times to be sure, but the drone just started up again in the same way. There was nothing to be suspicious about at all.

He hung up, wondering if his fussy mother was beginning to hallucinate. "Sorry, Mum, I can't hear anything. It sounds normal to me."

Standing in the doorway to the kitchen, watching him and looking a little nervous, she bit her nail. "Well, it was there. I booked in one of those engineers to come over in a few days. He'll know all about it."

"I'm sure he will," Bill agreed, briefly turning away to replace the handset and rolling his eyes at the same time. There was always something with his mother.

"So you're useless at this, too, then," his dad said from the back room where he'd been reading the paper. Typical him, doing nothing and leaving his mother to do all the work.

"I'm not sure why I'm surprised. You're useless at everything else."

"Graham!" his mother hissed. "That's enough."

"Don't you tell me when I've had enough," his father snapped back at her with real venom in his voice. "This waste of space has been an embarrassment to us for too long, and now he's gone and got himself fired from the police!" Back on his feet, his father stalked across the room towards the hallway where Bill stood. "I worked hard in the force and built up a reputation for hard work and fair policing, and this idiot is pissing all over it…"

"Please," his mother cried out. "Don't use language like that."

But his father was far from done and fixed him with a glare that could kill. "Are you proud of yourself, William? You could have had any job in the force. Any at all. I have friends there, and they would have loved to help me continue our legacy. But no, you couldn't do that, could you? You had to do your own bloody thing and associate the family name with anticorruption, a disgraceful department that targets its own. And now you can add failure and dismissal to that list. You're a selfish idiot who's thrown away a rare opportunity. You disgust me!"

With his hands on his hips, Bill quietly seethed while listening to his dad rant and rave about his so-called failure and the disgrace he'd brought to the family. He'd heard countless insults and tirades from his father, but they'd only intensified since his dismissal.

It had been years since he'd enjoyed visiting his parents, and if it wasn't for his mum, who was a lone beacon of light and support in the darkness, he'd have stopped years ago. Even after the dismissal, his mother remained positive and supportive, insisting that this was probably for the best and that he'd find his calling eventually.

Maybe policing wasn't for him, she'd said in an effort to appease him, and as the days passed, she'd asked him around more, giving him little jobs to do to keep him busy.

He agreed to do them because it was his mum, and she was the last person he'd ever want to disappoint. And yet, each and every visit led to at least one rude comment from his father, if not a full-on shouting match that felt on the verge of getting physical.

His mother tried to control him, but it was a pointless battle. His father subscribed to an outdated form of marriage, where the woman was his property, and she did as he wanted.

He boiled with rage at the way he spoke to her sometimes.

He honestly wondered what she saw in him, and as he looked at the old man standing before him, he wanted nothing more than to punch him as hard as he could.

Bill squeezed his balled fists, his nails to biting into his palms. Somehow, he managed to keep his arms clamped to his sides and his rage in check, but only just.

For a moment, as his father stared at him with unrestrained hate, Bill thought he might actually spit on him. But he didn't. Instead, he grunted and turned away, stalking back into the living room, grumbling and muttering something he was glad he didn't hear.

Bill watched him go, his own anger burning like a nuclear furnace deep inside him. One day, if his father kept this up, he'd release that rage, and then his father would see what kind of man he'd brought into this world.

"I'm leaving," Bill announced through gritted teeth and marched through the kitchen.

"But, Bill, you don't have to..." his mother pleaded, fussing at his heels.

"Too late," he snapped back and stormed out the side door, slamming it behind him.

Striding up the driveway, Bill grumbled to himself. "One day, Dad, one day. I'll show you. Just you wait."

20

Resigned to her fate, Roxy woke calmly, without drama or shock from a nightmare, but with a deep, aching hunger in her belly. Keeping her eyes clamped shut, she remained on her side and hugged her legs closer to try and stave off the hunger pangs that gripped her stomach.

She'd long ago forgotten about the foul state of the mattress in her cell, finding it far more favourable to lie on than the stone floor, dirt and stains be damned. She just didn't care anymore.

They'd fed her twice yesterday with what felt like scraps from the dinner table. They were meagre portions that wouldn't satisfy a small child, let alone a grown adult.

As she lay in the shadows of the cell that had been her home for two nights, she returned to a question that had plagued her since she'd been thrown in here.

Why her?

Why was someone doing this? What did anyone have to gain? Was it that hideous man, Truman? Was he somehow behind this? Was this his way of finally punishing her for what she'd done to him?

It was the obvious answer, and yet, it didn't feel right. There was something about the thugs, the man in the red mask, and this place that didn't feel like him. But she could be wrong about that. She could be wrong about a lot of things. It had been years since she'd seen Truman, and he could be a very different man to the one she'd known. Or was he always that man, but his true horrific self had remained hidden until now?

She opened her eyes at the sound of movement close by.

A rat, the size of her head, was no more than a couple of feet away, peering at her and sniffing the air.

Roxy yelped and sat bolt upright in fright, clawing at the wall and mattress to get away from it. Surprised by her sudden movement, the pest scarpered from the cell and ran right past the man in the red mask.

In his long, dark hooded coat, the man stared at her from the other side of the bars, the naked light bulb above him casting stark shadows across him. She could barely make out his eyes behind the mask, but what she could see chilled her soul.

She shivered in fear. Those were the eyes of someone at ease with violence.

"You're a lucky woman," he said in that gruff voice she'd come to hate. "The time of your grand performance has been delayed."

Roxy coughed once as she tried to find her voice. Her throat burned. It was so dry. "What… what do you mean?"

The man's eyes creased, suggesting a smile behind the mask. "You'll see."

Roxy forced herself to meet his gaze and hold it. She needed to show him that she wasn't scared of him. He was trying to break her, to terrify her, but she couldn't allow him that kind of satisfaction. She wouldn't play his game or be the damsel in distress. She needed to be stronger than him. She needed to be alert and be ready for any chance, no matter how small, to try and escape.

She would not die here.

She had too much to live for.

A door slammed, and hurried footsteps echoed up the corridor. The man in the mask looked up as another man appeared outside her cell. This one was new. She'd not seen him before.

He leaned in towards Mask and pitched his voice low, but she could still make out what he said.

"Urr, sir...?"

"What is it?" Mask asked.

The new man glanced into the cell. He met her eyes briefly before he returned his gaze to Mask. "You have a call. It's urgent."

"How urgent?"

The man whispered, "Code red."

There was hidden meaning behind those words, but it was lost on her.

"I'll be right there."

The new man nodded and disappeared back the way he'd come with a clatter of heavy footsteps.

Roxy wondered what had happened to cause that brief interruption. Had something gone wrong for them? She hoped so, and she hoped it might lead to some kind of opportunity for her.

"As I said, you're a lucky woman," Mask repeated, looking at her again. "It seems I have matters to attend to." He leaned closer to the bars and pitched his voice lower. "But rest assured, I will see you soon."

With that, he turned and casually walked out of sight.

She watched him go, and once that door slammed shut again, she buried her head in her arms and cried.

21

With their laptops out and a member of the station's staff connecting them to the network, Rob nodded at the room they'd been reluctantly assigned by Sergeant Susanna Parsons. The small meeting room had a central table, whiteboard, flip chart, and plenty of chairs. It would work perfectly well for their needs and even had a nice view of the town square below.

"Happy?" Susanna asked from where she stood, over the shoulder of the man working on their PCs.

"Very," Rob confirmed, thinking that she didn't look at all happy. "This is perfect. Thank you."

Susanna shrugged as the station employee who had hooked their laptops up to the network stood.

"You're all connected."

"Thank you," Rob said.

"No worries," the man replied and walked out.

Scarlett ended her call. "Tucker's on his way over."

"Okay, great. I think this will work well for us," Rob reiterated as he glanced over at Scarlett. "What do you think?"

"I like it. We can make this work."

Rob nodded. "I've been thinking about it, and I've decided that I'll stay local for a few nights. I want to be close to the action for this early part of the investigation."

"All right," Scarlett acknowledged. "I won't be joining you. Chris might call off the wedding if I keep having nights away. Besides, it's not that far from home. I hope that's okay?"

"That's fine," Rob confirmed. "I wouldn't want to miss out on your wedding because I made you work too hard."

"You should stay at the hotel around the corner," Susanna commented. "In the former police station."

"That's not a bad idea," Rob agreed. It felt like a fitting place for him to hang up his coat at night while on a case. "Is the food good there?"

"As far as I know," Susanna remarked.

"That's decided then." He turned to Scarlett. "I'd better call Erika and get her to look after Muffin."

Scarlett nodded.

"So, what's your plan of action?" Susanna cut in. "Where do you want to start?"

"All right, let's talk about this," Rob said and pulled out a chair.

The others joined him at the table, taking seats as he considered their next move.

"Let's go over the details, shall we? Right now, we have an unidentified male corpse on its way to Nottingham for a

151

postmortem. That should give us a cause of death once they've done their work. We'll also get fingerprints, DNA, and maybe even dental, but none of those are guaranteed to help us identify our man."

"Right," Scarlett agreed. "And given how this case looks right now, I'm willing to bet he's never been in trouble with the police and never given us his prints or DNA."

"That would just be our luck, wouldn't it," Rob groaned. "So, what else have we got going on?"

"The search," Susanna stated. "We've cordoned off both sides of the River Idle as it runs through Kings Park, and we have teams combing the area for clues, looking for anything that might help us. They'll let us know if they find anything."

"Like his phone or wallet," Scarlett added.

"Indeed," Susanna confirmed. "We're also going door to door, but there's not a lot of residential properties around there that could help us, so I think that might be a dead end, too, for now."

"I'm inclined to agree," Rob said. "So, let's widen the search a little more. I want to know about every incident that took place last night in the town and surrounding area. There's a chance that someone saw something, but we haven't linked it to this case yet, so let's go through the records and talk to the officers in the area and see what that throws up."

Now focused on the case, Susanna seemed to have forgotten all about being rude to them and concentrated on the plan of action. She liked being busy, it seemed. "Will do," she confirmed, making notes on her pad as Rob spoke.

"In addition, I think we can open this up to the general public more. A man went missing last night, and unless he was a genuine recluse with no friends, someone will probably be missing him by now. So, two things. First, let's look at missing person reports and keep an eye on any new ones. Secondly, let's also hold a press conference and appeal for either witnesses or for anyone who had a family member or friend go missing. Someone knows who this man is. We just need to find them."

"Indeed," Susanna said.

"Can you organise all that? I want to be speaking to the press in the next half hour. We'll hold it out front, on the square. Let's make some noise around this, shall we?"

"On it," Susanna said and left the room at pace.

Rob watched her go with a raised eyebrow. "Is it me, or was that the most agreeable she's been this entire morning?"

"I noticed it, too," Scarlett added. "Maybe she's come around to us being here?"

"Hmm. Maybe." Rob briefly wondered if Susanna would actually start to be cordial to them as he pulled out his phone.

She'd been nothing but hostile from the moment they'd arrived, but once they had her focused on the case and a plan of action, she had started to play nice. He ruminated on it for a moment more before dismissing that train of thought. He had stuff to do.

"Right. While I've got a moment, I'm going to make a quick call."

He got up and walked to the nearby window, scrolling through his contacts until he found the name he was looking for. He hit call on Erika's name.

After a couple of rings, she answered. "Rob, hi. What can I do you for?"

"I was wondering if you might be able to feed Muffin for me? Just for a few days? If you're free? I've got a case up in Retford, so..."

"Just a few nights?" Erika asked.

"If that's okay. If you can't, just say."

"No, that's fine. I can do that," Erika confirmed. "Shouldn't be a problem."

Relief flooded his system, knowing that Muffin would be fine and well-fed under Erika's care. "Excellent, thank you. You're a lifesaver."

"I know. Let me know when you're back."

"Will do," Rob said and said his farewells.

"Sorted?" Scarlett asked once he was off the phone.

"It is." His phone buzzed in his hand, making him jump. "Ooh, maybe I spoke too soon..." He glanced at the screen. "Oh, no, it's Nick. Hold on."

"Aaah, okay," Scarlett muttered.

"Nick, How's it going?" Rob said as he answered the phone.

"I thought you should know that I've decided to send Ellen down to Surrey to be there when DCI Pilgrim meets with Truman Collins. We should have at least one officer there at the interview."

Rob nodded. "Yeah, you're right. That's fine with me. Good idea, actually. Shame I couldn't head down there myself really. It's been a while since I've seen Pilgrim. It would be good to catch up."

"Yeah," Nick agreed. "I thought of going down there myself for that very reason, but I'm needed here, so it will have to be another time."

"Aye," Rob said. "Any other news?"

"Not really. We're trawling through CCTV to track this van, but we're not getting very far. We'll appeal for witnesses, too, to see if anyone in the area spotted anything. You never know. How about you? How's Retford?"

"All right, so far. I'll be staying up here for a few nights, I think, while this case gets going. We've got a bit of a mystery on our hands right now."

"Oh?"

"Yeah. We don't know who the victim is. Anyway, I'd better go, I have an appeal to write for my press conference."

"Sure. Catch you later," Nick confirmed and ended the call.

Rob made his way over to his laptop. "Right then, let's get this sorted."

22

Checking over his notes, Rob hung back behind the podium, leaving it vacant for the moment as the various members of the press and passersby waited for it to start.

The assembled press pack was filled with faces he didn't recognise from the local rags, TV, blogs, and online media channels and was bolstered by a small crowd of local residents who'd turned up to hear first-hand if the rumours were true.

As he waited, people muttered and made guesses about the nature of the talk, and it seemed that news of the body in the river had spread fast. This served to bolster his confidence that a resident might know the victim, and maybe this wasn't just a colossal waste of time.

After all, someone, somewhere, would know who that young murdered man was. They just had to reach them.

Susanna walked over to him. "Are you ready?" She was all business now they were actually making progress, and it was good to see that she could be a team player.

"As I'll ever be," Rob replied. He swallowed nervously. No matter how many times he did these things, he always got a little stage fright right before the event. He took a deep breath, in through the nose and out through the mouth, nice and slow to calm his nerves.

"When you're ready," Susanna said.

Rob turned to Scarlett and Holly, who were standing close by and there to show a united front at the Retford station. Holly, in particular, was keen to broadcast that they were taking this seriously and said it was vital for her to be visible. Rob agreed.

After a brief smile to the two women, he stepped forward and into the range of the mics that had either been attached to the podium or were held out by the assembled journalists.

"Good morning. I'm Detective Loxley with the East Midlands Special Operations Unit. This morning, the body of a young man was found in the River Idle, just a short distance from here, close to the Bridgegate bridge. It seems that he was attacked, and we're treating his death as suspicious. The reason I am speaking to you right now is because we need the public's help in identifying him. The victim is a white European man in his mid-twenties with short dark hair. He was found wearing dark-blue jeans, a grey top, and a black jacket. We believe he will have been in the vicinity of Kings Park, close to the River Idle, in the early hours of this morning. If you think you saw anything suspicious at that time, or you remember seeing a man who matches this description, I urge you to call and speak to us using the

Crimestoppers helpline. The sooner we can identify the victim, the sooner we can move forward with this case and bring peace to his family."

Rob finished off by listing the phone numbers to call.

"If anyone has any questions, raise your hand. Thank you."

Several people did, so Rob picked out what he hoped would be someone with a sensible question.

"Yes?"

"Do you know the time of death?"

"In the early hours," Rob answered. "A postmortem will be carried out today that will give us a better idea, but that's the best I can give you right now." He picked another raised hand.

"How did he die? Did he drown, or was it this attack?"

"Again, we're unsure right now, but we will have an answer soon. Thank you."

He went through several more questions as people clarified details or asked for information he either didn't have or wasn't going to give them until someone asked a strange, but perhaps inevitable question.

"Do you think the Red Man was involved?"

Rob grunted, but the crowd hushed slightly and waited for the answer. Whoever or whatever this Red Man was, he certainly held some kind of sway over the town.

"No," Rob answered. He saw no reason to be vague on that point, preferring not to encourage conspiracy theories that weren't helpful.

A ripple of hushed talk washed over the crowd, and as he was about to take another question, a new source of commotion kicked off to his right. It was the kind of thing he might expect if Brad Pitt appeared and walked into the crowd. Suddenly he wasn't the most interesting person there anymore, and the assembled press turned and looked for the cause.

Rob did the same and spotted someone moving through the crowd towards him. For a moment, Rob's hackles rose. He thought someone might be here to hurt him or cause some kind of problem. But the crowd parted, and he suddenly caught sight of the man's face, and his heart sank.

Rob sighed as his eldest brother, Sean Mason, parted the crowd like a modern-day Moses. Reaching the front, he smiled up at Rob and came to a stop. Sean stuffed his hands into his pockets and waited expectantly.

After a moment, when it became clear that everyone was waiting for him to say something, Sean spoke.

"Please, Inspector, carry on. This is your press conference. I'm here merely to listen, like everyone else."

"Okay," Rob muttered through gritted teeth. He glanced down at his notes, but he didn't want to be here anymore.

Whatever circus show Sean was planning, he wanted no part of it. He'd had enough of his family's antics to last him a lifetime. Luckily, he was right at the end of what he wanted to say. "Well, I think that's about everything for now. Thank you for coming, and please, if you saw anything or know anything, please call. We want to hear from you. Thank you."

Rob glanced at Sean who grinned back.

As he stepped back from the podium, the assembled press suddenly turned their attention to Sean.

"Sean. Why are you here?"

"Mr Mason, are you here to offer help to the police?"

The questions kept coming, so Sean moved closer to the podium and raised his hands to silence the crowd. "Thank you for the questions, everyone. As you know, my family are well-known philanthropists who support the town and its residents through charitable donations and outreach programmes, and our support extends to the police as well, especially during times of crisis, like this."

"Are you here to offer help?" someone asked.

"No, no. Not directly. The police have that covered, especially under the assured guidance of Inspector Loxley. We have total confidence in him. I'm here purely to show solidarity with the people of this town during this difficult period."

Rob had heard enough and turned away. He made a beeline for the station door and kept his gaze fixed on it as Scarlett fell into step beside him, leaving Holly back at the podium. Susanna was nowhere to be seen.

"Did you know he was coming?" Scarlett asked.

"No, I didn't," Rob grunted, annoyed. While it was certainly possible that the Masons appeared to show support for Retford, because they did do a lot of work here to hide their less savoury affairs, Rob couldn't help but think they'd come here purely for him and to remind him whose town he was in. It was a calculated move by his family, and he felt sure this wouldn't be the last time he saw them.

"Crap, I'm sorry," Scarlett stated.

"It was inevitable. I knew I'd see them sooner or later. It was just a matter of time."

"I know, but still, it's not nice."

"No, it's not." Rob reached the station door, where an officer waited and opened it for them. He thanked the young man and walked inside, a sense of relief filling him as he passed the threshold. "Where's Susanna?"

"She got called inside," Scarlett answered. "I don't know why."

"Oh, okay," Rob remarked.

But as he turned to move deeper into the station, Susanna suddenly appeared at the door.

She smiled at them. "We've found something."

23

Mary leaned against the wall, standing in the shadows, fidgeting with the collar of her shirt, rolling a button back and forth between her fingers as she stared across the way.

She'd walked around the main building of the Queen's Medical Centre to one of the back entrances that were not for public use. The entrance opposite consisted of a larger loading entrance and a smaller side door, both of which led to the hospital's mortuary.

After leaving the office following the call with her hacker contact, Mary soon came to a simple conclusion as to her next move. She needed information. She needed to know if her suspicions were correct about the identity of the victim, because if she was, then the logical conclusion was that her own life was in danger.

In a flash, she remembered being in Kings Park the night before, talking to her informant and seeing that group of men striding towards them in the dark. For whatever reason, her informant had recognised them right away and ordered her to run in no uncertain terms. She'd done as he'd asked, as he himself sprinted into the night in a different direction.

Luckily, his suspicions had been correct because at least one of those thugs had chased after her.

But she had been faster and had an escape route in mind.

The memory of that encounter was burned onto her brain. There was no forgetting it now. But was her informant the same man who had been found in the River Idle this morning? She had to know, and that led her here.

She'd been here before, doing the same thing she was doing right now, but she'd never felt this nervous, even on her first visit. But then, the stakes were so much higher now and much more personal.

Across the rear loading area, the sound of locks slamming into their housings sounded, followed by the rear door opening. The familiar face of pathologist, Katy Moors, appeared and waved her over.

Mary scanned around to check no one was watching and then glanced up at the CCTV camera. She pointed to it. Had Katy made sure they were disabled, like usual?

Katy nodded urgently and waved her over again.

Satisfied, Mary jogged across the courtyard and up the steps to the rear door.

"Get in," Katy whispered and shut the door behind Mary once she was inside.

"Thanks for this," Mary whispered.

Katy looked anxious and stressed. She held out her hand. "Charity only extends so far, you know."

Mary nodded and fished the cash out of her pocket. She peeled off several notes and handed them over. "I understand."

"Do you? You can't do this to me. You said you'd always give me time and space to fit you in. What's so urgent that you had to visit this morning?"

"It's personal and probably better that you don't know. But thank you anyway. I really appreciate it."

Katy narrowed her eyes. "I don't need your thanks, just your money. You might be Vanessa's housemate, but I don't really know you."

"I know, I understand. Can I see him?"

Katy sighed. "Come with me and do as I say. My boss has gone for a break, so you need to be quick."

"This won't take long," Mary reassured her and followed Katy along the corridors and through a couple of back rooms that smelled of disinfectant until they entered the familiar main room where they stored the adult bodies. The fridges were arrayed against the wall and looked identical apart from the name tags.

Katy didn't hesitate and marched straight up to one of the square doors labelled *John Doe* and opened it. A corpse, sealed inside a body bag, lay inside.

"What do you need to see?" Katy asked.

"Just his face," Mary stated and swallowed as Katy reached for the zip. She took a deep breath and did her best to prepare herself for what was to come. It wasn't the first dead body she'd seen like this, and it wasn't the potential for gore that was worrying her.

Katy pulled the zip. Mary closed her eyes and repeated a simple phrase in her head. *Don't recognise him, don't recognise him, don't recognise him...*

She opened her eyes on hearing Katy pull the two sides of the bag apart to reveal the head and looked down. The pallid, lifeless face inside the bag was covered in cuts and bruises that had long ago stopped bleeding, but beneath the damage someone had inflicted upon him was a familiar face that she'd seen just a few hours ago in the shadows of the Retford park.

It was him. It was her informant.

They'd killed him.

She kept a tight grip on her emotions and facial expressions, but inside, she felt like screaming. Instead, she muttered a quick thank you between gritted teeth as she turned away.

"Oh, okay," Katy replied and took a moment to reseal the bag and return the body to the fridge. Mary stepped away, back towards where she'd come in.

They'd done it, they'd actually done it. They'd murdered him.

"Is that it?" Katy walked over to join her.

"Yeah, I'm done. I've got to go. Sorry."

"Of course, no problem," Katy replied and led her back through the corridors to the rear entrance. "But next time, give me a little more warning, okay?"

"Yeah, sure," Mary answered absentmindedly. Right now, her worries about being discovered were the least of her concerns because her worst fears had been confirmed. Her informant had been killed. Those thugs had caught him and killed him, and it wasn't lost on her that she'd had a very lucky escape.

Would they have killed her in the same way if she'd not managed to get away?

Worse still, was her life now in danger?

Were those thugs searching for her?

She'd been quite open and vocal about her hunt for the Red Man, including publishing two articles on the myth, which had, in turn, led to death threats.

Did they know who she was? It wasn't unlikely.

Reaching the rear door, Katy stepped in front of her and opened it with her key. Mary waited patiently, doing her best to appear calm and collected as her emotions churned and roiled inside her.

As she stepped outside, her phone rang. She jumped and grabbed it while she walked away from the rear entrance and checked the caller ID. It was Britney from work.

Mary turned and waved goodbye to Katy before striding off and answering her phone. "Britt, what's up?"

"Are you okay?" her work colleague asked, a concerned tone to her voice.

"Yeah, why?" Mary was instantly suspicious. Something had happened.

"There was a man here looking for you. I've never seen him before, and, well, I just got a vibe off him, you know? I didn't like him. He was aggressive and was insisting on coming up. We had to get security involved."

"A man?" Mary asked with her heart in her mouth. "He came to the office and asked for me?"

"Yeah. Should I be worried, or…"

"Did he leave a name?"

"No. He refused. That was one of the red flags I got. He's gone now, but I thought you should know, okay?"

"All right, thanks," Mary replied.

"Is it anything I should worry about?" Britt pressed.

"Not right now. I'll let you know if something develops. It's related to my current story."

"I see." She sounded uneasy. "Okay. As long as you're sure."

"I am, thanks," Mary answered, and after a quick goodbye, she hung up.

Her worst fears were confirmed. They still wanted to find her, they know who she was and where she worked.

"Fuck."

24

After Ellen left the M25, her satnav guided her southwest, away from London and into the Surrey countryside. Everything was leafy green and lovely, very much in line with the county's reputation as both commuter belt and one of the more expensive areas to live outside London.

How much would a house cost around here, she wondered, as she made her way through the suburbs. She suspected she'd end up living in a crappy former council flat if she sold up and moved south.

Not that she had any desire to do that.

After nearly three hours in the car, she was looking forward to getting out and stretching. But it wasn't far now, so rather than stopping and taking a break, she continued on.

As she drove into the village of Horsley, she navigated through a dog-leg bend in the road, and on the second corner, a large brutalist building loomed into view, which her navigation app was leading her into.

"Finally," she remarked. She turned in, noting the sign at the front that proclaimed this to be Horsley Police Station.

She drove into the public car park and pulled into a space. After turning the engine off, getting out of the seat felt like heaven. Ellen took a moment to give her back a good stretch, enjoying the pop of her spine before taking a breath and gazing up at the unforgiving concrete structure. It wasn't subtle, that was for sure.

With a sigh, she made her way towards the entrance, her limbs loosening up as she walked.

Once inside, she approached the front desk and gave her name and the officer she was here to see. They directed her to sit and wait.

Her first impressions were very positive. The building appeared modern and clean, a departure from some of the stations the UK's police forces used sometimes. She found herself reminded of the new custody facility in Nottingham, which was purpose-built for their use, and how nice that building was, even though it was filled with suspects and criminals.

As she waited, officers and civilians came and went, passing through the reception or taking a seat like she had.

A couple of minutes passed. Then an auburn haired woman in a fitted suit with a police ID around her neck, strode into the reception and approached the desk. The receptionist pointed to Ellen.

The redhead made her way over. "Hi. Constable Ellen Dale?"

Ellen got to her feet and shook the woman's hand. "That's right."

"Nice to meet you, I'm DS Kate O'Connell. If you'd like to follow me?"

Ellen smiled and nodded, enjoying the Irish lilt that Kate had to her voice. It was subtle but attractive.

They moved through a security door and made their way upstairs.

"So you're on Loxley's team, right?"

"That's right, we're part of the East Midlands Special Operations Unit."

"EMSOU," Kate confirmed. "I've heard of it. It's good to have you here. I've heard a lot about Rob, Nick, and Nailer from Jon."

"They're a good bunch," Ellen said with a smile. "What's your unit called?"

"The SIU," Kate confirmed. "Special Investigations Unit. We were formed partially in partnership with the NCA to look into some of the area's most organised and serious crimes. Our remit actually goes beyond our county and could technically allow us to cover crimes anywhere in the country, but the reality is that there are usually local units that cover it."

"I see," Ellen replied as they reached the third floor, where she noticed the unit's name on a door.

Kate led her over and into a large, open-plan office. It was bigger than theirs back at Sherwood Lodge and much more modern. Several people worked at desks, but Kate led her to a nearby office separate from the collection of desks, where a man with short dark hair and a chiselled jawline worked. He saw them coming and got to his feet, stepping out from behind his desk to come and greet her.

"Jon," Kate began, "this is Constable Ellen Dale from Nottingham."

"Ellen, pleased to meet you." He offered his hand. "Thank you for coming down. I hope it's not a wasted trip."

"Me, too," Ellen agreed. "It's good to meet you finally. Rob's spoken about you many times."

"Has he? Nothing bad, I hope?"

"No... Well, mostly." She smiled. "I'm keen to get started. When will we be speaking to Truman Collins?"

"A little later on, he's got us booked into his busy schedule."

Ellen rolled her eyes at the answer and the way the rich sometimes treated the police. It seemed they were something of an annoyance to these so-called elites. "Typical."

"Yeah, I know. We'll deal with it, though. But in the meantime, you can set yourself up on one of the desks out there. Just keep your distance from Nathan unless you like conspiracy theories."

"Noted," Ellen answered, wondering who Nathan was.

"I'll grab you a drink," Kate said. "What would you prefer? Tea? Coffee? Something else?"

25

Rob perched himself on the edge of the table as Holly walked in to join Susanna, Scarlett, and himself.

"Well, that was unexpected." Holly closed the door. "We don't see much of the Masons, especially at random press conferences."

"I bet," Scarlett remarked, her voice deadpan.

"I take it you know about them?" Holly asked. "They're supposedly a local, charitable family who do good work for the town, but there's a dark core to them."

"We know all about them," Scarlett stated and gave Rob a knowing look.

"Yeah, we're well aware of their criminal activities," Rob agreed. "They've been a personal bugbear of mine for a while."

"Oh, okay. That's good then," Holly said and then frowned. "So, did *you* find that odd? Because I did. I'm not sure why they'd show up to a little press conference like that. It's weird."

"We have an idea," Scarlett muttered.

"Me, too," Rob replied. "That was likely because of me. Like I said, I have something of a history with the Masons. It's nothing to worry about, but I'm fairly sure Sean did that purely to get at me. It was personal and didn't have anything to do with the case… at least, I don't think it does." He shrugged. "I guess the case could have links to the Masons, but I doubt it." He glanced between the three women to try and get an idea of their thoughts on it.

"I wouldn't put it past them," Scarlett said with venom in her voice, born from the loss of her friend at the hands of the Masons. "They're scum."

"You'll get no argument from me there," Susanna added. "But they're not known to shit in their own backyard either, at least, not to any great degree. They enjoy their reputation as local celebrities and fund-raisers too much."

"I agree," Holly added. "But given the nature of their business, stuff goes wrong sometimes, and when it goes wrong in that line of business, it really crashes and burns."

"You think they're clearing up some mess they made?" Scarlett asked.

"I honestly don't know what, if anything, they might be up to. But I do think we should keep an open mind about their involvement with this case."

"Yep," Rob answered before turning back to Susanna. "Right then, don't keep us in suspense any longer. You said you found something?"

"We did," Susanna confirmed. "Last night, two of our officers attended a call in Kings Park. Apparently, a woman witnessed a group of men attacking a young man who broadly fits the description of our victim. But, by the time our officers arrived, the fight was over, and they couldn't find anyone."

"And this happened in Kings Park?" Rob asked.

"Yep. Just up from where the body was found. The attack took place on one side of the river, and our witness was on the other, hiding in the trees. She said it was quite vicious."

"And the two officers who attended the scene?"

"PCs David Morton and Russ Brewster. They've just made it in after being on the late shift last night. Would you like to have a chat with them?"

"Please," Rob said.

"All right," Susanna confirmed. "I'll go and grab them. One moment."

She left, leaving Rob to glance at Scarlett and Holly.

"Progress already," he remarked.

"Yeah, it's good. We should go and talk to the witness, too," Scarlett said. "Now we know what she saw, she might have useful info."

"Agreed," Rob said as voices sounded in the corridor.

Moments later, Susanna walked in with two uniformed officers in tow.

"In you come, lads." Susanna waved them in.

The two men looked a little unsure as they entered the room, glancing around at those assembled inside.

"Is this about the fight in the park?" one asked.

Rob checked the man's name tag. PC Morton. "It is. I'm DI Rob Loxley, with the EMSOU."

"Rob, Loxley?" David replied. "Really? That's your name?"

"Your parents must have had a sense of humour," Russ added.

Rob smiled. "My name's Robert, not Robin, and there's a story behind the surname, but that's for another time. So, tell me about last night's shift. You were called to someone who witnessed a fight in the park, right?"

"We were," David confirmed, and pulled out his pad to check his notes. "Yeah, it was late. We arrived after midnight, but I believe the call came in shortly before, around eleven forty-five. It was something of a busy night."

"Is it usually?" Scarlett asked.

"It can be," David said. "Anyway, the witness was Lois Carter. She'd been working late at a bar in town and walked home through the park when she spotted the fight on the other side of the river. She hid and called nine-nine-nine."

"And what did you find when you got there?"

"Not much," David answered. "We entered the park from the car park off Bridgegate and found the woman a short distance into the park. She'd moved away from the river's

179

edge and hid behind some bushes. Unfortunately, she didn't see what happened to the group of men."

"There was that one weird thing, though," Russ said, speaking up for the first time. "She said that one of the men was wearing a red mask. She said it looked like he was in charge."

"A red mask?" Scarlett asked.

Rob met her gaze and understood her line of thought right away.

"The Red Man," Rob muttered.

"You're kidding," Susanna said to the two constables. "You didn't tell me this."

David shrugged. "I'd forgotten about it."

"It didn't come to anything," Russ added. "Besides, it's not the first time some idiot's worn a red mask to capitalise on that urban myth."

"True," Susanna agreed. "I've seen kids in the area wearing them around town, trying to scare old ladies."

"Lovely," Scarlett remarked. "So the red mask might not mean anything?"

"Hard to say," Susanna replied.

"Let's not get too bogged down in that, shall we?" Rob added before he turned back to the two officers. "So what actions did you take once you found the woman and made sure she was okay?"

"I went to the other side of the river to hunt around," Russ explained. "I walked back to Bridgegate and along the other bank to where she saw the fight and had a good look around with my torch. I saw a tiny amount of blood on the ground, which confirmed that someone had been hurt, but I didn't see anything else suspicious. No victim, no attackers, nothing. But it was very dark, so I could have missed something."

"Like a body in the river," Scarlett muttered and fixed him with a stare.

Russ shrugged. "Sorry."

"So you found nothing?" Rob asked.

"Nope, nothing that deserved further action anyway. Nothing to indicate someone had been killed."

"Fights are not an uncommon occurrence after the pubs kick out," David stated. "Most of them are just drunken scuffles caused by kids getting rowdy. They don't usually merit a big investigation."

"We were going to follow up with the witness either later today or tomorrow," Russ said.

"That's okay. I don't think you did anything wrong. There was nothing to suggest something more serious had happened. I get it."

"We were also being called to other incidents and needed to move on. We're not exactly overflowing with staff, you know," David said.

"No, we're not," Rob agreed. "So, did you send the witness on her way?"

"After taking her details," David confirmed. "Here."

He showed them to Rob and Scarlett who took a photo of them with her phone.

"All right, thank you. Was there anything else that happened last night that you think might be related to the body we found in the river?"

"I don't know. There were a couple of fights in town, with one man arrested. We attended a robbery, some muggings, and a case of vandalism, amongst other minor incidents."

"I have the reports," Susanna confirmed, addressing Rob and Scarlett. "I'll make them available to you so you can have a read through to see if there's anything you think we should take a closer look at."

"Thank you," Rob replied, still surprised by how much she'd changed once they'd started to investigate the case. "Okay, I think we're done here."

"Cheers, guys," Susanna said and waved them out, only for another man in a tan suit with messy hair to appear at the door. "Oh, sorry. Can I help you?"

"Tucker," Scarlett called out. "You made it."

"Aye. So, what did I miss?"

26

Tired, anxious, and concerned for her friend's safety, Teri paced back and forth across the room, running her hand through her hair as she tried to think coherently about what she should do. After texting him all night with no answer, she'd finally decided to forget what her contact had told her and called him.

The phone rang, but no one answered, and it eventually went to voicemail. She'd left a brief message asking him to call as soon as he could but didn't mention why or what it might be about. She wasn't a total idiot.

That cycle had repeated itself more times than she cared to know, with each voicemail she left becoming more emotional and desperate until she was basically begging him to call her back.

Surely he wasn't ignoring her and following their contact's rules to the letter? There was no way. He'd hear her voicemail and see the messages. He would know she was freaking out, and if he was okay, if there was nothing to worry about, he would let her know. She knew he would. He wouldn't leave her hanging like that. That wasn't him.

But if he was ignoring her, she'd bloody well throttle him.

She stopped pacing and rechecked her phone. Nothing. No messages. No calls. Where was he?

In another fit of annoyance and impatience, she hit redial and called him again.

This time, it was different.

The line didn't ring. There was a series of tones and then an automated voice alerting her that the person she was trying to reach was unavailable.

She yanked the phone away from her ear and glared at it. "What? What the hell?" She hung up and called again but got the same response. "But that can't be right…"

She tried again and again, hanging up and calling time after time until a thought occurred to her. His phone had died. She'd called it so many times that it must have just run out of battery.

"Oh, shit." Why didn't she think of that before?

She blamed her current state of mind and her inability to think clearly about what she needed to do.

In frustration, she threw her phone into the sofa. "Bastard!"

She dropped into a seat and held her head in her hands, gripping her hair between her fingers and pulling at it. Somehow, the pain helped.

She couldn't leave it there. She couldn't just do nothing. Something had happened. She knew it had. It was the only reason for him not to get in touch. He was either in danger, hurt, or... No. She couldn't think about that. She wouldn't entertain that idea. He had to still be alive. It was just that wherever he was, he couldn't use his phone. That was the answer.

But if that was the case, then where was he?

Had *they* got to him? Her breath caught in her throat, and she tensed up at the thought. If *they'd* got to him, then they really were in trouble. There was no way *they'd* tolerate what they were planning, and she knew full well what they were capable of.

Teri shook her head to banish those thoughts. She couldn't give them credence. She had to remain hopeful, clear-headed, and believe that he was still alive somewhere and that she could help him. It was the only way forward. But she couldn't stay here if she needed to help him. She had to get out there and find him.

With her mind suddenly made up, Teri grabbed her coat and shoes and was out the door in a matter of seconds. Jumping into her car, she drove across town to Spital Hill and parked just a short walk from his house. She knew better than to park too close. She needed to be careful.

Pulling on her cap and then raising her hood over it, she looked around before getting out of her car, hunting for anything suspicious. But the road was quiet and calm. Would his road be the same?

Teri climbed out of her car and scanned the area again, just to be sure, but it was still clear. Satisfied, she locked her car, stuffed her hands in her hoody's pockets, and walked with her head down over the road. When she reached the end of his street, she paused to glance around. Nothing suspicious for now, she concluded, and set off towards his house. Keeping her face downturned, she scanned left and right, hunting for threats.

A few moments later, his house came into view a short distance ahead, but there was something off about it. Some people were hanging around, too. Were they his neighbours?

As she got closer, she realised she was right. It was his neighbours. The ones he hated. She wasn't exactly friendly towards them either and had suffered through a few encounters with them. They were idiots. She could make out the father in the front garden, drinking beer, and his teenage son on the road outside, riding his bike around like a hooligan.

She considered turning round and heading back the way she'd come for a moment. They'd surely recognise her and no doubt hurl abuse. She thought about giving up, but she realised there was no way she could. She needed to know what had happened to him. She needed to know if he was still alive.

Teri pressed on and approached the house. As she drew nearer, she got a better view of it and shivered. The windows had been boarded up, and there was graffiti all over the front face of the building. Most of it was insults. Teri stared in open-mouthed shock.

Who had done this?

"Oh, it's you," the neighbour grunted. "You can piss off, too."

Teri looked up at the father, Otto Frank, leaning against the dividing fence with a can of beer in his hand. He sported a large bandage across the right side of his face. She didn't know what to say to him.

Otto continued. "Stupid bitch. Lover boy's not here, and if he ever does come back, I'm going to break his face."

Otto's child, Bobby, laughed. It was a coarse cackle that scratched at her brain.

"You like my handiwork? Looks a damn sight better now, don't it?"

Teri glanced at the graffiti and then back at the kid. He, too, was injured. His nose seemed to be at on odd angle, and he had two black eyes.

Teri glared back at Otto. She hated them, but she had to know more. "So, he's not here?"

"Listen here, you dumb fuck. No, he ain't, because if he was, he'd be a red stain across the front of his house for what he did to my son." Otto pointed to Bobby and his broken nose. "Now piss off before I fuck you up for knowing him."

She glanced at the house and wondered if he might be hiding in there somewhere, scared for his life. She needed to be certain. Turning back to Otto, Teri clenched her jaw and gritted her teeth. "Are you sure?"

Otto stopped leaning against the fence and came to his full height. "Am I sure? Am I fucking sure? Who do you think I am? Yeah, I'm sure. The police went through there before they boarded it up to keep everyone else out. He ain't there. But you tell him from me, you tell him that if he comes back, his life won't be worth living. Got it?"

Satisfied, she nodded and turned away. She believed him, and there was no need to aggravate him further.

"Fucking stupid bitch," Otto called after her and followed it up with a series of insults that she ignored.

He wasn't here.

So, where was he?

27

Sitting in the dining room of the semi-detached house, Rob leaned back in his chair as he regarded the young woman sitting across from Scarlett and himself.

Located in Ordsall on the west side of Retford, the house belonged to Lois Carter's parents, who were sitting in the kitchen and probably trying to listen to their conversation. But this story needed to come from Lois, without her parents' influence.

They'd had a quick chat about her circumstances, and it turned out that Lois was a student attending a local college but was working evenings in a Retford bar to earn some money. On her way home from work, she'd encountered a fight in the park.

"So when you saw the youths heading your way, you diverted into the park?" Scarlett asked. She sounded surprised that Lois would make such a choice.

"Yeah. I've walked that way before," Lois confirmed. "It's not as bad as it sounds."

"Okay," Scarlett replied. "So what happened?"

Rob listened closely while Lois detailed her short trip along the riverbank before she'd heard the sounds of a scuffle and then spotted the assault on the opposite side of the river. She walked them through her actions. How she hid, sneaked away to some bushes, and then called the police. Unfortunately, while she was distracted, the fight ended, and when she finally went back, the group had disappeared. It was frustrating that she'd run away, but he couldn't blame her. She must have been utterly terrified that they would come for her if they spotted her.

"Can we go over what you remember the men looking like?" Rob asked. "The officers you spoke to mentioned that one of the men was wearing a red mask. Is that right?"

"Yeah," she confirmed without hesitation. "He was a scary dude. I think he was the leader. He watched and directed the men. It was weird."

"Can you give me some more detail? What else was he wearing?"

"It was difficult to make out in the darkness. It was some kind of dark coat, maybe. He had his hood up, too."

"Can you describe the mask?" Scarlett asked.

"Um, I don't know. It looked like a human face, I think. I just remember it being bright red. It stood out."

"And the others?" Rob pressed.

"Well, I didn't hang around. But they were wearing dark clothing for the most part. Black mainly. I remember at least one blond-haired man amongst them. I can't remember much more than that."

"And the victim?"

"Dark-haired, wearing a black coat and jeans. That's all I remember. I'm sorry, I'm being completely useless, aren't I? It all happened so quickly. I remember just feeling scared and helpless. I just didn't want them coming after me."

"That's understandable," Scarlett said, her voice soft and caring. "Don't feel bad about that. That's a normal human reaction."

Lois nodded but didn't seem too convinced. "So, do you think the man I saw getting attacked was the same man found dead in the river?"

"I think that's very likely," Rob answered. "We can't be certain yet, but I think it's very possible. Yes."

"So, I saw him being killed?"

"You were certainly one of the last people to see him alive, *if* it was the same man. And you're sure you didn't recognise him?"

"Sorry, no," Lois replied. "But then, I didn't get a good look at him either, so I can't help you identify him. I saw your press conference."

"Of course," Rob confirmed, disappointed that they weren't getting anything new from their witness. He'd hoped they could jog her memory, but it had probably been a long shot.

The detail of the red mask was interesting, given the graffiti he'd seen around the town, but it was probably little more than someone using the myth to try and strike fear into their victims' hearts.

Still, it might still prove useful yet.

28

"Do you think this will lead anywhere?" Jon asked from the driver's seat of the unmarked police pool car.

Ellen sat in the back of the vehicle after insisting that Kate take the front seat. She'd protested, saying that Ellen should take it, as she was the guest here, but she didn't give Kate any chance by just getting into the back.

"Honestly, I'm not sure," Ellen replied. "Roxanna Wells' rape was four years ago, and she's moved a long way from here. But the failed court case did have a major effect on Truman and his life. His wife left him, and he's lost a lot of contact with his children because of this, so that's got to hurt. I know I'd be upset if I were in his shoes. Of course, I wouldn't then conspire to kidnap them years later, but who's to say that Truman wouldn't do that? It looks like he was a serial philanderer with money and power that he used and abused to get what he wanted, and it was only when Roxy stood up to him that it stopped. She ruined a perfectly good thing for him."

"He's still rich, though," Kate remarked. "I mean, I know that's not everything, but that's kind of my point. He didn't lose everything. He kept his businesses and his affluent lifestyle."

"True," Ellen said. "But there are a lot of things money can't buy, such as happiness."

"How about revenge?" Jon asked. "Can money buy revenge?"

"It could certainly pay for a group of thugs to kidnap a young woman," Ellen replied. "Inflicting pain on the person who ruined his life might bring him a level of satisfaction that other creature comforts can't."

"Indeed," Jon agreed before getting distracted. "Here we are."

Jon pulled up to a gated property on a road filled with huge houses and lowered his window to speak into the intercom. Ellen listened to the distorted voice on the other end of the line check who they were, with Jon holding up his ID to the camera. Finally, the gate opened and they were let in.

The house was impressive and immaculate, with landscaped gardens, manicured bushes, and hedgerows pruned to within an inch of their life. Ellen almost didn't dare to get out of the car, just in case she ruined something by looking at it.

"Wow, that's a nice house." She craned her neck to take in the three-storey monster with its gleaming windows and cream-rendered exterior.

Once the car had stopped, she climbed out and joined Jon and Kate as they approached the main entrance, which opened to reveal a woman in a smart dress that wouldn't be out of place in an office. She smiled.

"Hi. I'm Sylvie, Mr Collins' assistant. You're here to speak with him, correct?"

"We are," Jon confirmed.

"Excellent, please, follow me."

They strolled into the entrance hall and waited while Sylvie closed the door and then led them past several beautiful rooms that looked like they'd only ever been cleaned but never been used until she came to a door that stood slightly ajar and knocked.

A male voice answered, "Come in."

Sylvie moved inside with Jon, Kate, and Ellen bringing up the rear. She entered an office large enough to serve as most people's living rooms and sported an ornate wooden desk and a seating area with comfortable leather chairs surrounding a coffee table.

As Ellen stepped into the room, Truman Collins walked towards them from his desk. He was all smiles and offered his hand to Jon. Jon shook it before Truman moved on to Kate and then Ellen, each introducing themselves in turn.

She felt briefly dirty after shaking the man's hand, but there was no need to be openly confrontational at this early stage. They needed him to cooperate, after all.

"I'm sorry I couldn't see you sooner." Truman led them to the nearby seats. "Things have been crazy busy recently, what with my conference in Spain. I've not slept much, so you'll need to bear with me."

"That's okay," Jon replied.

"So, what's this all about then?"

"I take it you remember Roxanna Wells?" Jon began.

Ellen kept her eyes fixed on Truman, trying to read his expressions and body language. Was he shocked by the revelation of what they wanted to speak to him about? Was he worried? He didn't seem it. In fact, he seemed quite calm as Jon had mentioned the name of the woman who did so much damage to his life. Had he expected this?

"Well, that's not a name I care to hear mentioned, I'm sure you'll understand. In fact, I've been doing my best to try and forget her as much as I can. But she seems to have a habit of showing up just when I think I've finally got away from her."

"Roxanna was the woman who took you to court for allegedly raping her," Kate clarified.

"That's what she claimed," Truman answered, his tone measured.

197

"Do you know where she might be right now?" Jon asked.

Ellen allowed a slight smile to curl one corner of her mouth as she enjoyed his subtle question.

"I imagine she's at work somewhere, ruining someone else's day."

"And where in the country might that be?"

"I'm not exactly sure," Truman answered. "I know she moved away up north somewhere. That's where her family are, after all. Why? What's happened? What are you asking me?"

Ellen leaned forward. "We're here because Roxy was kidnapped the night before last, and everyone we speak to is pointing the finger in your direction because of your history with her."

"Aaah," Truman replied, suitably shocked. But was it an act? "I had no idea. I'm sorry to hear that." He paused for a moment. "I see why you came to see me and why everyone would suspect me. That's to be expected, I suppose." He sighed.

"Do you know anything about her kidnapping?"

"Absolutely not," Truman said in calm but strong terms. "I had nothing to do with her kidnapping. When did this happen?"

"The night before last."

A triumphant smile spread over his face. "Well, there you go then. It couldn't have been me. I wasn't even in the country. I was in Spain. Do you want proof?"

"No," Jon stated. "We know you were out of the country."

Truman narrowed his eyes. "So what are you getting at?"

Ellen had an inkling that he knew full well what she was suggesting, but he was trying to drag it out of her. Well, she thought, why keep him waiting? "You're a rich man. Very rich. And you have something of a history with Roxy. I think it's fair to say you don't like her, right?"

"I'm not her biggest fan. I'll agree with that," Truman explained.

"She fairly ruined your life," Ellen stated. "Ended your marriage and separated you from your kids. I don't think it's unlikely that you'd want revenge for that, do you?"

"That was four years ago," Truman countered.

"Four years is nothing," Ellen pushed.

"That's a matter of opinion," he muttered. "What are you asking me?"

Time to come out and say it. "Did you pay to have her kidnapped?"

"Did I pay for a kidnapping?" Truman asked, sounding incredulous. "Are you for real? I wouldn't know where to start, even if I did want to, which I don't, in case that wasn't clear." He leaned forward. "What happened between Roxy

199

and I is ancient history. I have no interest in her or her life and want to forget the whole damn thing. But if you're asking if I could have paid for it? Then yes, I could. I have the money. I have the means, and I guess I have the motive, too. But would I do it? Hell no. That's crazy talk. I had nothing to do with this, okay?"

Ellen stared at the man opposite, searching his face for any hint that he might be lying to them.

"Do your research," Truman suggested. "Go on. Pull my bank and phone records. See what you can dig up. I guarantee you'll be disappointed."

"We might just do that," Jon countered.

"Please do. Especially if it gets you off my back. I'm a busy man, and I don't have time for this. So, if we're done here, I'd like to get back to my work."

"Of course," Jon replied. "We'll be in touch."

"I'll look forward to it," Truman stated, watching while they got up.

As if on cue, Sylvie appeared and ushered them out, guiding them to the front door and shutting it behind them.

"What do you think?" Jon asked as they climbed back into the car.

"I don't know." Ellen thought about the encounter and what he'd said to them. "I just don't know."

29

Mary sat in the shadows of the Nottingham Council House in the Old Market Square, surrounded by people going about their business, shopping, eating, meeting friends, or running errands. There were people everywhere, but that was exactly what she wanted. She needed the safety of a public space in broad daylight to hide in plain sight. There were some crazy people in this world, and some wouldn't think twice about attacking someone out in the open. But not everyone was like that, and the majority of people would at least pause before doing something too mad in the middle of a busy shopping centre.

In an effort to hide her identity and frustrate attempts to find her further, she'd bought a hoody and a cap, which she pulled low over her face.

Her mind had been a mess after learning at the Queen's Medical Centre that the man she'd met in the park the night before was also the victim who'd been found dead in the river.

They'd killed him for talking, and now they wanted her. That much was clear. Someone had already turned up at her place of work, which meant they knew who she was. They'd done their research, and now she was being hunted.

Fearing for her life, she'd left the hospital in a hurry and made her way into town using a bus before hitting the shops and picking up a hoody and cap.

She'd already called her family and told them to leave the house and stay with a friend, but try as she might, she couldn't get in touch with Vanessa, her housemate. Vanessa had undoubtedly turned her phone off or left it in her locker, neither of which was unusual. But right now, when she needed to get in touch, it was the most annoying thing in the world.

Surmising that the hospital was one place the thugs might be watching, if they knew the body was there, she'd departed at pace. But now she wished she'd tried to find Vanessa or her boyfriend, Ben, while she'd been there. Of course, that might not have worked, and it wouldn't have been the first time she'd tried and failed to find them. They were busy people, and the hospital was a labyrinth. But she should have at least tried.

There was no way she was going back, though. No way in hell.

Instead, she resorted to phone calls, voice messages, and texts in the hope of getting through.

Between calls, she hunted through the local and national news sites, looking for any update on the case, until she suddenly noticed a face she recognised.

"Rob?" she whispered. It was his face on a video. She popped an earbud in and hit play.

Rob's voice filled her head as she listened to him pleading with the viewers and the general public for help and leads. They needed to identify the body they'd found in the River Idle.

Mary bit her lip, aware that she had some valuable info to give Rob about the victim. She couldn't identify him formally, having never found out his full name, but she might be able to help. She needed to call him.

She marked it on her mental to-do list as she watched the press conference play out and how Rob seemed suddenly rattled after Sean Mason appeared. Mary grunted and turned the video off. She knew a fair amount about the Masons and their reputation. It was one of those secrets that hid in plain sight. Known but often ignored by many because the Masons could be fairly free with their money when it came to deserving causes. Of course, they could also be incredibly violent to those who stood in their way... if the rumours were to be believed.

Well, at least Loxley was handling the case, she thought, pleased. She trusted him after working with him on the Clipstone case and her story following it. He was one of the good ones.

Still, even skilled detectives needed a helping hand from time to time.

Returning her attention to her phone with the intention of calling him, she rechecked her messages, hoping Vanessa had phoned or at least seen her notifications. But no, there was nothing.

Distracted and annoyed, she called Vanessa once more. "Come on, answer," she hissed, but it went straight to voicemail again. She ended the call with an angry tap of her thumb.

"Miss Day?"

Mary looked up and instantly regretted it. She gazed straight into the face of a large man who loomed over her. Behind him, two more men glanced at her while watching their surroundings.

It was them.

She was instantly sure of it as her gut twisted in terrible fear. They'd found her.

Could she bluff them? "Um, who?"

The man smiled. He obviously wasn't fooled. "Don't make a scene, Mary, and come with me." He lunged for her.

Slapping his hand away, Mary rolled sideways off the concrete block she'd been sitting on. She sprang to her feet and sprinted like her life depended on it, because it literally did. With the hefty dose of adrenaline the scare brought her, she found speeds she'd never dreamed of as she charged up the side of the city council building, utterly terrified.

A quick glance behind only confirmed her fears. They were chasing her.

To her left, the cut-through known as Greyhound Street rushed up. She veered left and thundered into the tunnel, bouncing off the wall before slamming right back into fifth gear. Ahead, a couple of beefy guys stepped out of a barbershop. They looked like rugby players, judging from their size.

Perfect.

"Help," she yelled. She didn't need to try and sound desperate or scared, she already was. "Help me. They want to kill me."

"What?"

"Who?" the men asked, surprised.

"Them." She turned.

The three men barrelled down the tunnel with murderous expressions on their faces. Mary screamed and ran.

A second later, shouts and yells echoed up the alley behind her.

"Oi, leave her."

She didn't stop. Taking the left-hand bend at top speed, she charged along the final stretch of the tunnel to the sounds of shouting and a scuffle not too far behind.

"We'll find you, Mary," one of them yelled. "You can't hide."

Rushing out of the tunnel to see the majestic statue of Brian Clough standing on Speakers' Corner with his hands held high, she ran up Queen Street and didn't stop until she was confident that she'd lost them. She ended up in the Lace Market district, choosing to go somewhere public and busy. Leaning up against a wall, she took a moment to catch her breath and wondered how on earth they'd found her.

She'd been so careful, even buying the clothes with cash just in case they were *that* sophisticated.

It made no sense.

Her breathing slowed. She calmed down and pulled her phone out, hoping that Vanessa might have called or messaged... but no. She hadn't.

"Shit."

She stared at the illuminated screen in her hand, it suddenly hit her.

Her phone. It was her phone. That's how they were tracking her. They were far more sophisticated than she'd thought.

In that instant, the device that had, up until this point, been her lifeline, suddenly took on a whole new persona. It could get her killed.

Disgusted, Mary threw it to the floor as if it was some monstrous bug. Without thinking, she stamped on it over and over before picking it up and smashing it into the corner of a wall until it was destroyed. A few passersby gave her curious looks, but she didn't care.

Staring at the mess of metal and glass in her bleeding hand, she realised she'd not called Rob.

"Damn it," she grunted, annoyed she'd not called him first. Screw it, she had bigger problems. Rob could wait.

Mary walked to the nearest bin and dropped her phone inside. She needed to leave the area and clean up her cut hand, and then she needed to come up with a plan.

If those thugs couldn't find her, they'd probably go after someone they could use as bait, like Vanessa.

30

With latex-gloved hands, Guy checked through the clear plastic bags containing the postmortem exhibits and ensured they had everything they needed. He'd been here for a couple of hours, taking notes as pathologist, May Shephard, and her two assistants went about their work. Watching them slice the nameless body open and remove the various organs for examination and cataloguing was gruesome, but he'd seen quite a few of these by now and was used to the process.

Besides, he was usually busy scribbling down notes as the pathologist related her findings to him or receiving exhibits removed from the victim's body, which would need bagging and indexing for later reference and use.

They were pretty dull affairs usually, and this one was no different.

Satisfied that he had everything he needed, he pulled out his phone and quickly texted Rob: *All done.*

After hitting send, he noticed a reply from Erika and smiled at the reminder that he was going on a date with her tonight. He was looking forward to it. She was quite the catch, but there was more to this than simple attraction. She had secrets he needed to uncover, and tonight would be another chance for him to move closer to the truth.

He opened the text. *How about The Alchemist Bar? Have you ever been? It's fun.*

Guy frowned. He'd heard of it but had never actually been there. He shrugged and started to tap out his reply, only for the door to open, interrupting him. May Shephard walked in, drying her hands on a paper towel that she dropped in a nearby bin.

"Interrupting anything?" She eyed the phone in his hands suspiciously.

Guy raised an eyebrow at the comment, which was likely designed to make him feel like a naughty school boy, but failed. "Nothing that can't wait," he answered, and returned the phone to his pocket. "All done, then?"

"Of course," she replied stubbornly, refusing to give ground. She peered at him for a second more before relaxing. "Looks like your John Doe was beaten to within an inch of his life. He wasn't dead when he entered the water, but he might as well have been. He was in no state to save himself and succumbed to the water in short order. It was probably a mix of the cold and water inhalation. As for who he is, I'm no closer. Have you heard back about the fingerprints or DNA?"

Guy shook his head. "No. They were submitted a while ago, but as far as I know, there've been no matches. We're no closer to figuring out who he is."

May nodded. "All right. Well, that's all I have for you. Good luck."

"Thanks," he replied.

But she'd already turned and was walking out.

He watched her go, then grabbed his phone and returned to the text message he'd started to send Erika. He considered her suggestion and figured, why not? It sounded like a quirky place.

Sounds interesting, he replied. *What time works for you?*

He smiled at the message, keen to know more about the enigmatic Erika and just what her interest in Loxley might be. He'd find out one way or another. He was sure of that.

31

"So, our John Doe was beaten up and then drowned because of his injuries," Rob remarked, speaking to Guy on the phone.

Rob gazed out of the window he was sitting beside and let his attention roam over Retford's Market square below as people went about their business. The row of shops on the far side, beyond the war memorial and the road that ran along the side of the square, looked tired. Several of them were closed with To Let signs in their windows, but Rob wasn't sure how viable some were as places of business. The British high street was dying a long, slow, agonising death as a result of customers doing their shopping online, at retail parks or in the larger city centres where there was more choice. Small high streets like Retford's simply cou dn't compete and were haemorrhaging customers at an alarming rate. Only charity shops and coffee bars were left, and little else.

It was a sad state of affairs, and although he had mixed feelings about the town due to his personal history with it, it wasn't a pleasant thing to see. He would have preferred the town to thrive and find a way forward in this new digital era. But could it?

"That's what the pathologist said," Guy said. "He was so badly hurt from the attack that he couldn't save himself, whoever he is."

"And we've got no further in identifying him?"

"No, not yet," Guy confirmed. "There's no record of him either in the fingerprint or DNA databases."

"Dental?" Rob asked. It was a leap, but they were clutching at straws.

"Not so far," Guy replied. "But you know that works differently."

"Yeah, I know. Okay, thanks for taking this on for me," Rob said. "I know I just dumped it on you from a great height."

Guy laughed. "I'm used to being dumped on. Right, I've got a few things to sort out before I end my shift, so I'd better get on. Nick's working me hard on this abduction case, and I've got a date tonight."

"Aaah, yes. Erika, right? She mentioned you."

"Did she? Nothing bad, I hope." He sounded much more interested in Erika's opinion of him than in the postmortem results, but that was to be expected.

"No, nothing bad. Actually, she was asking my opinion of you."

Guy paused. "Oh? Well, you can't have said anything too bad, otherwise, I doubt I'd be going on a second date."

"Perhaps," Rob replied enigmatically. "But that's between me and Erika."

"She clearly trusts your opinion."

"Yeah," Rob answered, raising an eyebrow. "I'm not sure why. I'm hardly an expert on relationships."

"And yet, here we are."

"Aye. Now, don't you keep her out too late, you hear? She's meant to be looking after my cat, so I can't have her getting distracted."

Guy laughed. "Indeed not. I'll be sure to have her back before her curfew."

"You do that. Have fun."

"Cheers."

Rob hung up and turned to Scarlett who sat nearby at his laptop.

"Nothing new then?" she asked, still staring at the screen.

"Nope. We have a cause of death, but that's all. Still no idea who the hell this guy is."

"We'll find him." she sounded sure of herself. "Right, I'm about set up. You just need to join the call, and they'll be able to see and hear you."

Rob got up and stood behind Scarlett to peer down at the screen. She'd been setting him up on a video call with Nick.

"When you're ready, just click that, and you'll join the call," Scarlett stated.

"Perfect," Rob said. She vacated the chair.

He sat and got comfortable while Scarlett waited behind him, her reflection on the screen.

Once settled, he clicked the little blue button and waited for the program to let him in. Seconds later, one of the video windows sprang into life, and Nick appeared on the feed.

"Rob, you made it. Great."

"Was there any doubt?"

"Of course not. Your computer skills astound me."

Behind him, Scarlett coughed.

Rob grunted and decided to come clean. "Cheers, but it was all Scarlett's work."

"I guessed." Nick smiled. "Hi, Scarlett."

"Hi," she replied.

"Hey, Rob. Are computers still little magic boxes to you?"

"Absolutely. They've got these tiny critters inside them running around and making the screen work."

Nick smirked. "Did you speak to Guy?"

"Yeah. We're no closer," Rob commented and relayed Guy's findings to him. "I think he's heading back to the Lodge now."

"Great. Thanks for stealing one of my team during this simple abduction case, by the way. We were overstaffed and underworked," he replied sarcastically.

"Anytime," Rob said. "Are they gonna join us soon?"

214

A third video feed appeared below his and Nick's faces, revealing Ellen sitting beside Jon Pilgrim.

"Hello," Nick said.

"Hi," Rob joined in.

Ellen spoke, followed by Jon, but there was no sound.

"Huston, we have a problem," Rob remarked.

"Err, hey, guys? Guys? Hey?" Nick tried to interrupt them, but they continued to talk, unaware of the issue. He waved at them. "You're on mute. You need to turn mute off. We can't hear you."

"Yeah," Rob added in agreement. "We can't hear you. Come on, this is simple stuff that even I can do."

Scarlett punched him on the shoulder.

"That Scarlett can do, not me, obviously. I'm useless."

"Better," Scarlett grunted.

Rob watched them scramble around, trying to unmute themselves, finding their expressions of dismay amusing.

Suddenly a new sound channel came to life.

"Are we in?" Jon asked.

"Can you hear us?" Ellen said. "Ground control, come in, ground control."

"Yay, we can hear you." Nick smiled.

"Loud and clear," Rob stared.

"Excellent," Jon said. "Sorry about that. Technical hitch. Rob, good to see you. You, too, Nick."

"Thanks," Rob said.

"Cheers," Nick added.

"It's great to see you, too," Rob said. "It's been too long. We should meet up sometime."

"Yeah, that would be fun," Jon agreed. "We'll talk about that later, though. We're here for a reason, after all."

"Truman Collins," Rob muttered darkly. "How'd it go?"

"The interview went about as smoothly as I could have hoped, given why we were there."

"He kicked us out in the end," Ellen said. "But we got to ask a few questions and get a sense of the man."

"I take it he's denying everything?" Rob asked.

"Of course he is," Ellen said. "He correctly pointed out that he was away at the time of the kidnapping, with photographic evidence to prove it. So he couldn't have been the kidnapper. Which is fine. We're not disputing that."

"Indeed not. I wouldn't expect him to be," Rob replied. "Not when he can just pay for others to do it for him while he's off enjoying himself. You put that to him, right?"

"We did," Ellen confirmed.

"To his credit," Jon added, "he said that he *could* pay for such a thing, but didn't. All this is ancient history, according to him, and he's moved past it."

"He even insinuated that it was Roxy who kept harassing him," Ellen said.

"Did you believe him?" Rob asked.

Jon and Ellen swapped glances.

"Hard to be sure," Ellen answered eventually. "I can't say for certain if he was lying or not, for obvious reasons, but four years really isn't all that long."

"Not for a family grudge," Rob stated. "And I should know. So hopefully we aren't going to take his denial at face value?"

"Nope," Jon said. "We're going to pull his bank records, which will be a nightmare. He owns a bunch of companies and shell corporations all around the world, many of which have offshore accounts. So it's not going to be easy."

"It's going to take some time," Rob agreed.

"Yeah," Ellen affirmed. "We're also going to get a warrant to search his houses, of which there are a few."

"Ellen, what was your read of Truman?" Rob asked. "You drove down there so you could be in the meeting, so I'm curious what you thought?"

She frowned. "I guess the one word that came to mind in his office was slimy. I didn't like being near him."

"Because of how the meeting went or because he allegedly raped Roxy?"

Ellen shrugged. "I honestly don't know. I can't say if he was lying to us or not because I didn't get a sense of that one way or the other. But he isn't a man I'd want to spend any time with. And if you were to ask me if I think he's guilty, I'd

217

probably say that he was. But my personal feelings about him aren't gonna stand up in court."

"No, they're not," Rob said. "Well, it looks like you're at the start of a long road. Good luck."

"Thanks, we're gonna need it," Ellen replied.

"So, Nick tells me you're in Retford?" Jon asked. "Is that right?"

"Yeah," Rob confirmed. "On a murder case. Someone was beaten nearly to death and dumped in the river, which killed him. And so far, we have no idea who he is."

"Well, you go careful up there. I know you have history with that town. Let me know how it all goes, yeah?"

"Thanks, I will."

32

In the darkness and shadows of his home, Bill sat in the living room in his favourite armchair, resting his head on his hand and staring into the middle distance. But his thoughts were far away, in a sea of bubbling anger and regret as he ruminated on everything that had happened and how he could have done something different.

No matter what he did, he couldn't escape from an endless cycle of recriminations, thinking about how he could ruin Rob, just as Rob had ruined him.

Somehow, Rob had destroyed his life without even trying. This galled him no end. He'd worked so hard to try and expose Rob for who he was, only to end up jobless and ridiculed by everyone but his mother while Loxley remained untouched.

There was no way Rob could do that without being utterly corrupt. What strings had that scumbag pulled to get him fired? Which of the higher-up officers was beholden to Rob, or his family, the Masons?

Because that was where Rob was getting his orders from, wasn't it? He was the son of the Mason family kingpin and a key player in their multi-million-pound firm of criminality.

Why couldn't they see that? Why was he the only one who saw this rampant corruption? It was so obvious.

And yet, here he was, sitting in the dark as the afternoon wore on, having long ago forgotten what time it was.

The apartment stank, and he hated it. He was usually so clean and tidy, but all this with his job had driven him to distraction. Now he just left his mess where he dropped it. He didn't care. It didn't matter. Nothing mattered anymore. Nothing, apart from getting revenge on Rob, of course. That was the only thing that kept him going.

He needed that revenge. He needed to see Rob's face fall when he realised that the man behind his downfall was him. That was what drove him now. Nothing else.

But how?

How could he do that now that he wasn't an officer?

He thought back to his meeting with Guy earlier today and his insistence that getting revenge was somehow easier now that he was outside the police.

He understood what Guy was getting at, that he was no longer bound by the rules and ethics of the force, but that was a double-edged sword. The rules were gone, true, but so was the backup and resources that came with being an officer of the law.

He'd need to finance this himself. He'd need to cultivate his contacts and, somehow, manoeuvre things to his advantage.

Just the idea of it gave him a headache. Dejected and at a loss as to how to move forward, Bill sank further into the seat and dropped his head into his hands.

After several moments with his eyes closed, Bill's phone vibrated.

The shock snapped him out of his reverie and back to reality. He grabbed the device and checked the caller ID.

Mum.

He answered it. "Mum?"

"William," she gasped on the other end of the line. "Come, please. You have to help me. He's drunk…" Something smashed in the distance on the call. What was his father doing? "I'm scared. He hit me. Please."

"Mum, I'm coming. Lock yourself in the toilet. I'll be there as soon as I can."

"Okay. Yes, I can do that."

"Are you talking to our no-good son again?" his father yelled on the other end of the line. The call ended.

"Shit."

Within seconds, Bill was out the door and jumping into his car, all thoughts of Rob and his unceremonious exit from the police forgotten. His mother was in danger, and he was the only one who could help. She'd called him, and he wasn't going to let her down.

The tyres on his car squealed as he backed out of his driveway before changing gear and accelerating down the street. It wasn't far, just a few minutes' drive across Arnold to Weaverthorpe Road. Utterly focused on getting there as quickly and safely as possible, he soon pulled into his parents' road at speed, barrelled along it until he skidded to a stop, and rocketed out.

Had she made it to the bathroom and locked herself in? From what he'd heard at the end of their call, it didn't sound like it.

Bill ran up the path to the side door, grateful that they usually insisted on leaving it unlocked despite his protests, and charged inside. Shouting came from the lounge, and he rushed through.

"He's a bloody idiot." His dad loomed over his mother, dominating her into silence. "You know it as much as I do... Oh, look, he's here. The failure has arrived."

"Leave her alone, Dad," Bill rumbled as he glanced at his mother.

She had a cut on her cheek and the beginnings of a bruise surrounding it.

"William," his mum whimpered.

"Did you hit her?"

"Get out of this house," his dad snapped.

"Did you hit her?"

"So what if I did? She's my wife, and I'll do what I damn well like, especially when she's under the impression that you're not a goddamn prick."

"You touch her again," Bill threatened. He stepped closer and pointed his finger. "You dare touch her again…"

"And you'll do what, freak? Do you think you can take me? Huh? You think you're the big, strong man? You're nothing. You're a shit stain, nothing more."

Gritting his teeth, Bill squeezed his fists but held them in check. Turning his attention to his mum, he held out his hand. "Come with me."

His dad shoved her behind him, and she fell. She dropped to her knees and yelped.

"Don't you dare take her from me. She's mine."

"Don't you hurt her! Don't you dare hurt her."

"Make me," his dad thundered. He stepped closer and shoved him. "Go on, make me. Do your worst. Do it. Come on, make me listen to you."

"Don't push me," Bill growled.

His dad shoved him again. "Look at you. Weak. Pathetic." He punctuated each word with a prod. "You're no son of mine. I don't know who you are. What I do know is that you're a loser who can't help himself, let alone his mother."

223

Bill saw red. Somewhere, deep inside, the anger that he'd been bottling up broke free. The gates were suddenly flung wide. Bill roared and lunged at his father. He struck him hard in the chest. His dad stumbled and fell. A loud thud sounded. His dad's head caught the corner of the coffee table. He landed awkwardly, falling still.

Bill stared down, utterly transfixed with horror. Blood pooled behind his father's head, and his glazed eyes stared into nothingness. Somehow, Bill knew in that instant that things had suddenly changed.

His dad was dead... and he'd killed him.

His rage was gone as deep, primal fear gripped him, freezing him to the spot. All he could do was stare at the lifeless body and wonder how on earth he could have done such a thing.

Kneeling beside his dad, his mother sighed, closed her eyes, and leaned into her husband. She cradled his head and held him close while she quietly sobbed.

"I... I didn't..." Bill said, trying to say something but finding he had no words. He didn't know what to say or do. "He shouldn't have..." All his excuses or explanations just died on his lips. None of them seemed right or sufficient. Had hadn't meant to kill him... or had he? Maybe he did? Dad was an old-fashioned, belligerent fool who thought his wife was his property. There was no room for idiots like that in this society, none at all.

Maybe Bill had done the world and his mother a favour?

His mum got slowly to her feet and started to walk out of the lounge.

"Mum, I..."

"Quiet," she snapped. "You don't get to speak right now. You did this, Bill. I trusted you, and this is how you repay me? This is what you do to me? How could you?"

"But, no. He was hurting you. I couldn't let him."

"I was fine."

"You're not fine. You're bleeding."

She raised her fingers to her cheek and touched the cut. When she pulled her hand away, they were spotted with blood. "I've had worse."

"How...? What? Mum, I saved you. I couldn't let him..."

"I didn't need saving, Bill, I needed help. I was fine. I didn't need a knight in shining armour to whisk me away. I'm quite capable of looking after myself."

"What?" Bill felt confused. "You called me."

She sighed, and tears glistened in tracks down her cheek. "Yes, because I wanted help. I needed to get him to bed so he could sleep it off. And now I have this to deal with."

"I did it. I'll admit to it."

225

His mother rolled her eyes and pushed past him into the hallway, where she grabbed the phone and dialled 999.

Bill watched her do it, resigned to his fate. They'd come for him, and that would be it. He'd go to prison, and that would be his life. The end of his life. Rob had won.

"Ambulance, please," his mother said into the phone. "Hello, yes. I need some help. My husband has tripped and fallen and banged his head on the corner of the coffee table. I think..." She choked but soon reined herself in. "I think he's dead."

Bill watched in bewildered confusion. She gave the operator the details they needed before hanging up. She'd just lied for him. She'd covered for him. What was she doing? "Mum?"

"What?" she answered while placing the phone on the table.

"He didn't trip. I pushed him."

"He tripped," his mum snapped. "He tripped and fell after an argument with me. Then you came round, and this is how you found us, okay?"

"What? Are you sure?"

"Do you want to go to prison?"

Bill paused for a moment before shaking his head. Prison was no place for a police officer. "No."

"Then do as I say. The police will want to talk to you, so stay here for now, but after that, I want you out of here."

"What?"

"You heard me. I need you gone."

"You don't have to do this, Mum. He was an idiot. He hit you, for God's sake. You're better off without him."

"And you know that for sure, do you?" She shook her head. "He had his faults, I'll admit, but I had long ago accepted them. He was who he was, and no amount of work on my part was going to change that."

"What are you saying?"

"I'm saying that I loved him, William. You might not understand that or agree with it, but I did, and he didn't deserve this."

"Then let me take the blame..."

"No! You're all I have now. I don't agree with what you did, but I understand why you did it and I do not want you to go to prison. It's just going to take me a little time to process all this, okay?"

"Okay..."

"Good. Get yourself ready. They won't be long now."

Bill sighed and walked out the room. He didn't want to be in there any longer than he needed to be, and he had a lot to work through.

He'd killed a man. It was by accident, admittedly, but the fact remained that he was to blame for it.

Bill found a chair in another room, lowered himself into it, and closed his eyes as he waited for the emergency services to arrive.

33

Teri pulled up at the side of the road and tugged the handbrake on. Clicking it into place, she looked up. Shaken after her encounter with his neighbours on Spital Hill, she'd rushed home, terrified that she'd done the wrong thing. But she'd barely been there for more than a few minutes before she had to leave. There were so many reminders of what they'd had together in her flat. It was too painful.

Storming out, she'd jumped in her car and driven south to Markham Moor and the McDonald's on the A1. She needed to get away and try to clear her head. Plus, she was hungry. She needed a plan.

Time was going on, and she was at work tomorrow.

Work, ugh!

The very thought of walking back in there after all this chilled her to the bone. In theory, he was due to be there, too, but she was starting to question if she'd ever see him again. She'd continued to call and text, hoping he was still out there somewhere and might somehow see her messages if he charged his phone. But as the hours passed with no contact from him, she was starting to entertain some serious doubts.

What if something had happened? Had his meeting with this reporter gone so horribly wrong that, for whatever reason, he could no longer call? Was someone stopping him? Was he kidnapped?

Thoughts of her work and what they did there flashed through her mind. She thought of those rooms and the idea that he might be in one of them. They had broken the rules, and the punishment for such a breach was severe. They'd known that going into this, but somehow, they'd convinced themselves everything would be okay. They'd been super careful. They'd hidden their relationship from everyone at work, keeping their distance from each other the whole time.

But did someone know?

Was it Rubious? Did he know? Or maybe Crimson? Thoughts of her work colleagues sent a shiver down her spine.

She shook her head as she glanced up and down Chancery Lane. She was a short distance from the main entrance to Kings Park and was about to break another of her contact's rules.

Do not return to the scene of the meeting.

Their contact had been quite clear on this, saying that they should at no point over the next few days go back into Kings Park and visit the meeting place.

But Teri couldn't take it anymore. She'd had it with these rules. She needed to know where he was. Was he okay, or had something happened to him?

Taking a deep breath, Teri climbed out of the car, locked it, and strode along the side of the road beside the lush green hedgerow until she turned left opposite the Old Police Station and moved into Kings Park.

As she stepped through the entrance, she slowed. Beyond the gates was a long paved path lined with benches and a pond halfway up. The park's main footbridge over the River Idle was at the end of that path, but it was cordoned off with police tape, and an officer in a high-vis vest stood guard. Beyond him, she made out more officers walking in lines along the banks of the river. They were conducting a search.

Teri took a moment to take this in. The meeting point was on the other side of the river, but there was no way over there without going the long way around. But thoughts of navigating her way around there were overshadowed by the presence of the police officers.

What were they doing here?

Was it to do with him?

What was going on?

A sudden need to know gripped her. She sped up and marched along the path, around the pond, and over to the officer on guard.

"Um, hi," she began.

"Miss," the officer greeted her. "How can I help you?"

"What's going on? I wanted to walk over the bridge into the park."

"Sorry, you'll have to go around. This is an active crime scene now."

She eyed him suspiciously. "Why? What's happened?"

He raised an eyebrow in surprise. "A body was found in the river this morning," he replied. "A young man. You wouldn't know anything about it, would you?"

Teri's stomach dropped as the bottom fell out of her world. "A... young man?"

"That's right. It's been on the news. Have you not seen?"

"I didn't... I don't watch the news..." she muttered.

The officer gave her a pitying look. "Well, maybe you should. Were you near the park last night?"

Shock gripped her, and she answered almost on autopilot. "Sorry, no. I was at home."

"Okay. Well, if you think you might know something, feel free to get in touch."

"I will, thanks." She turned and walked out of the park in a daze.

A body? They'd found a body in the river. The body of a young man. Could it be? Was it him? Was it her partner? Her lover? Had something happened to him?

As she made her way back the way she'd come, she sped up, and once she was out of the gate, ran back to her car. She couldn't get into it fast enough. Slamming it into gear, she pulled out into the road, cutting up a car she'd not seen. He honked, but she ignored it and sped home, taking corners at speed and jumping several red lights.

Leaving her car on the side of the road, she charged over to the building's outer door, unlocked it, and rushed inside, heading for her flat.

Reaching her front door, Teri inserted her key and tried to unlock it, only to find it already unlocked.

Had she forgotten to lock it? Probably. She barged in, slamming the door behind her, and stormed into her living room.

After dumping her bag, she ran her fingers through her hair and paced back and forth. She suddenly found herself at a loss. What could she do? Was there anything she could do? One thing was for sure: she wouldn't talk to any police. No way.

She needed to know more. There was a chance, a slim chance, that the victim was not him. It could be someone else. There was no proof. Nothing.

Opening her laptop, she powered it up and logged in. It seemed a little sluggish, and it took ages to load up the browser. After a few moments, it seemed to speed up, so she started searching. It didn't take long for her to find several accounts of what had been found in the river, complete with a description of the victim and what he'd been wearing.

To her dismay, the description matched what he'd been wearing that day, including his favourite coat. Tears streamed down her cheeks while she stared at the screen in shock.

That was the last straw. Rules be damned, she needed to talk to her contact. Teri hunted for the number, found it saved in a separate unnamed file on her laptop, and punched it into her phone.

She'd done everything her contact had told her to do, taken every security measure, and now, it seemed like it had not been enough.

As she listened to the ringing line, waiting for the call to be answered, she noticed some trinkets on a nearby bookshelf had fallen over. She frowned at these out-of-place items. Had they fallen over while she'd been out? Had she unwittingly knocked them over?

The call clicked through, and a digitised voice sounded over the line, masking their real voice. "Hello, Cerise," the voice said, using her work-assigned code name.

"Riddle," Teri said. "You have to tell me, has something happened? They found a body in the river. Is it him? Is he dead?"

"Look, I don't know for certain, but yeah, maybe?" Riddle replied carefully.

"Oh Christ." Teri sobbed.

"I'm really sorry. I mean, I can't be sure, but yes, I think it might be Carmine," Riddle added, using his code name, too.

Teri sobbed as the emotion racked her body. "Goddamn it, Riddle. You said he'd be safe. You said this would work. What happened? Was it the reporter? Did they do this?"

"No. It's not the reporter. I trust her."

"Her?" Teri asked. It was the first time Riddle had referred to the reporter in a way that identified their gender.

"Shit, sorry. I shouldn't have said that. This is... stressful."

"No shit!"

"Sorry, I know this is worse for you. I can't imagine, but you can't let this get to you."

Teri waved her condolences away. She couldn't think about Carmine right now. If she did, she'd be an emotional wreck in a matter of moments. She needed to focus on the situation she found herself in and deal with that. She needed to know who'd done this and how they'd found out. "So, do you think this is them? Do you think they found out about the meeting?"

"Yeah, I do. I think they knew about the meeting."

"Just the meeting? Do they know about me? Am I safe? I'm going in tomorrow. I can't go in if they know about me, too."

"If they knew about you, you wouldn't be talking to me now. They know where you live, remember."

Teri nodded to herself. Riddle was right. If they knew she was involved, they wouldn't hesitate to come after her and kill her, too. But they hadn't, which meant they didn't know. "So, what do I do?"

"Act normal," Riddle replied. "If you're due in at work tomorrow, then go in. Do not give them any reason to suspect you."

"But he's dead! He... Carmine is dead. They killed him. Why would I want to go back in?"

"Because if you don't, you know what will happen. But if you do, you might be able to find out who knew about the meeting."

Riddle was right. She'd been warned about the repercussions if she acted against them in any way. They'd come for her, and they'd come for her friends and family. She couldn't risk that, which left her only one option.

"Pissing hell!"

34

Staring at the glowing screen of his laptop, he watched the slightly jerky feed from the spy camera he'd placed in the front room of Cerise's flat. Her internet wasn't the fastest in the world, and streaming video and audio over it while she was trying to use her PC was causing a few issues, but he got the gist of what was going on as she spoke to someone called Riddle about the meeting Carmine had been to.

He smiled until he spotted her noticing some out-of-place items on one of her shelves. He cursed his foolishness. He should have been more careful and not hunted around her home quite so much. Would she realise that someone had broken in?

He hoped not.

He watched her move away from the shelf to focus on the call. Breathing a sigh of relief, he relaxed again. He should have done this months ago, he surmised, smiling at the screen as she finally hung up.

She didn't look happy, but that was to be expected.

Maybe he could be a shoulder for her to cry on?

Maybe that was his way in? Either way, he'd have fun watching her tonight.

35

Approaching home after nearly an hour's drive, Scarlett sighed and wondered if Rob hadn't got it right after all. Maybe she should have stayed in Retford, too. Navigating through the chaotic rush-hour traffic had been the usual headache-inducing nightmare that she was getting depressingly used to by now. But in theory, she'd return home to Chris and have a lovely evening with him, making the journey worth it.

Thinking back over her day, she'd found her time with Rob in Retford fascinating. His history and baggage with the town was on show to anyone who cared to look, and she hoped he'd be okay over the next few days.

He seemed to be treating the case as his own personal rehabilitation course by throwing himself into the water to see if he'd sink or swim.

She had an inkling that he'd be okay. These things were often never quite as bad as you might think.

Interestingly, it hadn't taken long for one of the Masons to show up, which meant they'd known he was there before the press conference. But if that was true, how had they found out? The logical but frustrating conclusion was that someone in the force had told them. But Scarlett chastised herself for jumping to this conclusion. It was easy to believe that there was yet another corrupt officer around after everything they'd been through, but it could just as easily have been one of the reporters at the crime scene or just a random observer.

Whatever the case, it was probably better that she didn't start this investigation by looking suspiciously at her colleagues.

As for the case itself, it was being annoyingly stubborn about giving up its secrets. They still didn't know some basic details about who the victim was, which made forward momentum difficult. Hopefully, they'd clear that hurdle tomorrow and push forward in a more meaningful way.

One can only hope. She navigated her way through the Park Estate in Nottingham city centre and finally into her driveway. The tyres crunched over the pea gravel as she came to a stop and gathered her things. Climbing out, she caught some movement out of the corner of her eye and glanced over to the end of her driveway.

Nick's friend, Calico Black, walked across the front of her driveway and glanced up at her. The pair shared a moment of connection before Calico stepped out of sight and was gone.

She briefly wondered if she was seeing things but then remembered her earlier chat with Nick when she'd asked him to arrange a meeting.

It seemed that Nick had come through for her.

Scarlett glanced up at her house. Lights were on inside, but she couldn't see Chris. He wouldn't miss her for a few minutes, she reasoned. This was her chance to talk to Calico, and she wasn't sure she'd get another one.

Dropping her stuff onto the driver's seat, she shut the car door, hurried over to the end of her driveway, and peered up the road in the direction that Calico had walked. Sure enough, she'd stopped beneath an illuminated lamppost and leaned against it, minding her own business.

After a scan around the empty roads, Scarlett sauntered up the pavement and approached the stocky, solidly built woman with short, blonde, mussed-up hair.

"Hi," Scarlett began. "Thanks for this."

Calico glanced at her, appearing a little annoyed about being here and raised an eyebrow. She sighed. "Walk with me," she said quietly and turned up the street without waiting.

Scarlett fell into step beside her, stuffing her hands in her pockets.

"I really appreciate this," Scarlett added.

"You said that."

"I know. I just..." Scarlett bit her lip. Calico had done this as a favour for Nick, so it was probably best that she didn't waste her time. "Sorry. Um, yeah. I wanted to talk to you

240

because I was just so impressed with what you did the other week, on that drugs raid. You were incredible."

Calico grunted. "I was just doing a job."

"I know. But your skill set is amazing. I've never seen someone do what you did, especially a woman."

Calico gave her a sceptical look. "I think you need to get out more."

"Hmm, yeah, maybe..." Why did she feel so on edge and nervous around her?

"What do you want, Detective?"

Scarlett took a breath. "I don't know if you're aware, but recently, the Mason Gang kidnapped and killed one of my friends from university. They tried to blackmail me into working for them, but I refused, so they killed Ninette, my friend."

"I'm sorry for your loss," Calico muttered.

Scarlett briefly smiled and nodded in thanks. "I want to make the Masons pay. One way or another, they cannot get away with this, and I just feel like, if I had certain skills, I might stand a better chance of getting what I want."

"I see. And you want me to... what? Teach you?"

Scarlett withered under Calico's gaze. Her request seemed so silly and ridiculous now that she'd finally said it. Maybe it was one of those ideas that seem so logical and understandable in your head, but when you expose them to the cold light of day and the scrutiny of others, they crumple into ash.

Shuffling from one foot to the other, she shrugged. "I kind of thought so…"

"I see." Calico sighed and looked away.

"I'm sorry, I just… I miss my friend, and these gangsters can't be allowed to get away with this." As she spoke, the raw emotion from the loss of her friend surfaced, a tear falling over her cheek. "They're hideous scum of the worst kind. They need to pay for what they've done to me and others."

"I understand your frustration, Scarlett, and you clearly cared for your friend…"

"I did."

"I'd like to help you, but what you're asking…"

"It's a lot, I know."

"It's more than a lot," Calico replied. "It's not exactly something I can give you a crash course on over the weekend. I have years of training and experience, much of it hard-won in combat situations on distant battlefields where close friends died. That's not something I can easily teach."

"Yeah, I know, but I thought…" Scarlett paused. *Had* she thought this through, though? Because now she pondered it while talking to Calico, it seemed like she hadn't. "Okay. Obviously, I realise that I will never learn the full range of skills that you have, that's impossible, but I thought maybe you might be able to help me with anything you think might be useful. That's all."

"You're not a soldier, Scarlett. You're an officer of the law. Sure, there are similarities, but there's a lot of differences, too. I'm from a different world to you. It's not as if you can run around with a gun or beat people up, is it?"

"Well, no..."

"If you want to learn how to defend yourself, maybe take up a martial art or something? You can learn a lot from YouTube these days."

It felt like this chance was slipping away. No matter how she approached this or what she said, it seemed that Calico had an answer for her, and it was never the answer that Scarlett wanted to hear. "Please, Calico. Please. I need your help. I need you to help me with this. I can't do it alone. I need your help."

Calico turned and stepped in front of her, bringing Scarlett to a sudden stop.

Surprised, Scarlett backed off a step, putting some personal space between them. "Wha..."

Calico grunted. "You *need* this? I'm not so sure. I think you need therapy more than training, Miss Stutely. This conversation is over. Go back to your house and your hubby, and if you know what's good for you, you'll forget about me. Goodnight."

With that, Calico spun and marched off, crossing the road and disappearing down a side street without looking back once.

Scarlett watched her go, utterly defeated.

"Shit," she hissed before striding back to her house.

36

"Oh, hey, that's you," the young man behind the bar said with a smile. "Cool."

Sitting at the bar in the Old Police Station at the end of the day, Rob had a news report on his phone while sipping on his pint. The cool liquid felt refreshing as he watched the brief clip of him talking to the press. Annoyingly, it was followed by a clip of his brother, Sean Mason, and his statement to the assembled press.

As the seconds passed, he couldn't help but notice that they gave more screen time to his brother than they did to him. Nice way to rub salt into the wound, he grumbled silently to himself.

"So, are you a detective then?" the server asked.

Tapping the power button on his phone, Rob turned the video off and looked up. "I am."

"Cool. And you're here, in the Old Police Station." He said it as if it was the most novel thing in the world.

"It certainly seems that way," he remarked, adding a slow nod to his reply.

"So, you're on that case, with the body in the river, right? How's it going? Have you found who did it yet?"

After another soothing sip from his glass, Rob leaned back in his chair and fixed the young man with a glare. "I *could* tell you, but then I'd have to kill you."

The young man seemed stricken by the comment. "Oh, sorry."

Rob smirked. "Yeah, sorry. I can't go around talking about the case to any old person, so..."

"I understand. Well, I hope you find him... or her... whoever did it."

"Thanks," Rob replied before the barman walked over to serve a new arrival. He watched the kid go, smiling to himself. He shouldn't mess with people like that, but it was just too much fun.

It did make him think back over the day's events, though, and lament that they hadn't made better progress in the case. But the issue was the victim's identity, and until they knew who the hell the young man was that they'd pulled out of the river, they really weren't going to get very far.

Someone out there must know who he was. They just needed to keep pushing ahead until the truth was finally revealed.

A group of people entered and approached the bar, talking amongst themselves.

Feeling like he was in the way, Rob stuffed his phone into his pocket and got up from his stool. Spotting a curious photo, he ambled over to the wall opposite to get a better look.

It was an old black-and-white photo taken at the front of the building, back when it was a serving police station. It featured twenty-nine police officers in full uniform, sitting or standing in three rows. There were some impressive handlebar moustaches on display in the image, with only three of the officers without one. Maybe they were standard issue back then.

"That's a lot of facial hair," said a voice just behind him.

Rob turned to see a familiar but unwelcome face.

"Evening, Rob," Sean Mason said with a smile. "Pondering a new look, are we?"

Rob grunted. "What are you doing here?"

"It's a bar, Rob. I'm allowed to have a drink every now and then," Sean replied. "It's a free world."

"Yeah." Rob turned back to the photo and peered at the scruffy dog one of the officers on the front row had sitting before him.

"I hope I didn't steal your thunder at the press conference earlier today. I only wanted to help."

Rob sighed. "Help?" He turned to his brother. "How did that help?"

"I'm something of a local celebrity, Rob. People know me and my family. With me there, you had a little more exposure for the case."

"I see. Well, isn't that just wonderful," Rob remarked in an even tone. "I'd like to think that an unidentified body in a river wouldn't need promoting further, but you are, unfortunately, probably right."

"I know I'm right."

"So why are you here, Sean? Did you come to gloat and tell me how wonderful your family is for helping us out, or was there an even more odious reason?"

Sean grinned as if holding back what he really wanted to say before finally answering. "No, actually." Sean fixed him with a steely glare. "Father would like a word."

"Dear old dad is here, too, is he?" Rob asked. "How lovely."

"He won't keep you long."

"And what if I say no?" Rob felt unsure how to handle this and was sorely tempted to tell Sean where to go and disappear to his room in the attached hotel. But, as uncomfortable as this encounter with his father might be, there was a chance it could shed some light on the case at hand. Hell, his dad may even know who the victim was, and that would certainly be worth his time.

After all, it wasn't as if he could just pick and choose where his information came from.

"That's your choice," Sean replied. "He's round the back. Follow me if you want to say hello."

Rob watched as Sean turned and sauntered back around behind the bar and, for a long moment, remained rooted to the spot, unsure whether to go or not.

But in the end, there really was only one option open to him.

Rob followed in Sean's footsteps and walked behind the bar into a long corridor with several doors on either side. He couldn't see Sean right away, so moved along the hall until he reached the first door on his left. Inside what was once a former prisoner cell was a set of table and chairs, complete with a candle and menu. His father sat on the far side of it, looking out at him while holding a whisky on the rocks.

"Robert," his father said almost cheerfully. "Please, come in. Come and join me."

"Do I have to?" Rob muttered.

"You've come this far. Please, take a seat. No funny business, I promise. I just want to talk."

"And I'm supposed to believe you, am I?"

"You must do as you must."

Rob allowed himself a deep sigh, then stepped reluctantly into the room. Sean was in here, too, a little behind the door, waiting. He closed it with a smile and waved to the seat opposite their father.

Rob gave Sean a long glare before finally doing as he suggested and took the seat. Sean followed suit, sitting between them.

"Well, isn't this cosy," his dad remarked, smiling.

"Isn't it just," Rob agreed, but without the mirth.

"Thank you for coming to see me, Robert. I really appreciate it. Naturally, I understand if you were a little reluctant, given our history, but rest assured, I have no ill intent. I just heard you were in town and wanted to see you. I so rarely get to catch up with you these days."

"That is by design," Rob replied.

"I understand that, which is a shame, but I get it. You are my son, however, and despite what you might think of me, I still hold you in some regard and watch your career with interest. You've done well for yourself."

"Thanks." Rob found his compliments somewhat amusing, given his dad's alleged line of work. But he probably wasn't lying when he said he was interested in what he was doing with his life. He was Rob's father after all. He would probably be interested no matter what Rob's job was.

"I mean it, I'm impressed. You're an inspector now, right?"

"Right."

"That's great. I'm thrilled for you. It's just a shame you're here on a case rather than of your own free will or because you were interested in the town."

"I go where the cases take me."

"Of course, you do. Well, let me reassure you, just in case you get any weird ideas in your head, that my family and the firm have nothing to do with these events. Okay? Nothing at all."

Rob fixed his father, Isaac, with a piercing glare as he focused on the man's words. "You're sure about that, are you?"

"One hundred percent. Naturally, our competitors circulate outrageous rumours about the kind of business that we're involved with, which is only to be expected. But no matter what you might believe or have heard about our line of business, I can categorically reassure you that we have no links to the mess you found in the river."

Curiously, as Rob listened to what his father was telling him, he found himself actually believing him. His father's wording was unsurprisingly careful, but even with the couched terms and clever use of words, there was an honesty behind it all when it came to the body in the river. As far as Rob could tell, his father was not lying, at least on that point.

Rob sat back and thought about his answer. "You know a lot of people in this town."

"I'm well connected, yes," his father confirmed.

"Do you know who our victim is? Can you ID him?"

"I do not. Sean?" Isaac turned and looked at Sean, who gave him a subtle shake of his head. "No? Hmm. Sorry, it seems that we have no idea who he is. I wish I could give you some more positive news, but it seems that, at this time, we don't have any."

"That's unfortunate," Rob replied.

"Indeed. So, tell me, Rob, outside of your work, how's things? Are you well? Is there a woman on the scene?"

Rob stared back at the man, appraising him for a long moment. Was he trying to play happy families and have a casual chat? Suddenly uncomfortable with the direction this meeting was going, he shifted in his seat. "Do you really think I'm going to answer that? You might be my father, but you're not my dad. You haven't been that for a long time, Isaac, and you never will be again."

Isaac took a moment to process that and then shrugged. "I understand."

"I hope so."

"But you must understand, Robert, that no matter what you do or where you go, I will always consider you my son. I will always be interested in you and your life."

"I understand." Rob got to his feet and made for the door. But in the uncomfortable silence, a thought occurred to him.

He turned back. "What do you know about the Red Man? I've seen it plastered in graffiti all over the place, so I wondered if it might be connected."

In Rob's mind, following the statement by the witness of the fight, it seemed like it could very well be connected to all this, but there was no way he was mentioning that to his father and brother.

"The Red Man? I don't know who that is. I'm aware it's a thing, and I've seen the graffiti, too, but it's got nothing to do with us, and I don't know to what it refers. Sean?"

"I doubt I know any more than either of you," Sean stated. "But like Dad says, it's got nothing to do with the Masons. You could always ask Oliver or Owen, see if they know anything?"

"No thanks," Rob muttered. Again, he found himself believing what his father was telling him. "I think we're done here."

"Goodnight," his father said. "And good luck."

"I'll see you around," Sean added.

Rob grunted and left the room, pleased to be out of there. Once in the bar, he downed the last few gulps of his drink before making his way to his room. He needed an early night.

37

"What *was* that cocktail?" Guy asked, walking out of the Alchemist bar.

As they navigated the steps down to where Queen Street turned and changed into King Street, Erika reached out and took Guy's hand in her own to keep her steady. She sported a pair of shoes with skinny high heels and took her time down the steep steps.

"I have no idea." Erika giggled.

"It had dry ice fog or something coming off the top of it. I'd love to know how they do that."

"I know. It tasted lovely, though." She gazed up at him with those large dusky eyes of hers. She was clearly at ease with him if she was grabbing his hand to steady herself. This bodes well, he thought, and tried to keep track of what he was drinking. He needed to enjoy himself and drink enough so that she didn't feel like she should hold back, but not too much that he got a little tipsy and lost control.

He needed his wits about him if he was going to try and find out more about Erika, her family, and their relationship with Rob.

He wondered how Isaac was getting on over in Retford, meeting with Rob. He'd find out, one way or another, of course. Guy forced his thoughts back into the here and now. He needed to focus on the moment.

"Aaah, there he is, good old Cloughy," Guy remarked, pointing over the road at the back of the Brian Clough statue. "What a legend! I wouldn't say he was the best manager in the business, but he was in the top one."

"He was a football manager, wasn't he?" Erika asked. She clearly hadn't recognised his paraphrased quote.

"What? Don't tell me you don't know who he was?"

"I know who he was. Brian Clough. He managed the Notts Forest team."

"Nottingham Forest, not Notts forest. Notts is the county."

Erika threw up her hands in surrender. "Sorry."

"No, it's okay. I think it's the drink. It's making me a little more enthusiastic than I usually am. I like the beautiful game, but I'm hardly a die-hard fan."

"My dad is, but I'm not much of a fan. I'll watch an important England game and stuff like that, but that's it really."

"I'd guessed," Guy replied, giving her a knowing look. She'd mentioned her dad, perfect. He'd loop back around to that shortly. "So, where are we off to now? You said you had a surprise for me."

"Aaah, yes. I do," she confirmed. "It's, um, this way. Yeah, this way. Come with me, Mr Guy, sir." She led him off, over the road, and then east, towards the Lace Market district.

"Yes, mistress," he remarked and fell into step beside her. "Lead the way. I'm expecting great things."

"Um, then maybe lower your expectations."

"Really? After how you look and your choice of bar? How can I?"

"Aww, thank you. You scrub up nicely, too."

Guy grinned. "Thank you very much."

"Don't get a big head now!"

"Hey, you started it. Keep those compliments rolling in. I'll starve without them."

She smirked.

"So your dad's into his footie then? Forest fan?"

"How would you react if I said he supported someone else?" She gave him an appraising glance.

"I might have to rethink this date, I guess..." he answered jokingly. "Then maybe go home and cry."

She punched him playfully in the arm. "Good thing he supports Forest then. What about your dad?"

"He liked the game and supported Forest back when he was alive. My uncle even more so. He's got a box at the City Stadium."

256

"Oh, I'm sorry, I had no idea," Erika replied, clearly concerned that she'd said the wrong thing.

"It's okay," Guy said. "Both my mum and dad died a long time ago, when I was a kid. I'm fine with it now. Time heals all wounds. My uncle raised me from the age of seven, so I don't really remember them much."

"That's nice of your uncle."

"Yeah, he's been really good to me," Guy said. Isaac Mason wasn't really his uncle, but that's how Guy liked to think of him.

"And he has a box at the stadium? He's well-off then?"

Guy shrugged. Had he said too much? "I don't know. I guess." He needed to turn this around back on her. "Do your parents work?"

"My dad does," she answered. "He keeps himself busy. I don't get to see him much."

Guy furrowed his brow. He was treading on thin ice here, asking about her father. She would obviously realise that he worked with her dad, but he guessed she wouldn't want to talk about that too much, not before she got to know him. But this was why he was here. He wanted to know more about her family and their connection to Rob. So, given that he already knew who Erika's father was, he chose to focus on her mother instead.

"So, your mum doesn't work?" he asked.

"No. She used to, but not anymore."

"Are they local, your folks?"

"Yeah. I see them fairly regularly."

"You get on with them, then?"

"Did you not get on with yours?" Erika asked, turning the question back around. She seemed defensive, but a moment later, she realised what she'd just said. "Oh, sorry. I didn't mean... That was a little rude of me."

"Don't worry." He smiled. "You didn't mean anything by it."

"No, no, no, of course not."

"Then don't fret it. And I don't remember much about how I was with my parents, to be honest. I was very young, so..."

"Of course, yes. Tell you what, let's change the subject, shall we?" she suggested.

"If you like. I don't mind talking about it, though. I like hearing about other families. Especially from those with both parents."

"To find out what you missed?"

Guy shrugged. "Maybe. I don't know. I just like it, it's interesting."

"I get that," she replied. "I don't have much to tell you, though. My parents aren't that interesting."

"I'd beg to differ. All families are interesting."

Erika shrugged. "You work with Rob, don't you?"

It was a sudden change of subject, but not entirely unrelated, and a subject of interest to him. "I do. And you live next door to him."

"Yep."

"What do you want to know? Are you digging for dirt on him?"

Erika smirked. "No. Not really. He's nice. I'm looking after his cat while he's on a job."

"Up in Retford," Guy added.

"That's right. I've just got to know him a bit since living next door to him. He's a nice guy, and he's led me to you, so..."

"He did," Guy admitted and decided to push it a little more. "So, he's just a friend, then?"

She gave him a suspicious glance. "Yeah. Why?"

He shrugged. "I don't know. You seem close, so I was just wondering..."

She smirked. "I'm not interested in him in that way. He's a little too old for me. I mean, he's nice and all, but he's just a friend."

"A friendly neighbour," Guy muttered, almost not believing her.

"Yeah." She grinned. "Aaah, here we are."

Guy looked up at the front of the building. "Penny Lane Arcades," he read. "Cool."

"You'll love it. Come on." She grabbed his hand and led him inside.

38

Mary drummed her fingers on the steering wheel while she sat waiting in the dark. She'd been here for several hours, parked outside her own house like some stalker, waiting for Vanessa to show up after finishing work. She should have been here hours ago, but it wasn't exactly unusual for her to be late back, sometimes hours late. Her job as a nurse required her to be flexible, and when they needed her, she couldn't exactly say no. Lives depended on her, after all.

But as the minutes ticked by and turned into hours, Mary couldn't help feeling nervous.

After escaping the men who'd confronted her in town, she'd been terrified about returning to her car, in case they knew where she'd parked it and were watching it, waiting for her.

Scared and worried, she'd walked slowly back along a random path that included several loops, trying to keep watch for anyone following her, until she'd finally entered the car park.

Finding a secluded spot, she'd observed her car and the surrounding area for over two hours. Towards the end of that time, she'd ventured out and performed a couple of passes, wandering by her car to get a better look around while trying to draw out anyone watching the car.

But so far, she'd seen nothing.

On her fourth pass, she'd unlocked the car and jumped in, making sure to lock it from the inside before speeding out and heading home. Again, she'd driven in loops, backtracking and keeping a close eye on her rearview mirror, in case anyone was following her. But she'd seen no evidence of that by the time she'd made it back to her street.

Night was already falling as she'd parked up on the opposite side of the road from her house and settled in to wait for her housemate.

Ideally, she'd prefer to catch Vanessa at the hospital, but there were so many places she could park and end up missing her, not to mention the risk of the hospital being watched, that sitting here was the next best thing.

Sitting in the shadows of her car, she slowly developed a sinking feeling that the house was being spied on. She couldn't say how she'd come to that conclusion other than abject paranoia, but it felt likely.

She didn't even have much of a plan about what to do when Vanessa did turn up. Without her phone, she had no way of contacting her housemate to warn her off and hoped that she could somehow catch Vanessa before she entered the house.

If it was being watched, she'd probably need to make a quick getaway, but right now, she didn't care about breaking a few rules of the road. These people were out to kill her and probably her loved ones, too.

She could not let that happen.

Mary kept a close eye on the cars that passed. Her heart rate suddenly spiked when a car she recognised as Vanessa's rumbled past. It slowed and then stopped before her housemate reversed into a space.

Mary glanced left and right, hunting for anyone taking an interest, but on the darkened street, it wasn't easy to see much at all. Some people walked by on the opposite side of the road, but she had no idea if they were involved in all this.

Returning her attention to her housemate's car, the door opened and Vanessa stepped out.

It was now or never.

Mary opened her door, put one foot on the ground beside the car, and stood. "Vanessa!"

Hearing her name, her housemate seemed momentarily startled before turning to see who'd called for her. She spotted Mary and smiled.

"Come here." Mary waved her over as Vanessa raised her own hand in greeting.

"What?" Vanessa called out, confused.

A car door slammed shut, and Mary turned. A couple of men got out of a car up the street.

In sudden terror, she spun back to Vanessa. "Run! Now! Get in my car!"

"What?"

"NOW!" Mary bellowed at the top of her lungs.

Appearing confused and scared, she glanced up the street at the two approaching men, and started to cross the street.

Peering past Vanessa, Mary spotted another man coming the other way. All three were large, strong-looking thugs, similar to the men she'd seen in the park. All three wore severe expressions as they stalked towards them.

"Fucking leg it, Vanessa. Run!"

Mary glanced at the pair behind. The two men had started to jog towards them.

Vanessa saw them, too, and suddenly seemed to get it. She broke into a run. The men did the same.

"Shit!" Mary jumped into the car and twisted the ignition key, hoping that this wasn't the moment the car refused to start. But the engine purred into life without issue. Mary pulled partially out of the parking space while lowering the passenger window partway. "Get in," she roared.

"What the hell's going on?" Vanessa reached the door and yanked it open.

Ahead, the lone man ran towards the car. Mary glanced back. One of the pair sprinted back to their car while the other continued towards them. Vanessa jumped in, and the man behind reached them and slammed his fist against the bodywork as he tried to rush around her car.

Mary floored it, throwing them back into their seats. Her door slammed shut.

"Raise your window." Mary hit the lock button while accelerating towards the man ahead of them. To her horror, he pulled out what looked like a gun.

"Holy shit," she cried and braced herself as she bore down on him.

He tried to aim at them but was forced to jump out of the way before Mary ran him over.

"Was that a gun?" Vanessa's voice was high and squeaky with fear. "What the fuck?"

Mary didn't answer and barrelled down the road at high speed, slowing for the corner, but only enough to get round it. She slammed the accelerator to the floor again.

"Shit, slow down will you?"

"I can't."

"Why? What the hell is all this? What's going on? Who are those people?"

"They want to kill me," Mary said, getting right to the point.

"What? Why? What have you done?"

"I spoke to someone who was about to expose their operation. Last night, in Retford. I met someone who knows what those men are involved with. But we got interrupted and had to run."

"Oh, shit. The body they found in the river. I heard about that. Was that...?"

"The man I met, yes. They killed him, and now they want me."

"Holy fuck, Mary. This is insane... but, wait... Why were they after me?"

She caught on quick, Mary thought, and nodded. "I don't know. I think they might have tried to kidnap you or something to get to me."

"You're kidding?"

"I'm deadly serious, and right now, you need to direct me to Ben's. I don't know where he lives."

"Ben's? Why....? Oh, you don't think...?"

Mary shrugged. "I don't know, but I wouldn't put it past them. Can you call him?"

"Yeah. Hold on, I've not checked my phone." Vanessa pulled it out of her bag and turned it on. It beeped repeatedly as her messages appeared on her phone. "Wow. You've been calling me, a lot."

"Trying to get in touch with you, to warn you. I would have come to the ward, but they might have been watching you."

"I doubt it. I was assigned to another ward because of staffing shortages."

"So I wouldn't have found you anyway if I had come looking," Mary stated, glad that she'd not tried.

"You'd have found me eventually, but you would have needed to ask around. Right, hold on," she said as she tried calling Ben.

Mary could hear the phone ring, but it didn't connect.

"No answer?" Mary asked.

"No." Vanessa's voice sounded meek and worried. "Shit. What if they...?"

"Don't say it. Let's get round there."

"And what if he's gone? Then what? What do we do then?"

Mary hadn't thought too far ahead. They needed a plan, and fast. "I don't know. We need to regroup and work something out. I think we need help."

"We can call the police. They'll help."

"One step at a time, but yeah, we'll call them. I know who I want to speak to."

"Let's do it now. I can call nine-nine-nine."

"Wait," Mary said and peered at Vanessa's phone, realising it could be tracked, just like hers had. "Not yet. In fact, turn it off again."

"Why?"

"Because they tracked my phone earlier. They found me in the middle of town. Came right to me. It must have been my phone. There's no other way."

"You don't know that."

"Do you want to take that risk?" Mary asked.

Vanessa pulled a face. "All right, fine, we'll do it your way." Vanessa shut her phone off. "We still need to call the police, though."

"I agree, but we need to check on Ben first. We can be there before anyone else."

"And after that?"

"We need to get somewhere safe and get some rest. I need to think this through."

"Okay," Vaneesa agreed. She didn't sound too pleased with the idea, though. "We do this your way for now. Christ, I hope Ben's okay..."

39

Walking out of the hotel's front door with a belly filled with a Full English breakfast, Rob took in a long breath of the fresh morning air as he glanced across into Kings Park on the opposite side of the road. He sniffed, checked his watch, and then shrugged to himself. He had time to spare, so he wandered over the road and into the park. Ahead, the police cordon was still there with an officer on guard, but the scene was unnaturally quiet otherwise.

Wandering over the slabbed pathway and around the circular pond, he approached the bridge and the officer on the cordon.

"Morning." Rob held up his ID.

"Morning, sir. Anything I can do to help?"

"Nope. I'm just taking a butcher's. Mind if I...?" he asked, pointing beyond the cordon.

"Go ahead. I think they concluded the search yesterday."

"Thanks," Rob remarked, stepping over the fluttering police tape before walking up the slope and onto the bridge. He got halfway, stopped, and looked north towards Bridgegate, where the body was found.

After the witness statement put the point where the victim entered the water further downstream on the west bank, the search had been concentrated in that area. But, as far as he knew, it had been a fruitless endeavour so far. He'd get a further update this morning from the sergeant, but he wasn't hopeful.

They desperately needed a breakthrough.

With a sigh, Rob turned and gazed upstream. Below, a small weir tumbled, creating a constant, soothing white noise that he found relaxing. A row of trees lined each bank, framing the river as it flowed lazily beneath the boughs of the weeping willows on the west side.

It would be quite picturesque if it wasn't for the nearby crime scene and the strips of police tape.

Wondering what today would bring, Rob left the tranquil scene behind and returned towards the park's main entrance, thanking the officer on guard.

Pulling out his phone, Rob unlocked it and placed a call as he walked.

"Hello, Rob," Erika said at the end of the line.

"Morning," Rob replied. "Hope I didn't wake you."

"No, you're fine. Everything okay?"

"I'm good. I was just wondering if you'd popped in to see Muffin yet?" he asked.

"I saw him yesterday, and I'll be heading over to yours soon to check on him. He was fine when I saw him last night."

"That's good. Thanks for doing this on such short notice."

"Of course. Not a problem," Erika reassured him.

"So, go on. How did the date go?"

She laughed. "Jeez, you're worse than my mother. That was why you really called, wasn't it?"

Rob smirked. "Sorry. I don't mean to pry. Feel free to tell me to piss off. I was just curious, given that I know both of you."

"Mmm. Fair enough. Yeah, it was fun. Guy's nice. I like him."

"Good, good," Rob muttered.

She wasn't giving much away, and as far as he knew, Guy could be lying beside her in bed right now. But that was her business, so he chose not to push any further.

"All right, well, give the furball a stroke from me, won't you?"

"I will. See you later."

"Cheers. Bye." He hung up and smiled. He'd left the park behind and made his way towards the Shared Service station beside the Town Hall. His phone buzzed. It was Nailer.

"Morning, guv," Rob answered.

"Rob. How was your first night in Retford? Not too traumatic, I hope?"

"No, not really," Rob replied as he stopped by the gate into the station car park. "I did see my dad and Sean, though."

271

"I know, I saw the press conference. But I didn't know Isaac was there, too."

"Isaac wasn't, but he and Sean showed up at the hotel bar last night for a chat and a catch-up."

"A chat? Really?" Nailer asked. "Christ, the balls on these guys."

"I know, they don't give up easy."

"Did you glean anything useful from them?"

"Not much. They did, however, deny all knowledge and involvement in my case."

"And you believed them?" Nailer asked.

"Actually, I did, yes. I didn't detect any deception from them, not that my feelings have any bearing on the truth of their statements. And I'm not sure I'm the best person to be making such judgements."

As he spoke, Scarlet's purple VW Polo arrived. She drove past him and into the car park. Last night, she'd hitched a ride with Tucker back to the Lodge, having come here with Rob earlier in the day. Rob nodded to Scarlett and spotted Tucker in the passenger seat. They both smiled back before she drove in and parked beside Rob's black Ford Capri. Rob smiled, pleased that his pride and joy had survived the night.

"Fair point," Nailer agreed. "But I think I can trust your judgement on this."

"How's the abduction case going?"

"Slowly," Nailer answered. "We don't have anything new to add. But that's not why I'm calling."

"Oh? So why are you calling?"

"I thought you should know. Bill Rainault's dad was found dead in his family home yesterday after a fall. He was quite elderly and drunk, and it seems he was prone to knocking his wife around."

"Ugh, good riddance then. Hmm. I take it Bill is aware of this?"

"He was at the house when the services arrived."

"I see." Rob felt unsure what to make of this latest bit of news. "That's, um, that's interesting. I'm not sure what to say. Hopefully, he won't try to blame this on me, too."

"I doubt it. He didn't get on with his dad, who was a former officer, by the way. A superintendent by the time he got out. Worked his way up from being a raw recruit."

"Yeah, I've heard of him. Graham, wasn't it?"

"That's right. He didn't like that Bill joined the PSU. He saw it as something of a betrayal."

"That's sad." Rob wondered what kind of family life Bill had been suffering through these past few years. Had that contributed to his obsession with taking him down? "Thanks for letting me know."

"No worries. Good luck for today. Let's hope we have some kind of breakthrough."

"That would be nice," Rob said as he turned to see Scarlett and Tucker waiting for him. "Right, I've got to go. I'll see you later."

"Will do," Nailer replied and hung up before Rob walked into the car park.

"Sleep okay?" Scarlett asked.

"Yeah, not too bad. Sleeping wasn't the problem."

"Oh?"

"Dad showed up at the hotel bar last night," Rob answered and quickly described the encounter.

"They don't give up, do they?" Tucker remarked.

"Never."

"Well, at least they had the courtesy to tell you they didn't know anything about the case. That's something, at least," Scarlett added.

"If we believe them," Rob challenged. "Just because I did, doesn't make it true. If only life were so simple."

"If only," Scarlett agreed.

There was a weight to her words that had Rob wondering if something had happened since he'd last seen her.

They made their way inside and settled in, logging in to their laptops and checking through the updates as Sergeant Susanna Parsons appeared and greeted them, enquiring after Rob's night in the Hotel. He chose not to go into the details of his family and said it was fine before delving into the case.

"So," Rob began, "based on what we have so far, we still do not know who the victim is. His DNA and prints aren't on file, and so far, apart from the witness of the fight, we've had no one come forward."

"That's about the size of it," Scarlett replied.

"What about the search?" Rob asked Susanna.

"We've been up and down that riverbank so many times. We recovered blood belonging to the victim, but that's about it."

"Shit," Rob cursed. The door opened and someone from the main office appeared.

"I have a call for Detective Loxley. Line two." She pointed to the phone on the desk.

"Thank you," Susanna said. Rob reached for the phone.

With the handset to his ear, he tapped the button for line two. "Hello?"

"Rob, it's Mary."

He frowned, struggling to place the name. "Mary?"

"Mary Day, the reporter from the *Nottingham Echo*," she clarified.

"Oh, hey," Rob greeted her brightly as the voice suddenly clicked.

"Hi," she squeaked.

Sensing that something wasn't right, Rob narrowed his eyes in curiosity. "Is everything okay?"

"No, it's not. I'm really sorry, I should have called you yesterday, but things were just too crazy."

"Why? What's up?"

"I'll explain in a moment, but the reason I called is because I know the name of your victim."

"Our victim? You mean the body we found in the river Idle?"

"Exactly. Yes. His name is Dan."

"Dan?" Rob scribbled the name into his pad. "Are you sure? How do you know this?"

"I know because I met him the night before the body was found. We met in Kings Park. He was going to whistle-blow on the people he worked for, but they somehow found out we were meeting and showed up."

"Worked for?"

"I use the term loosely, because this isn't some supermarket or something. They're thugs, criminals and killers."

"I see. So, what happened?"

"We ran in different directions, and I lost sight of him. I got out and went home, but then this morning I heard about the body."

"And you're sure it's him?"

"One hundred percent. I visited the mortuary to confirm it. It was him."

"You did what?" Rob couldn't believe what he was hearing.

"Wait, that's not all," Mary continued. "The men who killed him, they're after me, too. They want to kill me, Rob. They were chasing me all day yesterday and went after my housemate. I got her out just before they reached her, but…"

"But what?"

"But I think they might have kidnapped her boyfriend. We went to his house after I picked her up, but we didn't dare go in, and we couldn't reach him on his phone."

"Jesus. Right, okay. So you met this Dan in Kings Park just minutes before he was murdered? So, who killed him?"

"Look, I don't want to say much over the phone, but have you heard of the Red Man? It's an urban myth in Retford about some mysterious man who's anything from a serial killer to a crime lord, depending on who you talk to?"

"Yeah. We've seen the graffiti all over town."

"Well, the myth has been something of an obsession of mine for a while now. I've written two articles on it already and received death threats after each. I've been convinced that the Red Man is real for years now, but I couldn't find any proof. But then, recently, one of my informants reached out. They'd been in touch with someone who works for the Red Man, and this person wanted to talk. It was the breakthrough I needed, so I agreed to meet the whistleblower."

"And that person was Dan," Rob stated.

"That's right."

"Okay. Are you safe?"

"We're safe."

"Where are you?"

"I can't tell you that. They somehow found me in the middle of nowhere yesterday, and the only thing I can think of is that they tracked my phone, so I got rid of it. They're sophisticated, and for all I know, they're listening in right now."

"I understand. So, did this Dan tell you who this Red Man is or what he does?"

"He did say something about it, but I want to tell you that in person, not over the phone. If you're happy to meet?"

"Of course," Rob replied, understanding her concern. But that left him with a dilemma. She didn't have her phone and was concerned about how secure this call was, but somehow, she needed to be able to reach him. He considered their next move for a moment, before continuing. "Okay. Get yourself a pay-as-you-go phone, something cheap, and email me your number. You have my email, right?"

"I can find it once I log in, yeah," Mary confirmed. "I can get that no problem."

"Perfect," Rob replied. "Use the working title of that article I wrote with you in the subject line, okay?"

"Will do."

"Okay, great." She was serious, he mused. Either that or paranoid. Whatever the case, she was scared, and maybe rightly so. "So you want us to check out your housemate's boyfriend?"

"His name's Ben Merrill, he a paramedic." She then went on to recite his address, which Rob noted down.

"Got it, I'll send someone round. And you're sure the man you met was called Dan?"

"Positive."

Rob nodded to himself as something fell into place in the back of his mind. "I'll look into that," he muttered. "Thank you."

"Rob, be careful. These guys are killers. They won't care if you're police."

"I'll be cautious," Rob reassured her. "I take it you're prepared to make a statement about all this?"

"Yes, of course. Whatever it takes. I want the Red Man taken down and my life back."

"Good. Take care of yourself, and I'll speak to you soon, okay?"

"Will do," Mary answered and hung up.

The line clicked off. Rob hung up and glanced up at his colleagues, who were already making notes and frantically typing into their laptops.

"Looks like we got the breakthrough." Rob quickly ran through the details of Mary's call. "Now, correct me if I'm wrong," he said once he'd gone over the details. "But wasn't one of the calls that your officers attended in the night of the murder to do with someone called Daniel?"

"Aaah, hold on," Susanna said and hunted through the database on her laptop. "Yes. The vandalism case on Spital Hill. The house belongs to Daniel Bolton, but he wasn't there when the officers attended the call, and they couldn't raise him. They still haven't been able to get in touch, it seems."

"Bingo, I think we have our lead." Rob turned to Scarlett and handed her the slip of paper with Ben Merrill's address on it. "Call Guy and get him to pay this address a visit. Tell him we have another suspected kidnapping."

"Another," Scarlett muttered and gave Rob a curious glance. "You don't think...?"

Rob knew what she was referring to, but it was too early to draw any links between Roxy's abduction and this case. "Let's not jump the gun, shall we?"

"Fair enough. What are *we* going to do?"

"*We're* going to pay a visit to Daniel Bolton's house, and if Mary's story holds up, then I'll be talking to *her* in greater detail."

"The Red Man might be involved after all," Scarlett said with a knowing expression.

"So, what's this Red Man malarky all about then?" Tucker asked.

"More important than that," Scarlett remarked and gave Rob another curious look. "Did you say 'bingo' a minute ago?"

40

Placing her hand on the door handle, Teri took a deep breath before she turned it and walked in.

The drive out here had been fraught with emotion. She was walking right back into the lion's den without Dan, knowing full well that the people who had likely killed him were the very people she worked for. She'd already been sick once this morning at the thought of returning, terrified someone might know what she'd done. If Crimson or the Cardinal knew, she'd be hauled off to one of the cells and left to rot, and that would be getting off lightly.

From what she could find out, the thugs who worked here had killed Dan and thrown him in the river like a dead animal. They didn't care who he was or who found him. They'd been told to kill him because he'd broken the number one rule of this organisation, and he'd paid the price.

But what few people knew was, it was her fault.

She hoped he hadn't suffered too much for her folly. It had been her idea, after all. Hell, she should be the one in that river, not Dan. She'd been the one to chicken out of meeting the reporter to spill the beans on this operation, leaving Dan to do it in her stead. And now he was dead.

Her fault.

Dan had given his life because she was fed up with working here and wanted the torture to end. He'd believed in the plan more than she did. He'd believed in her. But that just made him a bloody idiot. They should have known they couldn't get away with it. This was so much bigger than them, and these people were far too rich and powerful.

She had all the proof of this right in front of her as she stepped into the ops room. Several rows of tables, laden with top-of-the-range PCs hooked up to cooled server racks on one side while banks of TVs covered the far wall. There were tens of thousands of pounds' worth of kit in here alone, and that didn't include the salaries of their employees. It took a lot of money to keep people loyal and quiet.

Crimson looked up. He sat at his desk on her left and briefly acknowledged her appearance before returning to his work. Further in, she noticed Rubious. In early, as usual, most likely, the pathetic suck-up. He leered back at her, and beneath his leering eyes, his face split into a smug grin.

Ugh! God, she hated him.

She closed the door behind her, and her gaze slipped across to the empty seat in the middle, where Dan, or Carmine as he was known here, would have sat between her and Rubious, protecting her from the slimeball's advances. But Dan was gone, and no one would back her up anymore.

Teri took a deep breath and moved into the room. Rubious got to his feet and stepped into her path.

"Good morning, Cerise," he said, using her code name.

They all had one and were forbidden to find out each other's real names, or even get too friendly with each other. Another rule she and Dan had broken.

"Rubious." She approached, hoping he'd step out of the way.

"How are you, my dear?"

He didn't move, forcing her to stop in her tracks.

"Fine."

"Are you sure?" Rubious asked and inched closer. "You seem a little..." His eyes slid down her, eyeing her up before returning to her face.

She shivered.

"...morose."

"Well, of course I am. I'm back at work with you!"

Rubious smiled. "Were you unwell this morning?"

Teri narrowed her eyes. Did her breath smell from her earlier vomiting? "No, I was fine."

"If you need a friend, I could be a friend to you."

"I'm fine, thank you." She raised her hand and pushed Rubious gently back and out of her way. "Now, if you don't mind." She turned away and passed Dan's vacant station, her breath catching in her throat.

No, not now! She slammed the lid shut on her emotions and forced them down and away. She couldn't afford to let anything slip. She needed to be careful.

"You're late," Crimson said from the back of the room.

Teri froze and took a moment to compose herself. "Yeah, sorry. I overslept," she lied. She'd barely slept a wink since finding out about Dan.

"You need to run a complete system check," Crimson ordered. "There's been a leak, and we need to know if we've been hacked again."

Teri flushed and turned away. She knew all about that hack and who'd done it. It was Riddle, and it was how the hacker had first got in touch with her.

"What kind of leak?" As she asked the question, she scanned over the CCTV cameras showing the tunnels and spotted someone in cell one. A woman. How long had she been there?

"You don't need to know that. That's above your pay grade."

Teri glanced right to the empty chair. She could make a guess what this was in reference to. Rubious leered at her, grinning creepily. Did he know something? She turned away.

"Sorry, sir. I'll get right to it." Was no one going to mention that Dan was missing? "Who's in cell one?"

"Someone who won't be there for much longer. She goes into the Red Room today."

Shit. Another. She sighed. She cursed under her breath at the utter waste of life and the horrific nature of their business. She needed to get out of here and away from all this...

But as soon as the thoughts appeared in her head, she shunned them.

No. That was the sole reason why she'd lost Dan. She'd tried to fight them, and she'd lost. There was no winning here. There was no way out of this. Christ, just surviving the next few days without them finding out this was all because of her would be a miracle. She needed to keep her head down, do as she was told, and forget about her little rebellion.

She'd failed, and now Dan was dead.

It was over. She needed to accept that and move on.

At the back, the door opened, and a man in a dark hooded coat and red mask appeared and surveyed the room.

"Cardinal," Crimson said in deference.

She'd never seen him without his mask on, him and the Red Man. She had no idea who they were.

She watched the Cardinal lean down to Crimson and whisper something.

"Of course, sir," Crimson muttered, just loud enough for her to hear.

Seconds later, the Cardinal stood tall once more. His gaze briefly met hers. The glare chilled her. She turned away and, seconds later, heard him disappear through the door again.

Did he know? Did they all know? Was this a test? She had no way to know, and she had work to do. Pulling her water bottle from her bag, she took a sip to hydrate her dry mouth and did her best to focus on the job at hand. She had a busy day ahead of her.

41

With a marked police car behind them, Rob drove along Holmes Road near Spital Hill, approaching the house that, according to their records, belonged to Daniel Bolton.

Identical red-brick houses lined the street, each with a small, fenced-off front garden. It wasn't hard to pick out Daniel's house with the boarded-up windows and graffiti that covered the front of it.

Nonce, faggot, paedo, bastard. The insults were endless and scrawled in spray paint over the whole lower half of the building, including over the boards that the police had erected to cover the broken windows and door.

"Christ, they did a number on that," Rob remarked.

"Crap, yeah." Scarlett focused on her phone to read the report she'd accessed. "Apparently, the neighbour's kids and his friends did it because Daniel broke his nose. The kids were arrested and cautioned but released with 'No Further Action'."

"Well, they sound delightful."

"We'll need to talk to them," Scarlett added.

"That we will." Rob scanned the road ahead of them and then checked in his rearview mirror where PCs Morton and Brewster were already climbing out of their car.

They'd been the attending officers on the initial call-out, so it made sense to bring them along. The area seemed quiet this morning, with hardly any people about. The leaden sky added a morose feeling to the neighbourhood as they prepared to break into the house of what could be their murder victim.

"Do you think this is the same Dan who Mary met in the park?" Scarlett asked.

"That's what we're here to find out," Rob said, preferring not to commit. Although, he thought it highly likely that it was. "We need to find some photos or ID to confirm his identity against the corpse in the mortuary and then show Mary to see if she recognises him."

"Yep," Scarlett agreed. "No problem."

Rob climbed out of his Capri and the two uniformed officers approached from their car. PC David Morton hefted a mean-looking crowbar in one hand, ready to pry open the front door so they could gain entry.

"Ready?" David asked.

"Lead the way," Rob answered, waving him ahead. "Let's see those muscles in action, hey?"

"Oh, the girls love his muscles," PC Russ Brewster brayed. "They can't get enough of them, ain't that right, Dave?"

"If you say so."

"I'm sorry, I think I missed that memo." Scarlett joined them from the other side of the car. "But I shall wait in anticipation of being thoroughly impressed."

"I think you need to prepare yourself to be thoroughly disappointed." Rob directed his next comment at Dave. "Go on, hop to it. That door won't open itself."

"Guv." Dave nodded, approached the door and jammed the curved end of the bar beneath the edge of the board. Several yanks and squeaks of wood later, the corner moved. Dave continued on, working up quite a sweat as he working at the board, sticking the bar in at different points to get the best leverage.

With a loud final creak, the board finally came away with bare nails sticking out of its back side at odd angles.

His job done, Dave collapsed against the wall in a sweaty, panting mess.

"Well, I don't think I'll ever be the same after witnessing Dave and his muscles," Scarlett joked. "I think my wedding's off after that display."

"Har-di-har," Dave grunted between gasping breaths. "Now it's your turn to do some work." He jabbed his thumb towards the door. "I'm just gonna sit here for a bit and catch my breath."

"Good work." Rob pulled on a pair of latex gloves before leading Scarlett inside, being careful to keep his contact with any surface to an absolute minimum.

Inside the front of the house, stones and bricks surrounded by shattered glass still littered the floor beneath the windows and door. The debris crunched underfoot as they walked over it. Splitting up, they hunted through the house for anything that might be useful in identifying the owner. There was very little of use downstairs apart from some letters left on the side that were addressed to Daniel Bolton. But upstairs, in the back bedroom, they found an impressive gaming PC with dual monitors and a chest of drawers in the corner of the room. In the top drawer, they discovered a messy stack of papers and other bits of official letters and documents.

They focused their attention there and soon found a passport that belonged to Daniel Bolton.

"That's our victim," Rob said, peering at the photo inside. "I'm sure of it."

"Looks like him, which means we have a name, finally. Excellent." Scarlett agreed. "Hey, look at these." She'd found several printed photos of Daniel, including a few of him hugging a young woman.

"Girlfriend?" Rob asked, showing it to Scarlett.

"Maybe," she agreed. "We should take these."

"Right, how about we head next door and see what they've got to say for themselves?"

"Sure thing," she replied and followed him out.

As they descended to the ground floor, Scarlett checked her phone.

"The neighbour is Otto Frank, and his kid's called Bobby. He's the one who had his nose broken."

"Otto got into a fight in town the night Daniel hit his son," Dave said, joining him in the front room. "I don't know who with, but it might be worth looking into?"

"Sure. We should check his alibi, too." Rob led them outside. "Call in Forensics. We might as well get this place checked over. If his girlfriend's been here, we could find her DNA."

"It's odd she's not been in touch, don't you think?" Scarlett remarked. "Daniel's been missing for a couple of days now, and we've been all over the news trying to work out who he is. If it were me, I'd have called the police by now."

"Unless there are other mitigating factors," Rob countered.

"True. We also need to find his next of kin. He must have parents or family."

"Hopefully. One step at a time, though. Let's see what the neighbours have to say, shall we?" Rob led them round to the neighbour's house and knocked on the door. A TV, turned way up, blared inside.

It took several more rings of the bell to rouse the occupants. But after what seemed like an age, the TV decreased in volume and a voice called out.

"All right, all right. Hold your fucking horses. This had better be fucking vital." The door opened, revealing a teenager in a vest, jeans, and a scowl. He also sported a pair of impressive black eyes. "What?"

"Bobby, is it?" Rob held up his ID. "I'm Detective Loxley."

"So fucking what?"

Rob raised his brows at the comment but decided to play it calm. "I need to talk to you and your dad."

"He won't want to speak to you. Fucking pig."

Rob bit his lip in annoyance. "He can do this the hard way or the easy way, that's up to him. The easy way's better, though."

Bobby grunted, turned to the house and shouted at the top of his lungs, "Dad? It's the bloody police."

"I ain't got nothin' to say to no fuckin' pig," came the reply from deeper into the house.

"He's being a dick about it," Bobby added.

"I bet he is," was the reply before a stocky, overweight man appeared and walked up to the front door. Like his son, Otto also displayed signs that he'd been involved in a fight, with some Steri-Strips and scabbed-over cuts on his face. "Yeah, you look like a dick."

"Otto Frank?" Rob asked, to make sure.

"Yeah, what of it?"

"We're looking into the disappearance of Daniel Bolton."

"Who?"

"Your neighbour," Rob clarified.

"Oh, that little shit," Otto remarked, the penny finally dropping. "Why? What the fuck has he got to do with me?"

"Your son vandalised his house." Rob pointed to the graffiti.

"And?"

"He broke my fucking nose," Bobby blurted out, much to the annoyance of his dad. "It's the least he deserves."

"Do you know what happened to him? Where he might be?" Rob pressed.

"No fucking idea," Otto replied. "Don't care either. He can fuck off and die for all I care."

Rob raised an eyebrow at the unfortunate comment. "And where were you the night before last?"

"Having a drink with some mates in town."

Rob pointed to his face. "Did you have some trouble?"

"Just the usual cocksuckers. Nuthin' I can't handle. Why?"

"We have reason to believe that Daniel Bolton was murdered that night, and we were wondering where you were around midnight."

"Pissed, most likely. Why? Do you think I did it?"

Rob shrugged. He found himself amused by Otto's indifference. "Are you saying you didn't?"

"If he shows his ugly face around here again, I might kill him. But no, I didn't murder him the other night. I could barely stand up by midnight, let alone kill someone."

"Your record shows a history of violence, Mr Frank," Scarlett added.

"Does it, sweetheart?" He smiled and winked. "I bet you like a bit of rough, yeah?" He licked his lips.

Rob shuddered in disgust at his reply.

Scarlett grunted and then held up a photo showing Daniel and the mystery girl. "Do you know this girl?"

"Not intimately."

"But you do know her?" Scarlett pushed.

Otto sighed and leaned against his doorframe. "She was here yesterday, looking for shitface." Otto waved to the house next door. "I told her to fuck off."

"Do you know who she is? Do you know her name?" Rob asked.

"Nah, mate. I don't know who she is and don't care. But any friend of his can fuck right off, got it?"

Rob nodded. "Okay. We'll be in touch if we need to ask you any further questions, Mr Frank." He turned to leave, sure that Otto wasn't going to give them what they wanted. "Thank you for your time."

"Don't fucking mention it."

"Eeeargh! Go on, piss off," Bobby added. "Fuck the pigs."

Rob ignored him and turned to Scarlett as they reached the street and made for their car. "We need to find that girl, and I need to speak to Mary."

"We'll find her," Scarlett reassured him.

"I know." Reaching Dave and Russ waiting outside Daniel's house, Rob pulled out his phone. Mary had emailed with her pay-as-you-go number. "Aaah, here we go. I'll call Mary and arrange a meeting. See what we can find."

"Sounds good," Scarlett muttered

"What do you want us to do, guv?" Dave asked.

"Call Forensics in and wait here for them. I don't want any anyone else going in that house, so make sure it's secure once the place has been swept for DNA. Okay?"

"Got it," Dave replied and turned to Russ. "Make the call."

Russ nodded and reached for his radio.

Rob called Mary and put the phone to his ear. Seconds later, the call connected and Mary answered.

"Hello?"

"Mary? Hi. It's Rob. We need to meet."

42

Driving his pool car south from Sherwood Lodge into Nottingham, Guy turned east into Arnold. He needed to make a brief stop before continuing into the city to check on the address Nick had asked him to investigate.

He hadn't planned on making this stop until after getting into work this morning to hear that Bill Rainault was, once again, the talk of the station. The last time was after his suspension, just a few weeks ago, but now that he'd been gone a few weeks, he had not expected to hear his name uttered again within the halls and break rooms.

But on getting in this morning, he'd barely made it through the first security door before someone asked if he'd heard about Bill's dad.

Finding out that Graham Rainault had died after falling and smashing his head against the corner of a table, Guy couldn't help but wonder if he was hearing the full story. He knew about Bill's poor relationship with his father, and the rumours about Graham's violence towards his wife occasionally surfaced.

Had something a little less innocent happened in the Rainault family home, Guy wondered?

So when Nick had asked him to check out an address in relation to the Retford murder case, Guy resolved to pay Bill a visit on his way in and see what he had to say for himself. It wasn't too far out of his way and shouldn't take too long, all being well.

Having done his research on Bill a long time ago, he knew exactly where he lived and soon pulled up outside Bill's house. It wasn't far from Bill's parents' place, but there was no need for him to stop by there, too.

Wanting this to be a fleeting visit, Guy jumped out and strode up to Bill's house at pace, rang the bell and knocked. He made sure to put some urgency into it to try and get Bill to hurry up.

Sure enough, seconds later, Bill appeared at the door and gave Guy a curious glare. "What are you doing here?"

"Checking up on you," Guy replied. "You're the talk of the station, you know. Not something I expected after you left."

With a grunt, Bill turned away and wandered back into his house, leaving his door open for Guy. "You'd better come in then."

Guy pouted, shrugged and entered the house. The first thing that struck Guy as he stepped inside was the smell. It stank. A horrible, musty smell of unwashed clothes, body odour, and rotting food mixed into a cocktail nearly made Guy gag. "Jesus," he muttered and closed the door.

Bill was already out of sight in his living room at the back of the house, and as Guy advanced, the smell only got worse. He passed discarded shoes, bags, and scraps of rubbish on the hall floor, then turned into the pigsty that was Bill's living room. He didn't dare to look in the kitchen.

It took all of Guy's willpower to keep from pinching his nose. He hoped to get used to the smell while resolving to give himself a spray of deodorant back at the Lodge.

"Thought you'd check up on me then, did you?" Bill asked.

"I thought it would be wise, yes. I saw the report on what happened."

Bill grunted and turned away. "He fell."

"Did he?" Guy asked, his tone flat. He wasn't sure he believed him. "The statement given by you and your mother said he was drunk and being violent."

"Nothing new from him. He always treated my mum like shit."

"I'm sorry to hear that."

"He was a tosser. I'm glad he's gone, to be honest."

"And what about your mother? Is she okay? I thought you might be round at hers today."

"She said she needs some space, so..."

Guy detected a note of annoyance or petulance in Bill's words. He didn't seem pleased that he'd been sidelined. "Give her time. I'm sure she'll come round."

Bill muttered something. He didn't seem convinced.

"So, there was no fight or anything then? He didn't attack your mother, and she defended herself? Or maybe he attacked you?"

"What are you suggesting? Do you think me or my mother killed him? Are you insane?"

"You're a friend, Bill. We've worked together on trying to bring Rob down, and we've done it outside of the law. If there's something you want to share with me, you can."

"I've nothing to share," Bill snapped.

Guy raised his hands in surrender. "Okay? That's fine. I just wanted to be sure."

"And now you know."

Guy nodded. There didn't seem to be much point in pursuing this any further. Not now, at least. That would only serve to push him away, and right now, Guy felt that Bill was better placed and more useful as an ally. "All right, well, I'd better get going. I've got work to do. Call me if you need to talk."

Guy wasn't particularly interested in Bill or his feelings, but if there was dirt here, Guy wanted to know about it.

With no reply forthcoming, Guy turned to leave. "I'll let myself out."

"How did the date with Erika go?"

Guy stopped and turned back slowly. "All right."

"Did you learn anything new?"

"Not much of use, no. But Erika clearly cares about Rob. That much was clear."

"Yeah. Do you really think you can find anything out by going on dates with her? If you need to know something, then you need to force that answer out of her."

"Is that right? Well, given that I'm a police officer and her dad is my boss, that's not something that I'm going to be doing if I want to hold on to my career."

"Fair point."

"But maybe it's something someone who doesn't have a career could do."

Bill sank back into his chair as if he was trying to hide.

"Yeah, I thought not," Guy said. "Not as easy as all that, is it?"

"There's something between them," Bill muttered.

"I know. I'll find out what it is. I just need time."

Bill grunted. "Like I did, with Rob."

"Nothing's stopping you now."

"If you say so."

Guy sighed, annoyed at his pathetic, woe-is-me attitude. He'd never get anything done like this, and he didn't fancy staying here a minute longer than was necessary. "Right, I can't hang around here all day. I've got work to do." He took one last look around the room. "Piece of advice, Bill. Sort yourself out. Get all this shit cleaned up and stop living like a slob. You're not achieving anything like this, and the place bloody reeks."

"Piss off."

"Fine. See ya." Guy turned and marched out, slamming the door shut behind him before returning to his car and setting off into town and the address of Ben Merrill.

There was potential that Bill could be a useful asset at some point, but he needed to pull himself out of this pit of self-recrimination and probably grieve both for his dad and his job. It wasn't doing him any favours.

But until then, he wasn't going to be very useful.

Guy took a deep breath and forced those thoughts away. He switched his focus to the job he'd been assigned and followed the directions on his satnav. It didn't take him long to find the small terraced house. It was set back away from the road with a mid-sized garden at the front and seemed quiet enough.

Climbing out of his car, Guy approached the house, and as he got closer to the front door, it soon became obvious that it had been left slightly ajar.

With alarm bells ringing in his head, Guy gingerly opened the door and stepped back. Nothing happened. It was dark inside.

"Hello?" Guy called out, but no one answered. Seeing and hearing nothing, he stepped into the porch and turned right. Finding himself in the front room, he spotted several signs of a struggle. A table had been knocked over, and various items scattered over the floor in an otherwise clean and tidy room.

Being careful not to touch anything, Guy focused on the rest of the house. "Hello? Ben? Ben Merrill? Are you here?" Again, his calls were answered with silence.

Guy continued on through the house, going room by room, wondering if he might find a body or someone hiding. In the kitchen, he found a half-made meal, and upstairs, the bed remained unused. Ben was not here.

He pulled out his phone and called Rob.

"Guy. What do you have for me?"

"Rob. I'm at Ben Merrill's house, and he's not home. There are signs of a struggle in the front room and a half-made meal in the kitchen. I think I can guess what's happened."

"Shit, yeah. Me, too. Thanks, Guy. Good work."

"No worries, guv. I'll get Scenes of Crime here, pronto."

"Cheers."

43

"I know Rob fucking loves his Capri," Tucker said, sitting in the passenger seat of Scarlett's car. "But you can't beat a modern car with a Bluetooth digital radio and air-conditioning."

Scarlett smiled at his statement. "I'll take that as a compliment and firmly believe you're referring to my car."

"No need to believe because I am," Tucker remarked.

"Good," she replied. "I like Rob's car, though. It has a certain charm, and the retro look is very in vogue right now."

"I guess."

"But I agree with you. I'm a mod-cons girl, all the way. I feel the same about holidays, too. I need a bathroom with a shower and a comfortable bed. You will not get me going camping and sleeping on a groundsheet in the middle of nowhere."

"No pissing in the woods for you, then?"

"No way," Scarlett confirmed. She'd done her share of camping back when she was a kid with the Brownies and Girl Guides and had no desire to return to it anytime soon. But she meant what she'd said about Rob's car. While it wasn't something she'd want to own personally, she could understand the allure of it on a purely aesthetic level. But there seemed to be more to it for Rob. There was a personal connection there because it was a present from his mother, back before she'd disappeared.

There was no way he was getting rid of it.

"What's the deal with all this Red Man stuff? It's fucking freaky," Tucker asked.

"I know," Scarlett said. "And now there really might be something to it. We've got men in red masks killing people and a reporter saying it's all real and that the Red Man, whoever the hell he is, is behind it all. Hopefully, Rob's meeting with the reporter goes well, and we can find out what's really going on."

"And you weren't invited along, I see."

"The reporter's feeling paranoid," Scarlett explained. "She wanted Rob to go alone. I don't blame her. I think I'd be the same if I was being hunted by some murderous thugs."

"Oh, totally," Tucker agreed. "Means you get to piss about with me instead. Can't be bad."

"I lead a blessed life."

"You do indeed, my child. Blessed to fuck."

"Aaah, right, here we go, Park Lane. He lives along here somewhere."

Tucker grunted. "Not quite the Park Lane of London fame."

"Why is everyone so down on Retford?" Scarlett asked. "It's not that bad."

"Nah, it's all right for a backwater market town."

"Jesus."

"Don't take the Lord's fucking name in vain, Scarlett. That's my goddamned Jesus pissing job."

She laughed as they drove towards the far end of the road, to the last two-storey houses on the road, and pulled in. "Here we are. That's the house. The one before the bungalow."

"And this is where Daniel Bolton's dad lives?"

"Yup," Scarlett confirmed, taking a breath as she let a more sombre tone fall over her. They had to deliver the worst news a parent could ever receive, and she was not looking forward to it. "Right then, let's go and do this. Poor bugger. We're about to ruin his day."

"Yeah. Can't be helped. Let's get it over with."

She nodded, climbed out of the car, and walked around to join Tucker on the path before approaching the front door. She pressed the bell and waited. It didn't take long for the door to be answered.

Scarlett regarded the middle-aged man who opened the door and steeled herself, ready to deliver the news. "Mr Bolton? Myles Bolton?"

The man was a mess, in a crumpled tee shirt, shorts, and sliders. His hair clearly hadn't been combed in days, and he had an impressive amount of stubble on his jaw. "Yeah?"

"Hi. I'm Detective Stutely with the Nottinghamshire Police. I was wondering if we might have a word? Inside, if that's okay?"

Myles frowned. "Err, yeah." He stepped back and let them in. "What is this all about?"

"Let's go and sit down, shall we?"

Myles led them through to the lounge, which was nearly as messy as its owner. He quickly cleared a space for them on the large sofa and waved for them to sit before taking a seat himself. "How can I help you?"

"Well, I'm afraid we have some bad news, Mr Bolton." She took a breath and dove in. Best just to get it done. "Your son was murdered the other day. I'm sorry, but Daniel is dead."

Myles's face fell, and he dropped his head into his hands. "Oh God, no. Not Dan. Not Dan. No."

Scarlett scooted closer and placed her hand on his arm. "I'm really sorry for your loss."

"I knew it. I knew this would happen. Fuck. Oh God. How? What happened? Was it them? Did they kill him? What happened? Was it that body in the river? Was that him?"

"Yes, I'm afraid it was. We found him in the River Idle. The morning before last. It seemed like he'd been attacked."

"Jesus." He sobbed, but after a few moments, with tears still streaming down his face, he looked up again. "It was them, wasn't it?"

"Them?" He'd said that a few seconds ago, too. "Who do you mean?"

"Those thugs. The ones he worked for."

"Mr Bolton, we don't actually know who killed him yet. But if you have information that you think might help us, we'd love to hear it. Who are these people you keep referring to?"

"The ones who took him away from me... Well. Okay, this goes back a few years. Dan was maybe fifteen when I bought this house. I was a property developer back then. I was doing all right and bought this place to do up and sell on. I'd been working on it for weeks, with Dan helping. We pulled some late nights. Anyway, this one night, I was upstairs working on a bedroom, and Dan was downstairs doing something else. It was late. I was by the window, and I spotted a security light come on next door at the back of the house. And... well, I'll never forget what I saw." He sighed and took a breath.

"Take your time," Scarlett said reassuringly.

"Thanks. I saw three men drag another from the the house, through the pool of light. But this man they were carrying was naked and bloody, and I mean, like, *covered* in blood. Everything was red. They took him to the shed at the end of the garden. I was shocked and just stared out into the darkness. I couldn't believe what I was seeing."

"What did you do next?"

"I didn't know what to do at first. I moved away from the window and tried to concentrate, but my head was a mess. I thought about calling the police, but it all sounded crazy. In the end, I went downstairs and told Dan. I just had to get it off my chest. I needed to tell someone. I'd barely finished when the same thugs smashed our front door in. They grabbed us and started to beat me up. Christ, they would have killed me if it wasn't for Dan. He begged for my life. He asked them to spare me, saying he'd do anything for them. Luckily, the leader of the group seemed interested and, in the end, agreed. He said he'd spare me if Dan went to work for him."

Scarlett narrowed her eyes in curiosity. "Work for him?"

"Honestly, I never found out what he did for these thugs, and Dan would never talk about it. He always outright refused. But I've had a long time to think about this, and I keep coming back to something I saw when Dan was helping me with the house. Back then, he was very much into making little videos with his phone and short animations. He was always doing it, and the one previous time I interacted with the neighbour was when I caught him talking to Dan outside. Dan had been filming something, and this man was asking him about it. He seemed interested."

"He was interested in his video-making skills?" Scarlett clarified.

"That's the only thing I can think of. Nothing else makes sense."

"Okay. Was there anything else? Did he tell you his name or anything?"

"I didn't pay much attention because I didn't know it would be important. I think he was the owner of the house, though."

"The owner?"

"I think so. You might be able to look that up?"

"Yeah, maybe. Thank you." Scarlett scribbled some notes in her pad. "Did you never think that you should tell the police? We might have been able to help."

"Countless times. But the only time I got serious about it was a few months after Dan was recruited. I spoke to my wife about it over several days and was on the verge of calling the police, only to come home to find her dead in our bath. It looked like she'd taken her own life by slashing her wrists, but... I just couldn't believe she'd do that. That wasn't her. I think it was more likely a warning from them, you know? A warning to keep my mouth shut."

"But you're talking to us now."

"I know. But I don't care anymore. Dan's dead, Lia's dead, I don't care what they do to me. So fuck 'em. I'm done keeping their secrets. I'll help you in any way I can."

Scarlett nodded. "We appreciate it."

44

The drive down to Mansfield took about forty minutes, but it felt good to get out of Retford, wind down his window, and enjoy the breeze as he bombed along the country roads.

Rob's first twenty-four hours in the town hadn't been as bad as he'd feared, although he had been forced to endure a little more contact from his family than he felt happy about. That was undoubtedly a byproduct of the high-profile case they were on, which was attracting national media attention with TV vans parked up in the town and the local hotels benefitting from the influx of reporters.

Rob just did his best to dodge them as much as he could, preferring to keep his distance from reporters as much as possible.

Mary, however, was the one exception to that rule. He'd first met her during the Clipstone case and subsequently worked with her on a report she'd written up for the *Nottingham Echo*. Mary had remained professional and friendly throughout and had never overstepped her mark.

She was feisty, though, which probably worked in her favour as a reporter. She reminded him of Scarlett in that way.

Rob did his best to keep his expectations low on the drive down because, as promising as all this seemed, it was entirely likely that they were about to be thrown a curveball that would set them back. So far, everything had fallen into place following Mary's call. They'd successfully linked the name Dan to the victim in the river and to a call-out earlier on the night he was murdered. That led them to Dan's house, which in turn confirmed his full name and held some photos of him. Rob felt sure he recognised the man in the photos as the body from the river, and Scarlett agreed. The pathologist also said that the man in the passport was most likely the same man she had in her freezer.

So, with Scarlett and Tucker visiting Daniel's father to deliver the bad news, all that was left was to check if this Daniel Bolton was the same man Mary had met in the park and to find out what she knew about what was going on.

Was this, somehow, all to do with this mysterious Red Man, or was it something else?

Driving into the centre of town, Rob navigated his way around to Quaker Way and turned into the car park for the Four Seasons Hotel. He accelerated up the long ramp and bore right driving around the car park.

He was due to meet Mary on the top floor but decided to park up on the floor below and walk up. She was clearly trying to be discreet about this, so he decided to play along.

After parking his Capri, Rob strode along the row of cars and up the final ramp to the top floor. Wind caught his coat as he stepped out and made his way north to the far wall. Reaching it, he looked out over the roads and buildings below then scanned the car park to see if he could spot Mary.

The top floor was a split-level affair, and he was on the lower of the two, so he followed the wall up the nearby ramp to the higher section. At the top of the ramp, he could make out the entire top floor, but so far, he'd not spotted Mary anywhere.

Seconds passed as he watched a few people drive up, park, and then wander over to one of the stairwells and enter the main shopping centre.

A door squeaked open, and he turned to the closest stairwell in time to see Mary step out. She caught his eye, nodded and leaned against the same wall he stood next to.

She wore jeans, trainers, a hoody and a cap that she'd pulled low over her face. Her auburn hair had been tied back into a bun at the base of her neck to conceal its distinctive colour.

Rob wandered over. "Y'all right?" he asked once he was close enough. He smiled. "Sounds like you're having a tough time."

She peered up, tears forming in her glistening eyes. She yanked him in for a sudden hug.

"Oh, okay," Rob muttered, gently placing his hands on her back.

"Thanks for coming," she said, her voice quiet. "It's good to see a friendly face."

"Sure, anytime. I'm here to help."

"I know, thanks." She let go and put some space between them. "Sorry. I just... I think I needed that."

"That's all right. You seem a little strung out, if you don't mind me saying."

She had dark rings under her eyes and looked like she hadn't slept in an age.

She laughed. "That's fair. It's been a rough couple of days, that's for sure."

"I understand. I've got something to show you," he said, reaching into his pocket.

Mary flinched.

"It's just a photo," Rob said.

"Sorry. I'm just a little nervous, that's all."

"I understand." He produced a sheet of paper with a copy of Daniel Bolton's passport on it, as well as a couple of photos of him. "Is this the man you met in the park?"

Mary took the paper and had a closer look. She sighed. "Yeah, that's him. That's the man I met in Kings Park."

316

"That's also the man we fished out of the River Idle the morning after you met him. He'd been attacked and dumped in the river, where he drowned."

"Shit." She handed him the sheet of paper back. "I should never have met him."

"But you did, and he met you of his own free will. What happened to him is not your fault."

She smiled. "Thanks."

"All right, tell me what happened. What was this meeting about? Who is the Red Man? How was all this set up? I want to know everything."

"It all started with this legend. I wish I could tell you exactly when or where, but I honestly don't know. It seemed to have slowly spread over the last ten years or so, with the criminals and graffiti artists really taking it to heart and using it. I'm guessing you've seen all the graffiti around the town?"

"Yeah. It's hard to miss."

"Well, I got wind of it while researching another story in the town and looked into it, talking to anyone I could about it. I've spoken to some graffiti artists and kids who have worn the red mask when shoplifting, and no one knew anything. They all have ideas about who it might be or where it all began. It's all over the place really. I've interviewed so many people about this."

317

"I've spoken to a couple of people about it, too," Rob admitted. "They said the same thing. It could be the bogeyman, a serial killer, or crime lord. No one really knows."

"Yeah, that's what I always heard, too, but I feel like, if that was all it was, it would die a death. But it keeps going. It just won't die. Anyway, I've written two articles over as many years about the myth, and while most people don't care or just enjoy the reports for what they are, I have had a few death threats in the mail after their publication."

"Which suggests someone doesn't like you talking about it," Rob said.

"That was my conclusion. So I kept digging, and then a few weeks back, I got a message from one of my informants. They're a hacker, and they told me how they found a curious local server that seemed to have some crazy protections, so they decided to hack in and see what was going on. They didn't get much data from the hack, but they did manage to contact someone inside the group or organisation. Apparently, the person this hacker spoke to works for this mysterious Red Man, and they wanted to talk to someone. They were fed up with what they were doing and wanted to stop it and bring it all down. My informant reached out to me, and I agreed to help. That led to the meeting in Kings Park."

"Where you met Dan," Rob confirmed.

"That's right."

"How did that meeting go?"

"It was short," Mary replied. "We met, swapped the code words we'd been given, and started talking. But it wasn't even a minute later when the thugs turned up."

"Thugs?"

"That's right. I think there were four or five of them. They were walking right towards us, and if it hadn't been for Dan, I doubt I'd be here. I didn't know these guys from Adam, but Dan seemed to recognise them. He just shouted run and legged it. I didn't question him and did the same. One of the guys followed me, but I was too fast for him and already had my escape route planned out. I was annoyed because I didn't get what I wanted, but I didn't overthink it and went home.

"It was only when I went into work the next day, and I saw the news report about the body in the River Idle, that I realised what had happened. I left work, keen to find out if the body in the river was the same man I'd met in the park. And it was a good thing I did because I got a call later that morning saying that a large, rude man turned up at my work, asking for me."

"They came to your work?"

"Apparently."

"So what did you do?"

"I went to the hospital. I've built up a nice little network of contacts, and one of them works in the mortuary. She got me in so I could see the body."

"And that's when you recognised him," Rob guessed, impressed with her ingenuity.

"Yup. Scared me shitless. So I went into town, knowing I couldn't go back to work or back home, because apparently, they knew who I was. I was a little lost and just hung out in town, trying to work out what to do. That's when I saw your press conference."

Rob grunted. "Yeah. Not my best performance."

"You did all right."

"So what happened next? You should have called me or the police."

"I know. I wanted to. But I was interrupted by the same thugs. They tracked me down and chased me through the streets. I got away again with the help of some bystanders and realised that they were tracking my phone."

"Really? How did you know that?"

"Well, I don't, but how else would they have caught up with me and found me in the middle of town?"

Rob shrugged. "Blind luck?"

Mary pulled a face. "Yeah, right."

"You smashed your phone, didn't you," Rob said, guessing what she'd done.

"Aye. Chucked it. Then, I went for a long walk before returning to my car and heading home. Guessing they might try to go for my family or friends if they'd come for me, I'd managed to warn most of my loved ones earlier. But I couldn't get in touch with my housemate, so I decided to try to catch her as she got home. I did, but only just. They were waiting for me there, too."

"Christ, you've had a busy day."

"Yeah, you can say that again. Did you find out about my housemate's boyfriend? Ben? Was he at home?"

Rob grimaced. "Sorry, no. He wasn't there. We found signs of a struggle, though, and an unfinished meal. So I think we can guess what happened to him."

"Fuck."

"I've got one of my guys handling it back at Sherwood Lodge. They'll be letting his family know and dealing with all that."

"Okay, thanks. Shit. So, what do we do now?"

"Well, you still haven't told me what Dan said at the meeting you had." He gave her an expectant look.

"Well, the meeting was only brief. He introduced himself as Dan and asked who I was, and once he was comfortable, I asked him if he worked for the Red Man. He said that he did. So I asked who this Red Man was and what he did. And the only thing he managed to tell me before he spotted the goons was that the Red Man was running a Red Room."

Rob frowned. "A Red Room?" He was familiar with the urban myth. Online dark web video feeds of torture rooms where people paid to watch someone torture and kill someone. So far, they'd never been proven to exist. The bandwidth of the dark web was too low to allow them to run successfully. However, there were actual cases of people recording abuse done to others and then selling that footage to curious sickos.

"Yeah. That's what he said. A Red Room. We didn't have time to delve any deeper than that, though, because we were interrupted."

"And you believed him? You think he was telling the truth?"

She shrugged. "I've got no idea. All I know is that someone is going to some extraordinary lengths to stop me from finding out and publishing it."

Rob nodded in agreement as his mind reeled at the possibility.

Mary's phone rang. She pulled her pay-as-you-go from her pocket and checked the screen. "Aaah. Speak of the devil, my contact."

Nearby, an engine roared.

45

Riddle leaned back in her gaming chair, her eyes flitting between the numerous windows that were open on the array of screens on her desk. Below it, several high-spec PC towers whirred. Along with the hum coming from her server rack, they created a constant background hum to her open-plan apartment. But she couldn't hear the buzz of her equipment or the AC that was keeping her room cool either.

Instead, she enjoyed the thumping beat being pumped into her skull by her Bose earbuds, while their noise-cancelling feature cut her off from the outside world.

Apart from the slowly exploding mess of her Red Man hack, the day was like any other. She watched a couple of automated client hacks downloading the data they'd hired her to collect while another machine ran a security test on a company in Dubai. She'd been hired by the company to do this periodically and report back with any weaknesses. But so far, it seemed they'd implemented several of her suggestions, and their data vault was proving to be a good deal more secure this time.

But the file she kept on the Red Man mess was drawing her attention right now.

Mary was meeting with her detective friend, Loxley, in Mansfield, and Teri was back at work, hopefully surviving the day.

Riddle hadn't slept well since Mary's meeting in the park, and she still couldn't figure out how that had gone so wrong. Someone inside the organisation must have known something odd was going on. They had to have been keeping closer tabs on Teri and Dan than she'd thought.

The thought that Dan had met his grizzly end because of her sloppy preparation made her sick to her stomach. This was dangerous work, for sure, but she'd never even considered that someone might get killed, especially not because of her.

Riddle gave her head a shake to try and snap out of it. If things were as dangerous as this, Teri and Dan had to have done this knowing the risks. She'd not forced or blackmailed them, they'd agreed to talk because they both wanted out.

But there was a more worrying thought that she needed to consider, because if they were willing to kill Dan for talking, then these sickos would have no issues killing her.

They had to be looking for her, which meant she needed to be extra vigilant. It was why she kept her door triple locked at all times and refused to answer it to anyone she didn't recognise.

In her line of work, it paid to be vigilant and cautious. One day, someone would track her down and come calling. It was only a matter of time.

As she considered her options and what, if anything, she should do, a notification appeared on one of her phones. She picked it up to find a text waiting for her. It was from Teri. Riddle raised an eyebrow and read the message.

They know about the reporter's meeting.

Riddle's jaw fell open. "Shit, shit, shit." Dropping that phone, she grabbed another and called Mary.

Three rings later, Mary answered.

"Hey, what's up?" Mary said.

"Get out of there, they know."

"What?"

"Run! Now!" Riddle yelled into her phone, only for Mary yelp and shout, and then the line went dead.

"Fuck!"

46

It all happened so fast. One moment he was talking to Mary, getting valuable information about the case, and the next, they were running for their lives.

Mary answered her phone. "Hey, what's up?" she'd said before her face suddenly fell and a look of horror took hold. "What?" she'd snapped, turning to Rob.

Something was wrong.

Elsewhere, an engine roared.

Rob looked up. A large black 4x4 suddenly picked up speed and accelerated right for them. Taking Mary by the arm, he yanked her out of its path.

"Run, now!"

Mary yelped and sprinted after Rob. He charged down the double ramp, jumping the divider to get out of the way of the chasing car.

Mary followed suit. "Go, go, go."

Reaching the bottom of the ramp, he raced along the backs of the various parked cars. The 4x4 skidded down the ramp. He chanced a glance back. An armed man brandished a gun out of the open window. Rob grabbed Mary and threw her between the two closest cars. A single gunshot rang out.

"Shit."

Mary yelped.

A couple of shouts and screams echoed as other people panicked.

Keeping hold of Mary, he led her around the car and along the wall until they reached the down ramp to the floor below.

"Shit," Rob cursed. They'd need to break cover to reach it. "Okay. Run as fast as you can round the corner," he barked at her. "Get down the ramp and find cover. I'll follow. Go." He figured they'd be more likely to shoot the second person stepping out of cover.

She didn't question him and ducked around the wall. Rob followed close on her heels. Another gunshot and the *thwip* of it passing close by sounded, but they missed him. Tyres screeched somewhere. They charged down the ramp, turning right and then left into a cluster of parked cars.

"Get down," Rob whispered.

They crouched between the bonnets of two cars with pillars ahead and behind them. It was the best cover they could hope for. Rob pulled out his phone and called control.

He waited several painful, terrifying seconds. Shouts and tyre squeals filled the multi-storey parking garage until a police operator answered.

"Hello..."

"This is Detective Loxley," Rob cut in. "I'm at the Four Seasons shopping centre in Mansfield, in the multi-storey car park, and I'm taking fire. I've got at least one armed man trying to kill me and my informant. I need armed support here, right now. And get them to make some noise."

"Understood. An armed response team will be with you shortly. I'm routing the closest units to you now. They're blue lighting it."

"Thanks," Rob said.

Car doors slammed. "We know you're in here," a gruff man shouted. "You can't hide forever."

More screams from another direction.

"This way," Rob hissed and led Mary between the lines of cars to a nearby pillar. More shouts echoed through the garage.

They were yelling at shoppers, telling them to get out.

"Where's your car?" Rob weighed up his options.

"Mine?" Mary whispered. "Where's yours?"

"Over there." He pointed to the next row over. "We'd be exposing ourselves to get there. Yours?"

"Other side, that way." She waved. "Not close."

"Shit."

He could make out the rumble of idling engines and the squeak of rubber against concrete as new customers drove into the car park, and the sound of footsteps as the thugs hunted them. Occasionally, one of them shouted at shoppers that exited the stairwell to return to their car.

Seconds that felt like hours passed while they remained hidden between the rows of cars.

They needed to get out of here.

A cry went up.

"They're over here."

Rob turned. The head of one of the thugs popped into a gap between the nearby vehicles. He was looking right at them.

"Crap." Rob made to run when a thought suddenly hit him like a tonne of bricks. He recognised that man. But where? Where did he recognise that thug from?

"Oi!" The voice was new and came from the stairwell. "Security. What do you think you're doing?"

Forgetting about his revelation, Rob grimaced at the thought of a have-a-go-hero taking these guys on, but there was no stopping the security guard now.

"Let's go," Rob said and pulled Mary around the concrete pillar.

He rounded the corner and collided with a thug who'd been stalking between the cars on the other side. Had they waited any longer, he'd have found them.

The man recovered from the shock of their sudden appearance and tried to bring his gun to bear. Rob grabbed the arm with the gun and kicked. The man threw a punch back.

"You little shit." The man grunted.

Rob punched him back and Mary delivered a mean-looking kick to his side, the man huffed.

Close by, sirens wailed, drowning out the nearby screams.

"We're leaving now," a man yelled. "Forget them."

Rob punched the man's arm. He wailed in pain and threw a backhand at Rob. It sent him sprawling.

"Now!" the distant thug issuing orders cried out.

Holding his arm with a pained expression, the thug glared at Rob for a beat.

Meeting his attacker's eyes and getting his first good look at the man's face, Rob had the same shocking feeling that he'd seen this man before, too. That was two of this crew who he recognised. How? Who were these...

Then it hit him. The Roxy kidnapping! Both men bore a striking resemblance to two of the thugs he'd seen in the CCTV of Roxy's abduction.

"Holy shit," Rob gasped. The thug turned and ran, disappearing between the pillar and a car.

Seconds later, their 4x4's engine roared, and they were off.

Mary sighed and relaxed. "Are you okay?"

"Fine." Rob got slowly to his feet, his face aching from the two hits he'd taken. "Ooof. Christ, these guys are serious."

"You noticed."

"Are *you* all right?"

"I'm fine," Mary answered. "Thanks to you."

"Forget about it," Rob said, his mind still racing with the revelation about the thugs. "I'm gonna feel it tomorrow, though."

"I bet. Are you okay?" Mary asked.

Rob turned and met her gaze. She regarded him through narrowed eyes.

He nodded. "Yeah, I'm fine. I just. I think I recognised two of those guys from a kidnapping case we have surveillance video of."

"You do?"

"Yeah, I'm sure of it." Rob grimaced. "I'm gonna need to review the footage to be sure. I saw it a few days ago, but it seems to fit. Oh, and I'm sorry, by the way."

"Sorry? Why?"

"There's a leak somewhere, clearly. How else did they know we were meeting here? If I had to guess, I'd say it was most likely on my end."

"Your end?"

"I think we can assume that an organisation that operates like that," Rob waved to where the thugs had retreated, "has several officers bought and paid for. I'm working out of Retford Station, so I'm guessing we have a leak somewhere."

"That's a reasonable assumption," Mary agreed.

"Look, I was about to ask you before we were rudely interrupted if you knew whether Danial Bolton was working with anyone else, or was he operating alone?"

"I don't know for sure, but I think there was at least one other person involved," Mary answered. She didn't sound certain.

Rob nodded and pulled out the piece of paper again. He directed her attention to one of the photos that showed Dan with a young woman. "Could it be a girlfriend, maybe?"

"I honestly don't know, but yeah, maybe. I'll talk to my contact, see if they can help. Everything was done through them anyway."

"So who is this contact? This hacker?"

"I'm not sure. I think they're female and they go by the name Riddle, but that's all I know. Sorry. Besides, I wouldn't want to betray their confidence in me."

"You might need to if this goes to court."

Mary's lip curled. "We'll see." She nodded and sighed before moving closer and taking his hands in hers. "Thank you. You saved my life up there. I didn't see that car coming."

"That's okay. You're alive and well, that's the main thing."

"Yeah, I guess. I'd better hang around and give my statement to the plod."

Rob nodded. "That would be helpful."

He sighed at the thought of this latest incident, what it meant for Retford Station and the case as a whole.

This was getting messy.

47

Liz sat on the edge of the bandstand, watching her daughter run around in a world of her own, squealing and chattering away in delight as she enjoyed the park. They'd spent ages in the nearby playpark, but Maisie had demanded to be allowed on the hill.

Naturally, Liz had joined her and charged around like a mad thing, running and rolling down the hill with her a couple of times before pleading tiredness and taking a break on the nearby bandstand. Meanwhile, the bundle of endless energy continued to imagine herself in some delightful psychedelic adventure filled with fairies and unicorns while she ran, skipped, and cartwheeled with abandon.

Sitting back and catching her breath, Liz turned towards the river.

They'd opened the bridge, and the officers on guard had long since left, but there was still police tape hanging from the branches and several flyers posted to trees and park furniture, asking for anyone who might have seen something to come forward.

The thought that someone had been killed and dumped in the river, just a few metres away, was chilling. It made her think twice about walking through the more secluded parts of the park, but then, she already dealt with feelings like that on a daily basis anyway, so it was nothing new.

What was this town coming to, she wondered? Had it always been this bad? Was there always this rough element here? Sadly, she probably knew the answer to that question, and it wasn't a nice thought.

Nearby, Maisie crouched by the nearby stream between the bandstand and the river, playing in the long grass. Liz lost herself in the moment. She admired Maisie, innocent to the horrors of the world she'd been born into, playing in the grass. She sometimes wondered what kind of world she would grow up into? What were they leaving behind for them? What would this generation's legacy be?

She wasn't sure it was a good one.

Maisie stood, chattering to herself while holding her hand to the side of her head. She wandered over to her mother. Curious, Liz listened as she got close.

"Yes, hello. I am the mummy of Baby Rabbit," Maisie said, referring to her favourite soft toy. "He's a been a bad rabbit? Oh, that naughty rabbit."

Maisie got closer. Liz spotted something in her little girl's hand and frowned. What was that? It was small and black and thin...

Liz jumped down and waved Maisie over. "What have you got there?"

"I got a phone, Mummy. Can I keep it? It's like yours. But it's broken."

Liz stared at it, and Maisie held it up. "Let me have a look at that." She took it from Maisie and briefly examined the inert device. It was a discarded Samsung, a nice one, too. But it was utterly dead.

She tried to determine why someone might throw their phone away, until a thought occurred to her. She glanced back at the police flyer taped to the bandstand and suddenly linked the phone and the recent murder.

Was this something to do with that?

"Can I play with it? Please, Mummy?"

"No, sorry, sweety. I need to take this to the police."

Maisie's face fell, and her bottom lip trembled. "Please, Mummy. I found it, not the police. "

Never a truer word was said, she thought. "But it's not yours, darlin'."

Seconds later, Maisie was a mess of tears and tantrums as she demanded her phone back, but Liz refused, making the situation worse. Stuffing the phone into her pocket, she resolved to take it to the police once she'd calmed her daughter down.

48

Each time Teri ran the diagnostics check, it came back with nothing. There was no evidence of a hack anywhere in the system, and each time she reported it to Crimson, he ordered her to do it again and look harder. There'd been a leak somewhere, he said, and they needed to know where it came from.

But Teri knew where it had come from, and it wasn't through a hack. It had come from her. She was the leak, but there was no way she could ever tell them that, not if she valued her life.

Crimson seemed stressed, which wasn't unlikely, given the nature of this organisation. And if he was breathing down her neck, demanding that she find a hack that wasn't there, then it was only because the Cardinal, or maybe even the Red Man, was leaning on him to get some answers.

But she did as Crimson had asked because to do anything else would only incriminate her. She ran the automated tests and then dove into the system manually to check and see if there was anything wrong. Predictably, there wasn't. Even the footprints that Riddle had left on her last visit were gone.

As the hours wound on, Teri found her gaze slipping to her right, to the empty chair that Dan used to occupy. She

337

wondered if anyone was ever going to directly address the giant elephant in the room.

But, apart from a warning by the man she knew only as the Cardinal, where he reiterated that the secrecy of their organisation was paramount and that severe punishments would be handed out to anyone they found to be in breach of that rule, no one said anything.

Weirdly enough, Teri found this total silence on the issue the hardest to deal with. At several points during the day, she found she had to clamp down on her emotions so she didn't lose control and burst into tears.

Worse still, every time she glanced right, she could see Rubious on the far side of the room, and he frequently glared back, leering at her as if she were a particularly juicy meal that he wanted to gobble up.

She shivered at the thought.

The door to the ops room slammed open, and the Cardinal stormed in.

"Where are they? Where are the Red Team?"

"Just leaving Mansfield, why?" Crimson asked.

"Turn them round. Send them to Nottingham. I have a new job for them."

"Oh, okay. What should I tell them?"

The Cardinal glanced up at her and Rubious and then back down at Crimson. "Come with me. We'll discuss it in my office."

"Sir," Crimson confirmed and got up.

Teri watched Crimson leave and shut the door behind him before turning back to her desk. Her gaze fell on Rubious for a moment, who was giving her a smug, knowing look.

"Piss off," she muttered, just loud enough that he'd hear her say something without making out the words.

Returning to her work, she continued her latest useless scan, clicking the mouse and hitting return when prompted. All while a crushing pressure squeezed on the right side of her head. It was the feeling that Rubious was watching her, his eyes boring into the side of her skull, and she hated every second of it.

What was he leering at?

She glanced up at the CCTV screens and found her eyes drawn to the camera pointing into the only occupied cell. She felt sick. That poor woman didn't have long to wait now. She'd soon be dragged kicking and screaming from that disgusting cell into the Red Room.

A final indignity for her to endure.

Feeling suddenly sick, Teri got to her feet. "I need a drink." She turned and walked towards the central gap between the desks, heading for the back of the room where the sink and kettle awaited her.

As she moved, Rubious got up and rushed to meet her. He planted himself directly in her path and got in Teri's face.

"What?" Teri asked, suddenly shaken and worried. She hated being alone with him and usually tried to avoid it whenever possible. "What do you want?"

"I know what you did, Teri."

Her eyes bugged at the mention of her real name. He shouldn't know that. She had no idea what Rubious's name was. How had he found out? "What do you mean?"

"You and Dan. I know what you did. I know you talked. I'm not stupid, you know."

Her stomach did a summersault, her nausea suddenly much worse. He knew? How the hell did he find out? What does he know? Surely he can't know everything. Best to play dumb, she concluded. "I... don't know what you're talking about."

"Don't play coy with me, Teri Randell. I know you planned a meeting with a reporter. I know exactly what you did and how you got Dan killed."

"That's not true," Teri blurted, sounding about as convincing as... well... something not very convincing. "We didn't do anything."

Rubious stepped closer. "You can't lie to me, Teri. I know everything you did, and if you don't do exactly as I say, if you don't do everything and anything I want, I'll tell them. And you know what they'll do to you then."

Involuntarily, her body shook at the injustice and fear that gripped her. He should not be able to get away with this. This was so unfair. She hated Rubious but was acutely aware that Rubious seemed to have a crush on her.

As she processed what he'd just told her, the chaos of her confusion faded away, and she saw a bright path ahead of her as if her brain had suddenly kicked into gear to help her navigate her way through this.

"Go on then, do it. Tell them. I don't care. I'd rather face the consequences than do anything you might want me to do, you grotesque sicko. You disgust me."

"How dare…"

"Oh, but bear in mind that if you do tell them, I'll make sure to add in that you withheld information from them and used it to blackmail me for your own personal gain. I'm sure that will go down well with them. And then we'll both suffer the consequences, and you don't get to have me for yourself."

Rubious's lip quivered, and his left eye twitched in annoyance and frustration. "You think you're so clever."

"That's because I am," she replied. "Idiots like you think you're so clever, but you're just a moron with delusions of grandeur and a tiny dick. So go on, do it, and see where it gets you."

The door to the back of the room opened, and Crimson stepped through. "Everything okay?" he asked while returning to his desk. "I know it's been a stressful day for everyone."

"I'm fine," Teri replied, calmer now than she had been all day.

"We're good," Rubious agreed.

"Excellent."

"I thought I'd get a drink," Teri declared as she walked past Crimson, heading to the kitchenette. "Do you want one?"

"Sure."

49

Pulling into the car park at the back of the shared service station in Retford, Rob turned the engine off and allowed himself to fall limp, relaxing into the seat. He'd spent the rest of the afternoon dealing with the fallout from the attack at the multi-storey, answering questions from Mansfield police and talking to Nailer on the phone until they finally let Mary leave under Rob's supervision. Rob then promptly let her go, concluding that she was safer if the only person who knew where she was, was herself. He considered taking her to Retford, but the potential leak worried her, and he didn't fancy hosting her at his apartment when he was so far away. Instead, he settled on asking her to remain close to Retford should she get into trouble and need to call him.

She agreed and left.

Knowing that Mary was as safe as possible didn't make his feelings about the attack any easier to deal with, though. Whoever these people were, they were well-armed, powerful, and didn't care who they hurt or killed.

The entire multi-storey had been locked down as a crime scene while the boffins from the lab did their job. Like Mary, Rob had given as detailed a statement about the events as he could, complete with descriptions of the thugs and a clear timeline of events.

Hours had passed by the time he got out of there and back to Retford, giving him plenty of time to think about what Mary had told him about her meeting with Dan. Had Dan been telling Mary the truth about this so-called Red Man and the Red Room he supposedly ran? It sounded crazy, and were it not for the murderous thugs who desperately wanted to silence her, Rob felt sure he'd have already discounted the idea.

There'd been rumours of Red Rooms floating about the internet for years, but the traditional idea of one seemed to be a myth. A rumour given life by the power of social media and taken to its ultimate and extreme conclusion. It was fear-mongering created by contributions from conspiracy theorists and fiction writers, or so it seemed. But that wasn't to say that people didn't indulge in some sick stuff. It was just that the infrastructure for live-streaming video over the dark web was simply not there.

So, if Rob was to take Mary and Dan at their word, what form did this Red Room take?

He guessed they were basically snuff videos, where people recorded themselves doing some really sick things, and there were plenty of cases, some of them well-known, of people doing just that.

Was that what the enigmatic Red Man was doing? Was he recording videos for paying clients?

Whatever the case, Dan had taken that secret to the grave with him, and until one of their leads bore fruit, they'd remain in the dark as to who this Red Man was.

But things did seem to be falling into place.

Rob had explained to Nailer about recognising the thugs who had attacked him and Mary, but he couldn't be sure until he got back to the station and reviewed the abduction footage. But even if he did recognise them, what would that mean for the investigation, apart from them being able to join forces with Nick, Guy, and Nailer to try and bring this home?

As Rob thought about what leads they might find, he realised he'd not spoken to Ellen since this morning about her investigation into the disappearance of Roxy.

Rob grabbed his phone and called.

"Hey, Rob. How's things?" Ellen greeted him.

"Oh, just another day of getting shot at. You know how it is."

"Shot at?" Ellen asked, surprised.

"I was meeting with an informant and got ambushed," Rob explained. "These guys are serious."

"Bloody hell, Rob. They sound it. You need to be careful."

345

"I thought I *was* being careful," Rob replied. "Someone must have betrayed us."

"More corruption?"

"It's rife," Rob confirmed. I can't get away from it. I guess Bill had good reason to suspect me, given how much of it there is about."

"Are you feeling sorry for Bill now?" Ellen asked.

"Not quite," Rob answered. "So tell me, how are you getting on down south? Jon's not working you too hard, is he?"

"No, I'm good," Ellen replied. "But progress is slow. Really slow. Glacial, actually. Trying to access Mr Collins's company accounts is a nightmare, and by the time we do get that access, he could have covered his tracks."

Rob sighed. "Well, keep going. We need to know if Truman is involved in this while we explore other angles up here."

"And how's that going?"

"I spoke to Nailer and Nick earlier. They've been interviewing Roxy's friends and family, looking for anyone who might have a reason to do this, but so far, they have nothing. The trace on the van the thugs used to grab Roxy has been a dead end, too. But, there might be something new that could be useful."

"Oh?"

"I think I recognised the thugs who attacked us this afternoon from the Roxy kidnapping footage. I think they're the same people."

"Oh, really?"

"I need to review the footage again, which I'll do in a moment once I get in, but I'm fairly sure. It feels right. But if I am, that puts a whole new spin on this for us."

"How so?"

"The murder here seems to be linked to someone going by the name of the Red Man. It's a local urban myth, and according to my informant, this guy runs a Red Room."

"They don't exist," Ellen stated.

"The traditional idea of them streaming live video over the dark web doesn't as far as we know. Although I guess I could be proven wrong, technology is constantly improving, after all. But plenty of sick people record themselves doing some really disgusting things, like those paedophile rings and that Peter Scully case in Australia. It happens. We know it does. So it could be something like that, with people *paying* him to make videos..." Rob left the idea hanging to see if she made the connection that he had earlier today.

"Oh, you mean... Shit. So Truman could have paid to have Roxy kidnapped?"

"It fits," Rob suggested.

"It does."

"Something to consider as you're digging through Truman's accounts," Rob suggested.

"Definitely. But who is this Red Man?"

"Right now, I have no idea. We need to keep looking."

"Agreed," Ellen replied. "Right, I won't keep you.

"Thanks. I need to get on. I have some security footage to watch."

"Good luck with everything. I'll be in touch if anything turns up."

"Same here," Rob said and hung up before making his way into the building.

"Aaah, you're back," Scarlett said, getting up from her seat the moment she saw him walk in. She strode round the table and pulled him into a quick hug. "I'm glad you're okay."

"I'm fine," Rob confirmed, touched by Scarlett's concern for his health.

Tucker held out his hand, and Rob shook it.

"Glad you're okay, son. They probably had shit aim."

Rob shrugged. "Either that, or I'm just an action man."

"Yeeeah, right. Fuck off. Still, I'd rather have you back in one piece either way."

"I'm grateful for your concern," Rob said as Sergeant Susanna Parsons walked in behind him.

"I heard about the mess you made in Mansfield," she remarked. "I hope it isn't a sign of things to come for Retford."

"We will do our best to make sure it doesn't come to that," Rob reassured her.

"Glad to hear it. I'm pleased you're okay."

Rob raised an eyebrow. "You almost sound like you care." He smiled to take the edge off his words.

"Let's not get too carried away," Susanna replied.

Rob grunted. "Right then, we've got work to do."

"Nailer said you needed to see the Roxy footage again," Scarlett said. "I have it here."

"Yes, I do."

"Why?"

Rob explained how he'd recognised two of the thugs during the attack while Scarlett queued up the footage. "I just need to be sure."

She hit play, and he watched the brutal abduction once more, and sure enough, two of the kidnappers looked like a good match for the men he'd recognised. He couldn't be one hundred percent certain, but his conviction about this was easily in the high nineties.

"Is it them?" Scarlett asked.

"I think so. Which means Nick and I have been working on the same case."

"And we've not been idle either," Scarlett said.

"Go on," Rob urged as he took a seat. "What have you got?"

"Well, firstly, the forensics team went through Dan's house. They lifted a second set of prints and found several long hairs that seem to match the girl we've seen in the photos."

"And have you run those prints?"

"Absolutely." Scarlett smiled. "And we got a match."

"Brilliant. Who?"

"They belong to a young lady named Teri Randell. It seems she got involved with some petty crime when she was a teen, which is why we have her prints, and now we have her address."

"We sent someone round to pick her up," Tucker said. "But there's no one home, and we don't know where she is."

"We have a car sitting outside," Scarlett continued. "We'll get her."

"I've offered to take the evening stakeout shift," Tucker added.

"Excellent," Rob said. "We need to speak to her as soon as possible. Hopefully, she'll know more about what Dan was involved with. Hell, she might be involved, too. Great work."

"Thank you, but that's not all," Scarlett added. "Someone found a discarded phone in Kings Park today, close to where

Dan was dumped in the river, and handed it in. It was totally dead, so we charged it, and guess whose faces appeared on the lock screen?"

Rob smiled. "Dan and Teri?"

"Got it in one," Scarlett said with a grin, a wink, and a point of her finger. "We think it's Dan's phone, given he went to meet Mary, but it's locked, so we can't do a lot with it right now."

"Have you tried to unlock it? Guess the code or anything?" Rob asked.

"He's got it set to a pattern lock. We've tried some of the more common ones, but no, we've not had any luck yet."

Rob nodded. Locked phones provided a stumbling block in many cases, if you were unable to get the owner to unlock them. There were ways around it, using expensive, specialist, privately developed software to get around the lock and encryption, but even then, there was no guarantee of success, and bypassing the lock could take days, weeks, or even months. Sometimes more.

"I'll get someone from digital forensics to come and look at it," Susanna said.

"Thanks. If there's any chance of getting into that phone, take it," Rob stated. "There's bound to be useful information on there that could be the difference between solving this case and not."

"Will do," Susanna confirmed.

"Looks like it'll be another late one," Tucker said.

"I knew it," Scarlett said.

"Tucker, you take the early evening shift on the stakeout of Teri's. If she shows up, I want you to call us in. Don't go in there alone. Scarlett and I will take over later on and go through till morning."

Scarlett pulled a face. "Excellent. I'd better call Chris."

50

Climbing out of her car, Erika felt dead on her feet after a day's work, dealing with the public and their inane comments and requests. Whoever said the customer was always right had never worked in a shop.

However, despite her misgivings and the occasional rude customer, Erika enjoyed working in the coffee shop. She'd had several jobs over the last few years while trying to work out what she wanted to do for a career because, honestly, she wasn't sure. There was a strong police presence in her life, what with her dad working for them and her neighbour working with her dad, but she honestly wasn't all that interested in following in their footsteps. Not that her dad would want or allow her to work in the police anyway.

Too risky, he'd no doubt say.

Risky. Erika wasn't sure she'd agree with that assessment. It was no more dangerous than her living next door to Rob, and that had worked out fine so far. She knew the dangers of what she was doing and didn't appreciate her dad being so overprotective of her.

She needed to get out there and live her life!

Once she'd decided what she wanted to do with it, that was. She sighed, glanced up at the apartment block and thought over her plans for the evening.

First off, she needed to visit Rob's place to see Muffin. That poor cat had been left alone all day. It would need feeding and probably a scratch behind his ears. The thought of getting a soft cuddle from the feline warmed the cockles of her heart. She enjoyed caring for Muffin but wasn't sure if that was because of her genuine affection for cats or because of who the cat's owner was?

Afterwards, it would be time for some food of her own, then maybe a quick call to Guy followed by some trashy TV. She needed a relaxing night, so one of those silly reality shows would be perfect. What was that one called that was set on a luxury yacht and followed the crew as they sailed around the Med? Something like that would be perfect.

Besides, she couldn't go tearing up the town every night, she'd end up exhausted.

Nearing the door, she pulled out her key. An engine roared close by. She turned. A van swerved in and skidded to a stop right behind her. Its side door was flung open.

"What the hell."

Several men jumped out and lunged for her.

She screamed and tried to fight them, kicking and punching the thugs as they grabbed and lifted her off the ground. One of them clamped a hand over her mouth, muffling her screams while they carried her into the back of the van.

She bucked and kicked, doing everything to try and throw the bastards off, but they were so strong!

The van's side door was rolled shut. The vehicle revved and set off at speed, throwing them around the back. One of the men barked orders to the other three.

"Get that gag in place," he snapped. "Tie her up. Wrists and ankles. You know the drill."

The men used their greater strength and body weight to hold her down and secure her. She fought them as best she could until one of the men shouted at her.

"Oi, bitch face."

Erika glanced up and froze. The leader of the group pointed a gun at her. She stared at it and then at the impassive face behind it.

"Yeah, now you get it. If you want to survive this, I suggest you stop fucking struggling, or I will introduce the insides of your head to one of these bullets."

Erika grimaced and relaxed, sighing in defeat. "Fine."

With practised efficiency, they stuffed a rag into her mouth before wrapping the lower part of her head in tape. Interestingly, they took care to make sure she could breathe.

So they didn't want to kill her?

"Boss, here," one of the men said and handed him her phone.

She reached for her back pocket in shock, and sure enough, one of them had grabbed it.

The gunman held up her phone and then slammed it down onto the corner of the small bench he sat on, over and over, until the thing was falling apart in his hand. "No one's tracking you."

Erika grimaced. Who the hell were these guys?

Surely they couldn't be... them, could they? Had they found out and come for her? She frowned and thought back over the last few days, trying to work out if she'd slipped up and said too much. She felt sure she hadn't, but she couldn't be totally certain. The only new thing she'd indulged in recently were the dates with Guy Gibson, which had gone well. She'd had a few drinks with him and enjoyed their dates, but was it possible she'd let something slip and somehow that had got back to...them?

But if so, how? Had she said something, and then Guy let it slip somewhere else? Had someone been following them on these dates and listening in? Or was Guy somehow to blame...?

She cringed. No. Not Guy. Surely not, and yet, her mind seemed to fixate on him. Why?

She remembered the last date and the interest he'd taken in her dad. He'd seemed keen to know more about him and kept asking after him. She'd done her best to dodge the questions without arousing suspicion and remain vague, but had he read into it somehow? The identity of her father was something she wanted to keep to herself because it would change everything, especially where Loxley was concerned.

Had she been flying too close to the sun by dating Guy? It was something she'd considered a few times, and if her dad found out, he'd probably hit the roof.

Oh God. She'd got carried away with the excitement of it all and made a big mistake. One that might have somehow led to this, depending on who *these* idiots were.

No. No more. She was done. No more dates with Guy. His interest in her family was a little too concerning for her tastes in light of this latest predicament.

Glancing up at the men sitting around her, she silently chastised herself for worrying about her personal life. She had slightly more pressing issues to deal with right now and needed to concentrate and keep watch for any chance to escape.

Erika glanced up at the man with the gun. She wanted to talk to him, but there was no way to do that with this gag in her mouth.

The van drove on, its terrible suspension doing little to dampen the bumps in the road, leading to an uncomfortable and painful ride. There were no windows, and she had no idea where they were taking her, but the ride seemed to take a while. Maybe an hour, or just under? She couldn't be sure without a clock or watch.

In the end, she resigned herself to waiting until, finally, the van slowed. It sounded like they were driving over gravel.

"All right, we're here. Get her in, quick," the gunman ordered.

They sprang to life and grabbed her. She bucked once to throw them off until the gun pointed at her head again.

"Try it. Go on. I dare you. See what happens."

She screamed against the gag but stopped fighting the thugs who picked her up and carried her into the darkness. She glanced around. A large house surrounded by tall bushes loomed out of the shadows. They moved her around the side of it towards the back of the house and then into an outbuilding. The bare-brick interior was dirty and crumbling. They descended a set of stairs, walked along an underground concrete corridor, and then took a left. They dropped her to her feet. One of the men pulled open a barred cell door. The metal squealed and complained as it opened. Around her, she saw three similar cells, two of which were occupied. She spotted a dirty, broken-looking woman in one of them and a more animated, angry-seeming man in the other.

"Hey, what are you doing with her?" the male prisoner barked.

"Shut up," the gunman snapped back while another thug shoved her into the cell.

She stumbled and fell, landing on a thin, dirty mattress that saved her from hurting herself. Movement rustled close by. She twisted over. One of the men approached while the others stood outside, the leader still brandishing his gun. She lay still and compliant while the man cut the zip ties from her wrists and ankles before retreating from the cell and shutting the door.

"You're animals," the male prisoner railed against their captors.

"Shut the fuck up," the leader said, finally lowering the gun while laughing at the prisoner. He turned to her and grinned. "Sleep well, bitch."

She refused to give him the pleasure of a reply and just stared at him. The group strolled away as if this was the most normal thing in the world.

"Hey, are you okay?"

She looked up. Her cell was opposite the male prisoner who held his cell door bars and peered at her.

"You can take the gag off now. They don't care. No one can hear us down here."

Erika nodded and started to remove the tape. It was painful and pulled on her hair.

"Who is it?" said a resigned female voice from the next cell over.

"I don't know," the male prisoner replied. "She's got a gag on." He turned to her. "I'm Ben, by the way, and this is Roxy. I've been here since yesterday. Roxy was a few days before that."

Finally, Erika removed the tape from her mouth and removed the dirty rag, throwing it to the floor. She gagged briefly before coughing and getting control of herself. "Urgh, that's better."

"Are you alright?"

"Oh, fine and dandy," she snarked, and got to her feet. "What the hell is this? Where am I?"

"I wish I could tell you," Ben answered with a calmness that Erika found frustrating. "What's your name?"

"What the hell does that matter?" She grabbed the bars of her cell door and rattled them, trying to force it. "We need to get out of here."

Ben raised his hands, urging calm. "By all means, try, but I'd recommend saving your strength. You're not getting out of there."

"How do you know?" She kicked the door several times, yelling in frustration. After a full minute of this, she stopped to catch her breath. Her foot ached.

Across the corridor, Ben watched, his expression full of sympathy.

"Why are you so calm?" she asked.

Ben sighed. "I'm saving my energy. There's no way I'm breaking down my door, so why try?"

"What's your name?" Roxy asked from next door.

She sighed. "Erika."

"Well, welcome to hell, Erika." There was no hope in her voice.

Erika gave the dividing wall a dismissive glare and then turned to Ben, who shrugged.

"Where you from?" Ben asked.

Erika took a long breath and placed her hands on her hips while her heartbeat calmed. Ben was probably right. She wasn't breaking out of here by kicking the door, so why waste time and energy trying? She could do some serious damage to herself and ruin any future chance of escaping. She needed to be smarter than that.

Inside, her emotions were a stormy mess of fear and anger while her mind ran through countless possibilities about where she might be, who her kidnappers were, why they'd taken her, and who might realise she was missing.

She felt like curling up in a ball and crying, and probably would later on. But not now. She needed to try and get a grip, rein in her emotions and think critically about this. Panic and rage would get her nowhere.

"I'm from Nottingham," she said, deciding to engage and answer Ben's question.

"Me, too," Ben replied.

"I'm from Newark," Roxy added.

"Any idea where we are?" Erika approached the cell door and eyed up the crumbling dirty walls, rusty bars, and bare light bulb.

"No." Ben shook his head. "No idea."

"I think we're in the middle of nowhere," Erika suggested. "It was quiet outside, and all I saw were hedges and distant trees. But it's dark out there, so I can't be sure. Do you have any idea who these guys are? Why are they just grabbing random people off the street?"

"Is that what they did to you?" Ben asked.

With a shiver, Erika thought back to the moment they'd abducted. "I was about to walk into my apartment block, and the van pulled up. I've never been so scared." She shrugged. "Still am."

"Sounds like what happened to me," Roxy stated. "I was in a multi-storey car park, though."

"Mine was a house invasion," Ben added. "They just barged in and grabbed me."

"Shit," Erika hissed, shocked at the brazen way these guys were acting. "Have they talked to you? Have they said why you're here?"

"Not really," Ben answered. "There's a creepy man in a red mask who shows up sometimes, but he doesn't answer our questions. He just makes vague threats and disappears."

"Well, that sounds lovely," Erika quipped, doing her best to try and lighten the tone despite their circumstances.

Ben smiled. "Now you're getting it. No point in wallowing."

"Have they fed you?" Erika enquired. Her stomach rumbled.

"Just scraps. I'm starving."

"Me, too," Erika agreed. "I didn't eat much today."

"Well, don't hold your breath. This ain't the Hilton."

Erika grinned despite herself.

A door sounded nearby. Footsteps approached, and the thugs reappeared, followed by a man in a dark coat and a red mask.

Erika backed away from her cell door in fear. Were they coming for her?

Red Mask reached her cell and stopped, turning to face her. Behind the mask, his cold eyes looked her up and down.

"Welcome. I'm glad you could join us. I think you'll be most useful."

"Piss off," Erika hissed.

The man grunted to his men. "Get her."

Her bravado suddenly vanished, and she backed away from the cell door. "No, please. I didn't mean it..."

But the thugs went next door and opened Roxy's cell. A struggle ensued. Roxy shouted and pleaded with them.

"No. Please, no. Don't do this. Please. You can't."

The men dragged her from her cell with little difficulty. All her strength had gone, making her easy prey.

The man in the red mask regarded Roxy before reaching for her face and lifting her chin. "My dear Roxy. Your time has come. I'm sorry for the delay. I won't make that mistake again." He glanced at Erika with his black, shark-like eyes.

Erika shrank under his gaze, feeling a deep-rooted terror she'd never experienced before.

The masked man marched off the way he'd entered, deeper into the complex. "Bring her."

The thugs did as he'd asked, while Roxy screamed and wailed. Erika ran to the bars to try and see where they went, but they were soon out of view, leaving them with just Roxy's yells echoing down the hall. Soon, her defiant shouts descended into distant sobbing. Erika could hear voices but couldn't make out what they were saying.

Across the way, Ben remained silent and listened, too.

Several minutes later, a new noise started up. It sounded like a small motor, similar to what you'd find in a remote-controlled car or power tool.

"What is that?" Erika whispered. She tried to place it.

"I think…" Ben muttered. The colour drained from his face. "I think that's a drill."

A new fear rose inside her. Roxy screamed as the drill was suddenly forced to work harder.

Horrific images of torture and blood flashed in Erika's mind. Roxy's utterly terrified screams turned almost animalistic. Somehow, they didn't sound human anymore.

Erika backed away from the cell door, scared beyond words over what their fate might be.

She turned and vomited in the corner.

51

During her drive home, Teri kept the radio off and she stared out into the distance, doing her best not to think about what she'd seen tonight.

It wasn't anything new. She'd watched this happen countless times and had long been numb to the screams, gore, and horrific torture that occurred in the room downstairs from where she worked.

But tonight, something was different. Seeing the Cardinal and his thugs put that poor woman through nearly two hours of utter hell before finally granting her the merciful embrace of death, it was as if she was watching them do it for the first time all over again.

She was reminded of her reaction the first time she'd seen them use the Red Room and how that had made her feel. And somehow, Dan's murder at their hands had stripped away her defences and allowed her to objectively view what she was a part of. She hated every moment of it, and that poor woman's cries of pain would haunt her for the rest of her life.

But even with this fresh perspective, she felt helpless to do anything. They'd tried to go public and shed the cold light of day on this secretive operation by using a sympathetic ear, only for Dan to end up dead.

Somehow, Rubious had found out. He'd known what they were planning, and must have told the Red Man and the Cardinal that Dan was behind all this and conveniently left her out of it because he didn't want her to be killed. Instead, he'd hoped to use his knowledge of their plan as blackmail.

She'd poured cold water on that idea for the time being, but she wasn't sure how long that would hold him off, and Rubious might try and call her bluff. She wasn't sure how she'd react if he did go down that route. Would she let him tell all and suffer the consequences, or would she relent and do whatever Rubious wanted? She couldn't answer that right now, nor did she want to think about what Rubious would like her to do. Some sick sexual stuff, most likely.

She nearly gagged.

The time would come soon enough, though, and one way or another, she'd be forced to choose.

Pulling into the car park around the side of her apartment block, she pushed thoughts of her future away, preferring not to think about it. She hated everything these sadists were doing but saw no way to stand up to them. There was no way she trusted the police, knowing full well that they could not protect her from these maniacs. She'd seen enough evidence of that during her time working for the Red Man, and knew full well that some of these officers took bribes from him and might report on her if she spoke.

Instead, she'd agreed to speak to a reporter sympathetic to her plight, who had not been bought and paid for by the people she worked for. That way, she could remain anonymous but still bring them down.

That had been the hope, anyway, until Dan had disappeared.

Leaving her car behind, Teri walked round to the front of the block and into the building. She made sure to lock her front door once she was inside, hoping that it might provide some protection should they come looking for her, and collapsed into the softness of her bed.

To her left, her second phone buzzed.

Sighing in annoyance, Teri reached over and picked it up. A quick look at her messages revealed that Riddle had been texting her.

We need to talk.

Call me.

I can help.

Don't do this alone.

Please, call me when you get home. I can get you out. Please.

Teri read them all and, for a moment, considered not replying. Riddle had been the one behind these meetings, making her wonder if the hacker had somehow left a clue before for Rubious to follow? Was Dan's death her fault?

She couldn't know for sure, and it was quite possible that she was barking up the wrong tree with that line of thought.

No, she decided, she needed to reply and started composing the message

Sorry, but no. We're done. I'm not risking mine or anyone else's life trying to bring these guys down. I'm done. Don't contact me again.

She hit send, dropped the phone to her bed and buried her head in her hands. It was the end of a very long day that had taken a huge toll on her physically and emotionally. Utterly drained and shattered, she rolled over and drifted off to sleep.

When the sound of heavy knocks on her door snapped her back to the waking world, she could have sworn she'd been asleep for barely a minute, but a quick glance at her clock told her otherwise. She'd been home for nearly an hour.

She sat up. The person at her door knocked again. There was an urgency to it. The doorbell sounded, too. They really wanted in. She frowned, wondering if this was the Red Team finally coming for her. Her stomach briefly flipped at the idea, making her feel sick, but a moment's thought had her doubting this was the case. The Red Team didn't mess about. If they wanted in, they smashed your door down.

So who was it?

Sliding off her bed, she got to her feet, crept to the bedroom door, and peered down the hallway to the front door at the far end. She made out shadows through the crack beneath the door.

Curious, she tiptoed partway up her hallway. "Hello?"

The shadows moved. "Hello. Is that Teri Randell?" asked a male voice she'd not heard before.

"What of it?"

"I'm Detective Loxley with the Nottinghamshire Police. We'd like to talk to you if you have a moment."

Shocked, Teri stared at the door for a long moment. How could this be? How had they found her? She'd been so... No, obviously, they hadn't been careful enough. Rubious had found out, so why wouldn't the police have done the same? Maybe Rubious had called them?

"Are you there?" asked the detective. "We just want to talk to you."

Teri approached the door. She padded right up to it and put her eye to the peephole. She spied two people. A dark-haired man with plenty of stubble standing beside a striking blonde woman with fierce eyes. Both were clearly detectives. They just had that look about them. The man kind of reminded her of a younger Hugh Jackman in appearance, something she found somewhat attractive. But now wasn't the time to get too distracted.

"It's a little late," Teri answered, unsure what she should do. Glancing to her right, she gazed through her kitchen window and out into the dark. She wondered who else might be out there, watching her. Was that how Rubious had found out what they were doing or...? She turned and stared into the adjoining rooms. Was he watching her now?

Were the Cardinal or even the Red Man watching her?

"I'm sorry, I can't talk," she blurted out as a sinking terror gripped her. "I've got nothing to say to you."

"We need to talk to you about Daniel Bolton," the man answered. "We won't take much of your time, and you're not in trouble. We just want to talk."

"No, I can't. I'm sorry, but no. I'm not talking to you. Please leave."

There was a brief silence from the other side of the door.

"Teri, please reconsider," said the female detective. "We only want to help. We can protect you."

"No, you can't. We're done here. Please leave," she pleaded. She strode back to her bedroom, and slammed the door shut.

She perched on the end of her bed and she tried to figure out if she'd done the right thing. She couldn't be seen talking to the police. If *they* saw her doing that, if *they* found out, they'd kill her. There was no doubt in her mind about that at all. She had to keep her distance. After a minute, the knocks and bell rings from her front door ceased, leaving her in silence.

Suddenly filled with curiosity, she got up and flicked off her bedroom light. She crossed the hallway into the spare bedroom at the front of the building and peered out the window, keeping the lights off so anyone outside wouldn't see her.

The two detectives crossed Moorgate Road and approached a car parked just up from the end of Tiln Lane. They got in, but the car remained stationary. She watched for a while, but they didn't move and didn't seem like they were going to.

With mounting horror, she realised they were staking out her house.

"Shit, shit, shit," she hissed. Her mind flailed about, wondering what to do. They might try to follow her into work tomorrow if they stayed there all night. But that would be a disaster. They couldn't do that. People would die, including her.

Desperate for a solution, she spent the next twenty minutes pacing the room, and talking to herself while she considered all the options. She thought about running away, talking to the police, or sneaking out somehow, but there were no easy choices here. The option that she kept returning to was to call in and alert the Cardinal that her place was under surveillance. That way, she was showing her loyalty to the organisation. She was showing she was trustworthy and meaning she might escape any punishment. She also wouldn't be putting her family at risk.

Grabbing her phone, she contemplated calling, but threw it back onto the spare bed and went back to the pacing. But after another ten minutes, with the detectives still in their old black car, she really didn't see an alternative.

Feeling sick, she concluded that there was simply no other option.

She had to tell her boss.

She had to warn them.

Strung out and desperate, she made the call.

52

Rob woke with a jump. Something buzzed and rang loudly. He glanced around in shock and he tried to work out exactly where he was. For a brief couple of seconds, he found himself at a loss as to why his back ached so much and why a young blonde woman sat beside him, giving him a curious look.

Then he remembered the stakeout with Scarlett. His phone continued to ring. He groaned in annoyance. "Ugh, why did I agree to this?"

They'd arrived last night after Tucker called, saying that Teri had returned home. After relieving Tucker, they'd decided to pay Teri a visit and knocked on her door, but she'd refused to answer it or even talk to them.

Annoyed, they'd retreated back to their car and decided to wait for her to emerge.

Rob had taken the first shift, letting Scarlett get an uncomfortable couple of hours of sleep until he'd woken her in the small hours, and she'd taken over.

It felt like he'd been asleep for about thirty seconds, although several hours had passed by this point.

"Morning, sleepyhead," Scarlett remarked with a sly grin. She held on to her insulated mug with both hands and sipped at the fragrant contents. The coffee inside it smelled divine.

"Mmm, that smells lovely."

"Get your own," she replied begrudgingly. "Just because I came prepared and you didn't."

Rob grunted in frustration.

"Are you gonna answer that?"

"Yeah, yeah, I know." Rob lifted his phone and saw a number listed with a single letter above it. M.

Rob answered. "Mary. Are you okay?"

"Fine, I'm fine," Mary said. "Don't worry, there's nothing wrong. I'm in town and wanted to come and see you."

"You're in Retford?"

"Yeah. Is that a problem?"

Rob considered this for a moment. "Not as long as you're keeping a low profile, no."

"Then we're good. Are you at the station? I'm close."

"No, sorry. We're on Moorgate hill, near Tiln Lane. You can come and meet us here if you want."

"Alright. See you soon." She hung up.

"Rob," Scarlett called out, urgency in her voice.

Rob looked up. Scarlett pointed over the road to the flats. Teri was running into the car park, glancing their way.

"Shit." He dropped his phone and turned the key in the ignition, firing up the engine.

Seconds later, Teri's hatchback flew out of the parking area, screeching over Moorgate and speeding down Tiln Lane.

"Bloody hell," Rob exclaimed, shocked at her recklessness. "Right then, hold on to your knickers." Checking his mirror, he pulled out and quickly turned into Tiln Lane, piling on the speed to catch Teri up.

They flew along the residential street, past the terrace houses on the right, before taking the bend in the road at speed.

"There she is," he remarked.

"She's slowed down," Scarlett said, sounding confused.

He was quickly catching her up. Rob slowed to match her speed.

"Yeah..." Rob didn't understand why either.

He was several seconds past the bend when a large 4x4, sporting a set of bull bars, followed and closed the distance between them.

"Huh," Rob muttered. He glanced into his rearview mirror. "I think we have company."

They pressed on and drove past Carr Hill Primary School on their left and approached the edge of town. In the distance, trees and fields.

"Where's she taking us?" Scarlett asked.

"No idea." Rob checked his rearview mirror again. The 4x4 was getting close.

He frowned in annoyance as they cleared the school and passed the last few roads to either side. The houses on the right gave way to fields with a farm in the distance. Teri suddenly braked.

The manoeuvre snapped Rob's attention to the car in front, forcing him to pump his brakes to avoid hitting Teri's car.

"Shit."

An engine revved behind them.

"Look out!" Scarlett yelled

A loud bang sounded through the car. He was forced left. Rob slammed the brakes on and tried to turn out of it, but his wheel caught the kerb. Everything twisted and spun, and for a brief moment, he was weightless.

Scarlett screamed. Rob yelled, and then the car landed upside down with an excruciating thud. Rob's head hit something, and the seat belt dug into his body. Rob's beloved Capri slid over the grass, into a gully along the side of the road and stopped at a Dutch angle with a splash of water.

They'd ended up in a stream.

"Bloody hell," Rob muttered.

Somewhere in the distance, engines roared and faded into the distance.

377

Rob's head swam while he hung upside down. Everything hurt, but as far as he could tell, he still had use of all of his limbs.

He tried to make sense of what had happened, and suddenly remembered his passenger.

"Scarlett?"

He turned. She hung from her seat with a single trickle of blood falling from the corner of her mouth. She wasn't moving.

"Scarlett? Scarlett!"

53

The rest of Teri's drive to work passed in a blur. Her heart pounded and she struggled to keep hold of the steering wheel with trembling hands. Every last drop of strength seemed to have seeped out of her, making it difficult to manoeuvre the vehicle, even with power steering.

With the enormous black 4x4 right on her back bumper, she drove calmly out of Retford, navigating the country lanes towards her place of work.

She'd done everything the Cardinal and the guys on the Red Team had told her to do. She'd sped out of the car park and down Tiln Lane to draw the police out, then slowed to let the Red Team get close, and as soon as they were in position, she'd braked.

Seeing that old black car hit the curb and flip over had been a heart-stopping moment. But she'd done exactly as the Cardinal had asked, which should hopefully buy her some respect and time.

That was what she hoped anyway.

Deep down, though, there was a niggling doubt that gnawed at the edges of her mind, causing her to wonder if this would end well. It wouldn't be the end of what the Cardinal would want her to do. She felt sure of that. He'd require more from her to secure the organisation now that the police were after her. But she was prepared for that. She'd picked a side, and that came with certain responsibilities.

After finally reaching her destination, Teri pulled into the gravel driveway out front of the large, dark stone-brick house and stopped in her usual place.

Turning the car off, she gripped the wheel momentarily, clenching her fists and flexing her fingers, trying to banish the shakes that had gripped her. Someone was playing the drums inside her chest. Her heart hammered and refused to slow down.

Closing her eyes, she took a few deep breaths before checking her wing mirror. The four members of the Red Team exited their vehicle with Stammel on his phone. He quickly ended the call, nodded to his team and strode over.

Teri took another long breath, opened her door and climbed out. She smiled at the approaching man mountain. "Hi. Thanks for that."

"He wants to see you," Stammel stated, his eyes cold.

He gave her the creeps.

Expecting as much, she nodded. He directed her around the side of the house. They passed between the house and the double garage towards the courtyard at the back. On her right up ahead was the small outbuilding that led to the underground tunnel. They stepped out from the side of the house, and the larger L-shaped outbuilding she'd worked in for several years came into view on the left.

Teri hesitated on seeing the four people standing outside of it. Were they waiting for her? She spotted Crimson and Rubious at the back. Rubious was biting his nails and averted his eyes.

At the front was the Cardinal, staring at her from behind his plain red mask. But more worryingly, beside him was the leader of the organisation.

A man whose face she'd never seen.

He rarely visited, but when he did, he was always masked, just like the Cardinal, except his red mask was shaped like a skull.

The Red Man.

A wave of fear washed over her. They'd never done this in all her time here. Why were they out here waiting for...?

The thugs of the Red Team grabbed her arms.

"Agh, hey. What are you...?" She glanced at the men who held her.

They marched her closer to the welcoming committee.

"Stop it, what are you doing?"

"Thank you for letting us know about the police outside your home, Cerise," the Cardinal said. "It was greatly appreciated. But I think it's clear to us that you've become something of a liability."

"What?" She looked past the Cardinal to Rubious, who glanced furtively at her.

He seemed ashamed of himself and embarrassed. Suddenly, the jigsaw puzzle fell into place.

"You. You've done this."

"Take her," the Cardinal ordered.

"No, wait," Teri yelled in sudden panic.

"He knew. Rubious knew what I'd done, and he hid it from you. He wanted me to himself," she ranted while the men dragged her across the gravel and into the smaller outbuilding.

She tried to fight them, but they were far too strong. Their hands were like vices around her upper arms, allowing them to force her easily into the building and down the stairs. They crossed the short distance up the corridor and took the left-hand ninety-degree bend onto the long section with the four cells. They marched her closer, and she spotted the two new inmates in their cells, staring at her from behind bars.

"No, please don't. Don't do this," she wailed. She knew what being locked in these cells meant and was desperate to avoid it. "I'm begging you, please."

She was thrown into an empty cell, the one that had been left vacant just yesterday. She landed awkwardly before they closed and locked the door.

"No," she sobbed. She scrambled to her feet and ran at the door. She slammed into it, reaching through to try and grab one of them. "Please, no. Not this. No."

She knew the fate of the unlucky souls who ended up in these cells and was overcome by a sudden wave of regret about her life and the decisions that had led her to this point. Well, there was only really one choice that had led her here, and in recent weeks, there wasn't a day that went by that she didn't wish she'd made a different one. She should never have tried to hack into that server. Had she chosen a different one, and not been discovered, these sickos might never have come for her and threatened to report her to the police if she didn't work for them.

Or maybe she should have called their bluff? They were criminals, after all. Would they actually have reported her to the police for hacking into their server? Perhaps not, but these thugs had more persuasive methods at their disposal anyway. Knowing what she knew now, she'd probably been lucky.

But it seemed that her luck had run out.

Teri cried out, the men stalked next door and opened the other girl's cell.

She screaming at them. "No, get away. Get away."

"Leave her alone," the young man in the cell opposite shouted, but to no effect.

The four strong men carried the young woman from the cell while she yelled in protest.

Teri watched her go, knowing the fate that awaited her.

"Erika!" the man in the cell opposite shouted. "Goddamn it, no. Erika!"

54

Bracing his legs and using one hand to lift himself, taking the strain off the seat belt, Rob finally reached and clicked the button on the clip, releasing it. It snapped loose, and he fell to the roof of his car.

"Jesus," he cursed and righted himself. He turned to his partner.

"Hey, Scarlett." He gripped her shoulder and gave her a gentle squeeze. "Scarlett. Are you okay?"

Her eyes snapped open. "Agh. What the hell? Oh my word, that hurts."

"Are you all right?" Rob repeated.

"Yeah, I'm fine. Bruised and battered, but otherwise, I'm okay." She clicked the buckle of the seat belt and dropped to the roof with a thud.

"Ow! Awww, I think I fell on my keys."

Rob smiled. "You're okay then."

"Oh, yeah, never better. Next stupid question."

Rob shook his head and tried to open the door. It took a few shoves, but it finally shifted. He climbed out before offering a hand to Scarlett. "Here, let me help you."

She took it, and he helped her from the wreck. They scrambled to the top of the bank by the road. Rob stretched and looked back at his ruined car.

"Well, shit."

"Oh, Rob. I'm sorry," Scarlett said. She put her arm around him and pulled him close. "I know how much it meant to you."

Seeing Belle, his pride and joy, and the only remaining thing he had from his mother, scratched, dented, and on its roof in a ditch was heartbreaking. But he'd already made up his mind. "I'm getting her repaired."

"What, are you sure?"

"Absolutely. This is *not* how she goes out. No way."

"I dread to think how much that will cost you."

"I don't care." He was resolute. This was not the end of Belle. Not by a long shout.

His phone rang. Rob answered it. "Hello?"

"Sir? It's Heather Knight."

"Heather," Rob said in greeting.

She was one of the EMSOU's Family Liaison Officers and a damn good one, too. She'd been assigned to Myles Bolton after meeting with him about his murdered son, Daniel.

"What can I do for you? Hopefully, you're going to cheer me up."

"It'll try, sir. I paid Myles Bolton a visit yesterday before Daniel's phone was found to check up on him and introduce myself. All was well. Then, this morning, I went back to update him. I told him that Daniel's phone had been found and handed in and that we were interested in getting into it, but Myles questioned me on the facts of this. He said we couldn't have Daniel's phone because, this morning, he'd remembered that he could track Dan's phone, and the tracker reported that the phone was not at the station."

"Not at the station?" Rob frowned.

"I was confused, too, so I called to check while Myles showed me the tracker on his phone. Dan's phone is still at Retford Station. Tucker said he had it on his desk and was looking right at it, and yet the tracker on Myles's phone was pointing to a house just north of Retford."

"North?"

"That's right. Out on Tiln Lane, I think."

Rob froze and then looked up the road. They stood on Tiln Lane at the north end of Retford, and that was also the direction Teri and the 4x4 had left. An idea formed in his head. "Okay, send me a copy of the map on the tracker. Take a photo of it on your phone or something. I need to know exactly where it's pointing, okay?"

"Got it."

"All right, do that now. I need to make another call."

"Of course. Bye." She hung up.

"A lead?" Scarlett asked.

"Maybe." Rob thought things through. He had one idea why this might be the case, but they'd need to investigate further to know for sure. "One moment." He called Nailer.

Nailer answered after a couple of rings. "Rob. Hi. I'm in Retford. I'm sending Tucker back to you. You guys need to take a break from that stakeout. You've been there all night."

"Nailer," Rob snapped. "We've just been rammed off the road."

"What?"

"Teri left her flat and drove off at speed. We followed, but a large four-by-four tailed us and knocked us into a ditch."

"Are you okay?"

"We're fine. Don't worry." Rob gazed down at his Ford Capri 2.8 Injection. A classic that was now a mess in the ditch.

Nearby, a passing car stopped to check they were okay. Scarlett dealt with them.

"Something's not right. We paid Teri a visit last night, but she didn't want to talk to us. She wasn't interested. Then, this morning, she tears off like a bat out of hell, just asking to be tailed. So we did and got run off the road. Not only that, but DC Knight called. Dan's father has tracked Dan's phone to a place north of Retford, on Tiln Lane. It says it's there right now, but his phone is in Retford Station."

"North? And where are you?"

"Tiln Lane. We were heading north, following Teri before we got rammed."

Beside him, car tyres screeched. He turned. Another car had stopped just as the first set off again. But this second car had Mary Day at the wheel. She glanced past him at Belle.

"Need a lift?" Mary asked, raising an eyebrow.

"You read my mind," Rob said. He waved at Scarlett to join him and climbed into the front passenger seat.

"I take it you're going to visit this address?" Nailer asked.

Rob's phone beeped. "Yeah, hold on," he said and moved his phone away from his ear to check the notification. It was a message from Heather Knight, with a photo of the map attached.

He smiled, pleased she'd come through for him. "Perfect." He turned to Mary, pointed out the front window and put his phone back to his ear. "Head north."

"Will do," Mary replied and set off.

"Sir, yeah, we're going to investigate now. Send backup as soon as you can. I have a hunch…"

55

They drove north out of Retford. Rob finished emailing the map to Nailer and tilted his head to peer into the rearview mirror at the upside-down remains of his beloved car.

He'd had that beautiful hunk of metal for twenty years. They'd been through thick and thin together, and apart from the occasional scratch he'd made sure to repair, he'd managed to keep it in pristine condition until now. He sighed, annoyed that he'd been using it rather than a pool car. He wouldn't care if it had been a pool car, and the repairs wouldn't need to come out of his pay packet.

The image of the black 4x4 that had rammed him off the road flashed in his mind's eye. He'd make them pay. There was no doubt about that. No one hurt Belle and got away from it. No one.

He couldn't let these thoughts consume him, though. He needed to concentrate and see this latest lead through.

Based on her behaviour, Teri clearly had something to hide. That much was clear, so he'd want to investigate further without the phone pointing them out here. The tracking data only served to seal the deal.

"Christ, Rob. You don't do things by halves, do you? What happened?"

Rob jabbed his thumb back the way they'd come. "That was not my fault. We were rammed off the road."

"Rammed? By who? No, wait, let me guess, the same guys who attacked us in the car park."

"That would be my assumption. The car they were in was very similar to the one we saw in Mansfield, and the girl we were following was, we think, Dan's friend or partner."

"If it's the same guys, that means they're probably armed," Scarlett said, a note of warning in her voice.

"Probably." Rob was quite aware of the risks involved in doing this, but there was something about this lead that felt different. It felt like they were onto something. Something big.

"So, what was the phone call all about?" Scarlett asked.

"Dan's dad tracked his son's phone, and it pointed to a house up here, north of Retford."

"But isn't it back at the station?"

"It is, they checked."

"So, how...?"

"It was cloned," Mary cut in. "Right?"

"That would be my guess," Rob agreed. "Sometimes, when a phone is cloned and you track it, it can show you the location of the cloned phone rather than the original."

"So someone cloned Dan's phone?" Scarlett replied.

"Right," Rob confirmed. "Someone was spying on him, so I think it's time we pay a visit to whoever was doing the spying, don't you think?"

"Absolutely."

"Which way?" Mary asked.

Ahead, the road split. They could follow it right or take the lefthand spur.

Rob double-checked his map. "Go left. It's not far. A house up here on the left."

"Got it," Mary said and pushed on.

A short distance up the back road, he spotted a driveway up ahead, which seemed to lead to a house peeking over the hedgerows.

"Here," Rob said. "Pull over."

Mary drove up and into the driveway before backing out again to face the way she'd come and then moved to the side of the road.

"There. Ready for a quick getaway."

"Good thinking," Rob complimented her before climbing out.

The women joined him with resolute expressions on their faces.

"Ready," Mary confirmed, already turning towards the driveway.

Scarlett narrowed her eyes. "I take it we're not waiting for backup?"

"No." Rob grimaced. "If my suspicions are right, every second counts."

"The Red Man," Mary muttered. "That's what you're thinking, isn't it? You think he's in here."

"I don't know, but it makes sense, and if I'm right, then there could be people in here whose lives are at risk, including Teri. And if he smells the police coming, he'll run."

"What are we waiting for?" Mary asked, egging Scarlett on.

"Okay, fine. Let's do this." Scarlett lifted the extendable baton from her belt and snapped it out.

Rob did the same.

Mary eyed the weapons. "Not going to do much against a gun, though, are they?"

"Best we've got," Rob said with a smile.

Mary was right, but it wasn't as if there was another option.

Rob led them to the driveway. A large, ragged expanse of gravel spread in front of a looming, dark house that seemed like it had been here for decades. The windows were unlit, and the building seemed quiet, but there were several cars parked in front, including Teri's car and the black 4x4. Rob eyed the huge vehicle. It was a large black Toyota Hilux. A mean-looking thing, Rob thought. None of the smooth curves of his Capri, that was for sure.

"I think we have the right place," Rob muttered and pointed the cars out.

"So, what do we do?"

Ahead was the house itself, a separate double garage, and Rob made out more buildings around the back.

"You two take the house," Scarlett suggested. I'll check out the garage and meet you round the back."

"Are you sure?" Rob asked.

"I'll shout if I see anything. It's just a garage."

Rob glanced at Mary who shrugged.

"Fine with me," she said.

"Okay," Rob confirmed. "Shout if you see anything, anything at all."

"You know I will." Scarlett grinned. "Go on. See you in a moment."

With a grimace, Rob approached the house's front door. He turned the handle. It opened easily.

"Not locked," Mary remarked in hushed tones.

"Apparently not." Rob pushed the door, and mercifully, it didn't creak.

He stepped into a silent house, and Mary followed close behind. He found himself standing in a long hallway leading to a kitchen at the back. There were stairs just ahead of him and doors to his left and right. Turning left first, he leaned into the room to find a drawing room filled with furniture, boxes, and general mess. Papers and books were everywhere. Whoever lived here didn't take much care of this place.

"Could do with a clean," Mary commented.

Rob grunted and turned back, crossing the hall to step into the room on the opposite side of the house. Through the windows on the side of the building, he spotted Scarlett having a good nose around the garage, trying the doors. He felt better now that he could see Scarlett and focused on the room. Like the drawing room, this sitting room had the same musty, messy feel to it.

Rob wrinkled his nose at the smell and the general detritus and made for the next door, leading deeper into the house.

"Rob!"

He spun. Mary stood near a window and stared out in shock. He rushed over. Two men had accosted Scarlett. One held her around her waist with a hand over her mouth, while the second held her at gunpoint. They were dragging her to the outbuilding behind the garage.

"Shit," Rob hissed and bolted across the room.

Mary followed, but as he reached the door for the hallway, he stopped and raised his hands to stop Mary.

"Wait here. Let me deal with this."

"But…"

"No. If I don't come back, get out of here and wait for backup. Don't follow me."

Mary pulled a face. She didn't seem pleased, but after a beat, she nodded in agreement. "Okay, fine. Go get her."

Satisfied, Rob charged through the front door, and sprinted around the side of the house. Racing for the outhouse, he could make out movement within. Scarlett was struggling against the two men.

"Stop struggling," one of the men barked. "Where's your mates?"

Rob put on a last burst of speed and clattered in through the door before swinging his baton. He caught the man's hand keenly. The thug dropped the gun and wailed in pain.

"Hey," the man holding Scarlett shouted.

Rob swung the baton again. It caught the first guy across the face. He fell to the floor and stopped moving.

"You bastard," the second thug hissed.

Raising her knee, Scarlett stamped on the man's foot as hard as she could.

The man roared in pain, loosening his grip in shock. Scarlett twisted and backhanded the man across the face.

"Oof," he grunted. She slipped his grasp.

Rushing in, Rob swung his fist. His punch connected and hit the man solidly on the cheek. He staggered to one knee.

Stepping in, Rob kneed him in the face, knocking him to his back.

"Cuff that one," Rob said, pointing to the first thug, who'd been holding the gun.

The second guy twisted and rolled left. Rob rushed over and grabbed him, but the man dragged Rob to the floor.

The thug got a swift punch into Rob's gut, making him gasp. He wrestled against the goon. The snap of cuffs rang out. Scarlett had secured the first man, but this second guy was putting up a fight. They rolled across the dirty floor, kicking up dust in their fight for dominance.

"Rob, careful," Scarlett yelled.

He managed to get a grip of the man's arm and twist it behind his back. The man roared in fury. Rob twisted it further, threatening to dislocate it.

"Stop struggling," Rob rumbled and he got on top of the man. "I'll pop it from its socket."

"Aaargh, you git."

Rob heard the sounds of a scuffle to his left. He glanced up. A third man had appeared, coming up from a lower level. He had his hand around Scarlett's throat and a gun to the side of her head. He must have caught her by surprise.

"Let him go," the man ordered.

Rob froze but kept hold of the second thug. "Wait."

"Do exactly as I say and let him go. Or do you want me to show you the inside of her skull?"

The ice in the man's steely eyes chilled Rob to his core, and he didn't doubt for a moment that he meant it. But if he let this man go, he was giving up control of the situation.

"Don't do it," Scarlett grunted.

The man squeezed her neck. Scarlett gagged and he jabbed the gun into her temple. "Shut up."

"Okay, you win," Rob said. He let go of the man below him, raised his hands, and got to his feet. "There's no need for anyone to die here."

The man Rob had restrained scrambled to his feet, giving him the evil eye.

The third man sneered at him. He stepped out from the stairwell. "We'll see. Roon?" He was addressing the second thug. "Bring him. Go in front. Check his pockets."

Roon shoved Rob towards the stairwell. "What about Blood?"

The third man scoffed at the cuffed man. "You can come back. He can take a nap for a while."

Roon rummaged in Rob's pockets and around his belt, removing his phone, baton, spray, and everything else. He tossed them to the floor before forcing Rob down the stairs.

Passing Scarlett, Rob glanced over at his partner. She met his gaze, her face calm and resolute. There was strength there that he admired. She was not giving up. Roon jabbed him between his shoulder blades again, urging him forward. Rob did as Roon wanted, descending the steps and into a short tunnel. At the end, it made a sharp left turn into a much longer section with four doorways partway up, two on either side. Further up, there seemed to be a junction with tunnels leading left and right and a closed door facing them.

Roon jabbed him again. Rob walked up the corridor to the doorways, which revealed themselves to be cells, two of which were occupied. Two faces peered back at him from behind the bars, and he recognised both. He knew Teri from Dan's photos and the old mugshots from her previous arrests. He recognised Ben from pictures he'd seen of him after Mary had asked them to check out his house, but this was the first time he'd seen them both up close.

They were scared, but Ben was in a worse state than Teri.

Roon opened the first empty cell and shoved Rob inside. He didn't resist as he glanced back at Scarlett. She mouthed the word 'sorry' to him.

Roon closed and locked the cell door before opening the last empty one.

The third thug then jabbed the gun into Scarlett's back. "Get in."

"I'm going," Scarlett said, annoyed.

Roon closed and locked the door, and once they were secure, he lowered his weapon.

"That's better," the third thug muttered. "Right, I need to report in."

"No worries. I'll go wake Blood," Roon said. "Catch you later."

The third thug continued on towards the junction while Roon turned to head back the way they'd come.

He glanced at Loxley and winked. "Fucking pigs. Gonna get what you deserve." And with that, he was gone.

Rob watched him go, then stepped closer to the door to check on Scarlett. "You okay?"

"I'm fine. Don't worry about me," Scarlett answered.

Rob nodded and turned to the cell with Ben in it.

"Welcome to the club," Ben quipped.

"Ben, isn't it?" Rob asked.

"Yeah, how'd you know?"

"Not that I can do much right this moment," Rob waved to his cell, "but I'm Detective Loxley. We've been working this case."

"Aaah," Ben replied. "Going well then, I see."

"I've had better days. But backup's on its way. Is it just you and Teri?"

"No, there's one other. Erika. They've just taken her to the Red Room."

"Erika?" A sinking feeling of gut-wrenching horror washed over Rob. No. It couldn't be, could it?

He glanced up at Scarlett who was clearly thinking the same thing as she stared at him, open-mouthed.

"Yeah. Roxy was before that. She went to the Red Room yesterday. She didn't come back."

Damn it, they were too late. Rob grabbed the cell door bars and tried to yank and rattle them loose, but they wouldn't budge, no matter how hard he pulled at them.

"Fuck!"

56

Mary watched Rob run out the door and around to the outbuilding towards the back of the house. Standing in the window, she peered out into the darkness, shifting anxiously from one foot to the other.

She spotted movement through the door twice until Rob and one of the thugs rolled into view at the entrance.

He seemed to have him subdued for a moment, but suddenly, the fight stopped, and Rob got up, holding his hands aloft.

"Shit."

They had him. They had both of them, and now she was on her own. Suddenly vulnerable, she glanced towards the driveway entrance through another window, willing the police backup to appear, but nothing stirred in the darkness.

She looked back to the outbuilding and then the entrance again. "Bloody hell." She clenched her fists in frustration. She should do as Rob had ordered and get out to the road. She could lock herself in her car and wait for backup to arrive, but in the meantime, what would happen to Rob and Scarlett?

She gazed one last time at the driveway and shook her head in frustration. "No. I can't do it. I'm not leaving them."

Mary marched outside, and turned left towards the outbuilding. On reaching the first corner of the house, she stopped, peered around, and checked the coast was clear. Seeing no one, she dashed to the outbuilding and threw her back to the wall beside the door.

Movement came from within, but not close.

Taking a chance, she peeked around the doorframe. On the far side of the small room, a passage descended into the earth, the backs of several people walking down it. She made out Scarlett's shock of blonde hair and grimaced.

They needed her help.

Mary ducked inside and jumped in shock at a prone body on the floor. She thought it was Rob for a heart-stopping moment but quickly realised it was one of the thugs who had attacked Scarlett, the one who'd been carrying the gun. He was bleeding from his temple with his wrists cuffed behind his back.

Mary sneered at him. "Serves you right," she muttered in low tones. She was about to follow the thugs when she spied the gun on the floor.

"Huh. Don't mind if I do." She picked it up. She knew enough to check the safety was off, but wasn't sure what she was looking for and shrugged. Hopefully, she wouldn't need to actually use it.

Crossing the room, she found a couple of discarded batons, a pair of cuffs, and several other bits that had been thrown on the floor, including Rob's and Scarlett's phones. Working as quickly as she could, she stuffed their phones into her pocket, followed by the cuffs, and finally picked up one of the batons.

Satisfied, she hurried to the steps and descended to the short corridor. Ahead, around the corner, she heard movement, voices, and doors being shut and locked.

At the bottom of the steps, she paused to listen.

"Right, I need to report in," said a male voice she didn't recognise. It was probably one of the thugs.

"No worries. I'll go wake Blood," another said. He sounded closer. He must mean the unconscious man behind her.

"Crap," she whispered and charged back up the steps. She ducked right into the opposite corner from where the unconscious thug lay and crouched. She held the gun up and ready in shaking hands.

Footsteps approached along the corridor below, then trudged up the steps.

"Right then, you lazy fucker," the thug said as she stepped into view.

Doing her best to steady the gun with both hands, she kept it trained on his head.

He wandered over to his friend. "Fucking pigs."

Still shaking with nerves, with her heart pounding, Mary stood and took a careful, creeping step towards the man.

"Right, where's your gun..." the thug muttered.

"Right here," Mary answered, doing her best to sound confident and not at all utterly terrified.

The man froze.

"Don't make a sound, and I won't need to use it."

The thug raised his hands and slowly twisted to get a look at her. "Are you sure you know how to use that thing?"

He was trying to call her bluff, but he shouldn't mistake her nerves for weakness. The man before her was the worst kind of scum and didn't deserve to live. She needed to project that confidence to him. She took a long breath before answering. "Point the shooty end at the bad man and pull the trigger thingy. Then, the bad man dies. Is that about right?"

"Close enough." He gulped, narrowed his eyes and peered at her. "But having the balls to actually use it is another thing entirely."

His disbelief only served to turn some of her nervous energy into anger.

"Dude. You're nothing but a waste of good oxygen, and after what you've done to my two friends, do you think I care what happens to you?" The pent-up rage bubbled up inside her, she felt certain she could have shot him right then and there. "Go on, try me, see what happens. I might be nervous, but I sure as shit don't care if you live or die." Sure, some of it was bluster, but right then, she felt perfectly justified in shooting him.

Having turned around fully, the thug stared into her eyes. He grimaced as if he'd seen something in them and then sighed. "Fine. What do you want me to do?"

Forcing herself to remain calm, Mary reached into her back pocket and pulled the cuffs out. She threw them to him.

The man caught them easily.

"Put them on, cuff yourself to... that," she ordered, pointing to some pipes running along the bottom of the far wall.

The man grunted but did as she'd asked, threading the cuffs behind the old pipe before securing his wrists to it.

She watched in simmering anger, furious at the man for what he'd done to her friends and for what he was making her do. Without thinking about it, while he finished cuffing himself to the wall, she swapped the gun to her left hand and lashed out with the baton, striking him across his ugly face. He grunted and looked delirious, so she hit him again, finally knocking him out.

With a white-knuckled grip on the baton, she stood over the idiot goon, breathing hard. Her heartbeat slowed, but she felt no regret, only justified satisfaction. He deserved that and worse, as far as she was concerned, but true justice was for others to hand out. In the meantime, she took a moment to enjoy the power she felt.

Having twisted as he'd fallen, she saw another gun stuffed into the back of his belt.

"Shit, how many guns do these idiots have?" She took it and put it into the back of her jeans. Who knew when it might be of use?

She scanned over the scene and found a dirty rag. She shook off the worst of the dirt, and rammed it as far as she could into his mouth. Tape would have helped keep it there, but she didn't have any of that on her.

Shrugging, and with the gun ready, she crept back down the steps and along the corridor. At the left-hand bend, she slowed and peeked around the corner.

The next section of corridor was longer, with what appeared to be cells partway down. Luckily, it was deserted. Taking the corner slowly with the gun up and ready, she stalked down it until she saw Rob in the first cell on her right.

"Rob! Are you okay?" She stepped over to him.

"I'm fine," he replied. She turned to see Scarlett, then a woman she didn't recognise, and then her housemate's boyfriend.

"Ben!" She dashed over and reached through the bars to take his hand.

He was in a terrible state. Pale, drawn and weak, with bloodshot eyes.

"Are you okay?"

"Hey. Good to see you," Ben said. "I'm fine. Nothing a shower and a good meal won't cure."

She stepped back to take a better look at the barred doors and the chunky padlocks that secured the bolts. "I need to get you out. How do I?" She grabbed one of the locks and rattled it.

"They're secure," Ben said. "Believe me, I've tried."

Mary glanced at the locks again and then at her gun. "Could I?" She wiggled the gun towards the locks.

"No guarantee of success, risk of injury and very noisy," Rob said. "This isn't the movies."

Mary pulled a face.

"There's a key upstairs in the office," Teri said.

"Upstairs?"

"Yeah." She pointed towards the junction and the door. "Through the door, up the steps. They're on a peg on the office wall. You can't miss them."

While Mary stared up the tunnel, the door at the junction opened, revealing stairs leading up and a man about to step through into the corridor. He spotted Mary and froze in place.

Their eyes locked for a heartbeat. He glanced down at her gun and then back up to her face. He visibly swallowed.

"Who is it?" Rob asked. "I can't see."

Mary kept her eyes on the intruder. "Company."

The man yelped and ran back up the stairs.

"Shit." Running on adrenaline and pure instinct, Mary sprinted after him. If he raised the alarm, this was all over.

She reached the junction and briefly made out short corridors leading to closed doors on either side of her before barrelling through the open doorway and up the steps. She reached the top and twisted to face the room with her gun up and ready. The space had been well decorated, with nicely plastered walls painted to a professional level with a tiled floor. It was quite the contrast to the shabby tunnel below them. To her right, the man she'd seen, a tall, thin person with mussed hair, rattled a door handle while banging and kicking the door it was attached to.

"Let me in, now!"

A young man fighting to keep the man out was on the other side of the door, with his face right up to the inset window.

"No way."

"Let me in, she'll kill me," the tall man bellowed.

"No wa....oh." The kid inside the room saw her. He backed away from the door with his hands up.

The man with his back to her tensed and then turned to her. "Don't kill me, please."

409

Planting her feet, Mary took careful aim. "Hands up, both of you."

Terrified, they both did as she asked.

"You're going to do exactly as I say."

57

Scarlett watched Mary charge off down the corridor, out of sight. She glanced over at Rob. "Do you think she can do it?"

"She's got guts, I'll give her that," Rob answered. "We've got as good a chance as any."

Scarlett smiled and turned to the ruin of a cell behind her. The place stank to high heaven. A hole in the corner reeked. She didn't dare walk over and look inside.

The only other piece of furniture was an old, stained mattress. Frayed at the edges with a massive dent in the middle where the foam had started to give way, it didn't appear terribly comfortable.

"Jesus."

Was this indignity what Roxy had to live with before they'd finally taken her to this so-called Red Room and inflicted whatever horrific tortures upon her? Poor girl. No one should have their last days be so nightmarish. When Scarlett got out of here, she'd take great pleasure in finding this Red Man and bringing her own form of justice to bear.

"Pretty grim," Rob remarked.

"You're not kidding," Scarlett agreed and glanced over at Teri who sat on the floor of her cell, her back against the wall. "Hey, Teri? Are you okay?"

"What do you care?"

Scarlett grimaced at the girl's bolshy attitude. "We want to help. That's why we knocked on your door last night. You should have spoken to us."

"You can't help me," she said and finally. "Look at you. You can't even help yourself. You're in no better position than I am. You can't win, you know."

"I beg to differ," Rob said.

Teri scoffed. "Well, you keep telling yourself that."

"They threw you in a cell, Teri," Rob pressed. "Is that how a good boss treats his employees? I'm guessing you did as they asked when you sped away from your flat this morning, no doubt to lure us after you. Right?"

She said nothing.

"Thought so. You did as they asked, and this is how they reward you?"

"I betrayed them. I broke the rules. I spoke to someone outside of the organisation about what they do here. It's my fault."

Scarlett shook her head at the mental knots the girl was tying herself in as a door sounded further up the corridor.

"Mary?" Scarlett muttered. She wanted to call out, but just in case it wasn't her friend, she decided to say nothing and wait.

She looked nervously at Rob who nodded to her.

Seconds later, a hooded man with a plain red mask strode into view. Scarlett frowned at the curious man and watched him carefully while he glanced between her and Rob.

"Well, well, well, what have we here? New guests? We will be spoiled for choice."

"What have you done with Erika?" Rob snapped at him.

The man turned to Rob. "Oh, you know her, do you? Heh, so he was right. Interesting. You know, I'd love to take you in there and let you watch. I'm guessing all kinds of goodies would come tumbling out… if he's right… We can be quite persuasive when we want to be. Isn't that right, Cerise?" The man said to Teri and shook his head. "It's a shame you turned on us, after everything we did for you."

"Did for me?" Teri asked. "What are you talking about? You're not some kind of charity. You blackmailed me into working for you. Just like you did with Carmine."

"Aaah, so you were friendly."

"You're damn right. He told me how you threatened to kill his dad unless he came to work for you."

"Aww," the masked man mocked. "And were you just as honest with him? Did you tell him all about your troubled past? How very cute, and pathetic."

Teri grunted.

"You really should have known better and kept that pretty mouth of yours shut. Look where it's got you."

"Piss off," Teri muttered.

The masked man laughed.

Another door sounded up the corridor. Scarlett twitched but kept her eyes on the masked man who turned towards the noise.

"Hey, Stammel...oh..." The masked man tensed and took a step back. "Wha...? What the hell? Crimson? Rubious? And who the hell are you? What's going on?"

"Stay right there, don't move," Mary called out.

The masked man glanced into Scarlett's and Rob's cells briefly. Scarlett smiled back as smugly as she could.

"Checkmate."

The masked man grunted in annoyance. "Fuck." He ran, sprinting out of sight.

"Don't... Damn it," Mary cried. "Shit. Right, you two, up there. Now."

Scarlett frowned, wondering who Mary was talking to. Moments later, two men with their hands raised walked into view with Mary behind them, holding them at gunpoint.

"And don't even dream of trying to run like he did," Mary added.

"Mary, let me out, quick. I'll go after him."

She nodded and addressed the taller of the two men who held a set of keys. "Unlock that cell, get out of her way, and hand the keys to him." She pointed to Rob while keeping some distance between her and her two prisoners.

The man started to unlock Scarlett's cell.

"Scarlett," Rob called out, "are you sure you want to do that?"

"I'll get Mr Mask. You go after Erika. I'll be fine." With the door unlocked, she yanked the door open and stepped out.

"Hey," Mary said, attracting Scarlett's attention. She held out a baton and a set of cuffs. "You might need these."

Scarlett grabbed them. "Cheers." She sprinted up the corridor, taking the corner at speed and charging up the steps. Reaching the outbuilding, she noticed that lights glowed outside, and there were voices. Was the backup here? Finally?

She rushed outside, the masked man silhouetted by the headlights of a police car in the dark. Its flashing blue lights strobed over the house and driveway.

"Get on the ground," a man called out from the shadows, close to the police car.

415

"I'm police," Scarlett called out with her hands up, just in case. She didn't want to get tased.

As she approached the masked man, two officers stepped into the light, holding batons and tasers. It seemed like it was just the one patrol car for now.

"I said get on the ground."

Scarlett recognised them as PCs David Morton and Russ Brewster. She couldn't repress the smile that spread over her face as she breathed a sigh of relief.

"Finally."

"Aaah. Morton, Brewster," the masked man in a smug tone. He lowered his hands.

Scarlett frowned. What was going on?

"Be good lads and let me pass, will you?" the masked man suggested. "There's a hundred grand each in it for you."

The officers stopped but kept their weapons trained on the masked man.

"What? No. Arrest him," Scarlett called out. Her heart rate spiked with worry.

The masked man turned to her, the light from the car catching in his soulless eyes. "I'll make it two hundred grand each if you teach her a lesson she won't soon forget. We can take it from there and get rid of the mess, but the spectacle will be worth the price."

David and Russ glanced her way, then back at the masked man, and at each other.

"What?" Scarlett couldn't believe her ears. Were these two working for this gang? "Guys." She raised her hands as the officers peered over at her. "Let's not get silly now."

58

With the two men in the cell, Rob clicked the padlock into place and gave it a rattle to confirm it wouldn't open. Satisfied, he stepped back and regarded the two men in the cell. They were both built very differently to the goons they'd tangled with earlier.

These two were slim and pale, with bloodshot eyes, and didn't look like they'd do well in a fist fight.

"Happy now?" the taller of the two asked.

"Ecstatic," Rob muttered. He glanced to his right and saw Ben free Teri from her cell.

Mary lowered her firearm and took a breath.

"Good work," Rob said. "Well done."

"We'd better get after Scarlett," Mary suggested.

"No, she can handle herself," Rob answered. "I need to find Erika. I just hope I'm not too late."

"I'm coming with you," Mary stated, her tone resolute as she met his gaze.

"Are you sure?"

"Of course. Oh, and here, take this." She pulled another gun from the back of her jeans. "Might come in useful with this lot."

"Aaah." Rob hesitated. He preferred not to use firearms. He was also a serving police officer, so waving a gun around probably wasn't a good look. He had completed his firearms training, though, and kept it up to date.

"Rob, they're all armed, and they won't hesitate to kill you if you get in their way," Mary said.

"She's right," Teri added. "They don't give a fuck. Take the gun."

"You don't need to fire it," Mary added.

Rob sighed. He didn't like the idea, but he couldn't argue with their points. He took the gun. "Thanks." Rob turned to Teri. "Where's the Red Room?"

"That way." She pointed up the corridor to the junction. "Take a left, and it's ahead of you. Can't miss it."

"Thanks." Rob said, and addressed Ben. "Now, get out of here and take her with you." He gestured to Teri.

"No way." Ben shook his head. "I'm with you all the way. These twats can't get away with this shit."

"Fuck it," Teri exclaimed. "I'm with you, too. I've had it with these arseholes." She wandered over to the cell with the two men inside. "Hey, Rubious, how's it feel to be the one locked up? Well, you'd better get used to it because you're fucked." She spat at him. "You, too, Crimson."

"Ugh, piss off," Rubious snapped. "I think you'll find I'm a little more valuable than that. I won't see jail time."

"Are you sure? You bugged my flat, didn't you? That's how you were spying on us. What do you think the police will think when they find those bugs?"

"He bugged your place?" Rob asked.

A look of worry crossed Rubious's face with Rob's comment.

"Yep. I'm pretty sure. And then he reported back and got Dan killed."

"Huh." Another puzzle piece slotted into place as Rob made a connection. "I'm willing to bet you cloned Daniel's phone, too, right? Meaning, it was your phone that led us here."

"You did what?" the taller man snapped. Rubious flushed in embarrassment. "You bloody idiot. Of all the hare-brained idiotic screw-ups!"

Rubious said nothing but wore a guilty expression.

"Thought so," Rob muttered. "We'll deal with you later."

"Laters," Teri added with an extended middle finger.

Rob started up the corridor. "So, if that was the Red Man Scarlett ran after, who's in with Erika?"

"That wasn't the Red Man," Teri answered.

Rob paused at the junction. "Oh?"

"That was the Cardinal. He's second-in-command. The Red Man's probably still in there."

"Do you all have code names?" Rob asked. "I noticed the Cardinal called you Cerise earlier."

"Cerise, Rubious, Cardinal, Crimson. They all mean red," Mary said.

Teri nodded. "Yeah, we all have them. I was Cerise, Dan was Carmine. It was to preserve anonymity, so we couldn't grass anyone up."

"Clever," Rob muttered taking the left-hand branch at the junction. "Come on."

He stalked towards the Red Room. Gripping the gun awkwardly, he took a deep breath to steel his nerves. Rob grabbed the handle, threw the door wide, and rushed inside.

He found himself in a large oblong underground room, slightly deeper than it was wide, with a solid-looking chair bolted to the concrete floor two-thirds of the way in.

Strapped into it was a woman Rob barely recognised behind the cuts, bruises, and swelling that covered her face. It was Erika, his neighbour, and she'd been badly beaten.

After seeing his good friend subjected to such torture, Rob had no trouble pointing the gun at the four men in the room. "Hands up, right now. You're all under arrest!"

The men twisted towards him in surprise and annoyance. He could see three of their faces, but the fourth was masked, like the Cardinal.

Two of the unmasked men were large, powerful thugs, one wore a denim jacket, and the other a black leather one. Rob recognised Leather from his fight with Rob in the outbuilding. He'd been the one to surprise them and hold a gun to Scarlett's head.

The third man was tall and skinny with slightly greying hair and a drawn face. His blood-stained surgical gown and tray of cruel torture instruments, including several power tools, on a trolley beside him sent shivers up Rob's spine.

The final man wore a long dark coat, and in the shadows of its hood, his face was covered by a bright-red skull-shaped mask that leered out at him.

"Hey," Denim called out and went for his gun.

"Don't," Mary shouted, standing beside Rob with her gun up and ready. "Don't you dare."

"What is this shit?" the torturer hissed.

"Loxley," the Red Man muttered, his voice distorted by a device hidden behind the mask.

Rob frowned. The Red Man knew who he was? What the hell?"

"I take it you're the Red Man?" Rob asked.

"That's him," Teri confirmed.

The Red Man scoffed at Teri. "The worm that turned."

"All of you, up against the far wall! Go, now," Rob ordered, waving his gun around as he entered the room. "Now!"

With their hands raised, the men took slow, careful steps towards the far wall, leaving behind the instruments of torture, the three cameras trained on Erika and the video lights that lit the scene.

Rob walked over to where Erika sat, his heart breaking as he got closer and got a better look at the injuries they'd inflicted upon her. Her face was swollen up so much that one eye was almost totally hidden. Blood covered her face and soaked into her top. Rob winced; they'd pulled a couple of her nails out of her right hand, her fingers were bleeding.

"Jesus, Christ," Rob whispered. "Erika? Can you hear me?"

"Rob?" she gasped and tried to look up. "Is that you?"

"I'm here. We're getting you out."

"I'm sorry," she muttered.

"Shush, don't talk."

He placed a hand on her arm while Ben and Teri released the straps and helped her to her feet. Erika tried to take her weight, but her strength failed, and she stumbled. They all jumped to catch her.

Sudden movement snapped Rob's attention back up, just in time for the skinny torturer to tackle him. The man might be thin, but he was tall, wiry, and a whirling dervish of energy. He hit Rob with quite some force. Rob fell, smashing into one of the lights and the trolley with the knives on it. He hit the floor on his back, and the skinny man landed on top of him. His attacker went for the gun, clawing at Rob's hand with his long nails.

"Aaagh, get off," Rob roared.

A short distance away, Mary shouted, "Back off."

With his left hand, Rob scrambled around to find something he might use as a weapon and cut himself on one of the fallen blades. He hissed in pain and tried to shove the man off instead. He loosened the skinny man's grip and brought the weapon to bear.

He wanted desperately to be rid of this idiot, but hesitated to pull the trigger. The skinny man went for Rob's throat. Rob shoved and kicked him. The thug in the leather jacket loomed over and threw a punch, hitting Rob on his cheek.

"Not so cocky now, are you Loxley?" the Red Man said. He wandered closer, looking imperious.

Rob struggled against the seemingly countless hands and fists that were trying to restrain or hut him. He caught a glimpse of Mary with Ben, Teri and Erika behind her. She pointed her gun at the Denim thug, fending him off.

"Keep the fuck away," Mary barked. Denim aimed his own weapon at her.

The skinny man went for the gun again. The thug punched Rob in the face a second time. Rob yanked his hand free, his finger slipped, and the gun barked.

"Urk," the skinny man grunted, an expression of sheer shock and surprise appearing on his lined face. He pulled away and tried to get to his feet but stumbled and dropped to the floor.

Leather lunged in, taking advantage of Rob's surprise, and ripped the gun from Rob's hand before stepping back and aiming the weapon back at him.

"Damn it, Loxley," the Red Man swore in his distorted voice. "You killed Sanguine. He was not easy to find."

Rob scooted back, away from the Red Man and Leather, and got to his feet.

"Don't you fucking move," Leather spat.

Rob raised his hands.

Behind Leather, the Red Man started to stalk around the room, focusing his attention on the others. "Mary. Be careful with that thing."

"Fuck you."

Rob glanced over. Mary stood with her feet planted wide with both hands on the gun she kept trained on Denim. But her hands trembled. Briefly, she met Rob's gaze. He saw only fierce determination behind her eyes. She wouldn't go easily.

"Is that any way to talk to someone you've written so eloquently about, Miss Day? I thought you might want to take this opportunity to interview me and get some answers to your questions." The Red Man tilted his head. "That *is* why you met with Carmine, isn't it? Oh, but you'd know him better as Dan, wouldn't you."

"You're a cheap thug, nothing more," Mary snapped back.

"I think you'll find I'm a little more than that. And as for cheap? Well, you're clearly unaware of the eye-watering amounts of money people will pay for my services."

"Sick fucks, all of them," Teri sneered.

"Oh, for sure. But who am I to judge what other's 'get off' on when there's money to be made?"

"Drop the gun," Denim ordered Mary.

"Piss off," Mary replied.

"Ruddy, please," the Red Man said, holding a hand out to the thug in the denim jacket. "We're talking here. Take a page out of Stammel's book." The Red Man pointed to the thug wearing leather, aiming his gun at Rob. "He's keeping Loxley covered but not interrupting our nice conversation."

"Sir," Ruddy obeyed.

"That's better. Now then, let's move on because you still haven't answered my question, Erika."

Held up by Ben and Teri, Erika peered at the Red Man through the one bloodshot eye she was still able to open. But she didn't say anything.

"What is going on between you and Loxley? Who are you to him? Huh?"

Rob frowned. "What are you talking about? She's my neighbour."

The Red Man jabbed a finger towards Rob. "I wasn't talking to you."

Rob pulled a face and shrugged.

"Erika, please," the Red Man continued. "Tell me what I need to know."

"Shove it up your arse," Erika muttered. "I've got nothing to say to you."

The Red Man grunted. He stared at Erika for a long moment, then took a step towards them. Mary twisted and switched her aim from the guard to the Red Man.

"Don't you dare," Mary warned him.

"Fine," the Red Man answered. He turned, marched over to Stammel, took the gun off him, and strode across the room to Rob. The Red Man gripped Rob by the scruff of his neck and jabbed the gun into the side of his head.

The cold steel bit into his temple. Rob tensed. Was this the end?

"Tell me what I want to know right now, or I will kill him."

Erika stared at him and then glanced at Rob. There was something there, behind her eyes that he couldn't quite get a handle on. What was the Red Man going on about? What was Erika hiding?

"Don't," Erika said, her tone less defiant.

"This is down to you, Erika. You can stop this right now. I'll count down from five, and then I'm going to kill him."

"No."

"Five."

"No, please," Erika begged. "Please don't."

"Four."

"It's all right," Rob said, his voice calm. "Tell him what he wants to know. It can't be anything too terrible."

"Three."

"Goddamn it," Erika snapped.

"Two."

"All right, all right. I'll tell you. I'll tell you anything you want to know. Just stop."

The door slammed open, and a stream of armed officers rushed into the Red Room. Scarlett was with them.

Two gunshots rang out from the far side of the room.

Rob grabbed the gun, and twisted it loose. It fired, catching Rob's skin as the slide racked back, but it came free of the Red Man's hand. He threw it to the floor and tackled the masked man. He stumbled and fell back. Rob went with him and pinned him to the floor while the armed officers rounded up the remaining people.

The Red Man raised his hands. "You got me."

"Who are you?" Rob muttered and reached for the mask.

"Take it off and find out," the man said, the mask still distorting his voice.

Rob narrowed his eyes. He peered down at the mask before gripping it and lifting it from the man's head, simultaneously pushing his hood back.

"Holy shit," Rob hissed.

Owen Mason, his brother, stared back at him.

"Owen?"

"Rob."

"You're the Red Man?" Rob's mind suddenly raced. He thought back over the investigation, wondering how this could be possible.

"Have been for over ten years," Owen answered. He shrugged. "It was a nice little sideline while it lasted."

"But Sean and Isaac, they said the Masons weren't involved." Had Rob misjudged their comments?

"They're not, they don't know. I'm sure this will come as a surprise to them." Owen sighed. "This will change everything, you know that, right?"

"You utter bastard. You were going to kill me! For what?" Rob turned to look across the room, hunting for Erika.

He found her with Nailer, who'd brought up the rear of the firearms team. They were hugging tightly. Rob frowned as Erika spoke.

"I love you, Dad."

What the hell? Dad? What on earth was going on?

"Sir?"

Rob glanced up to see two armed officers. One of them had a pair of cuffs ready.

"Do you want us to take him?"

Rob glanced down at Owen who stared into the middle distance, apparently contemplating his life and future.

Getting up, Rob stepped back and nodded to the officers. "Yeah, you can take him. Get him out of here."

Rob watched the officers get Owen to his feet, cuff him, and then march him out of the room with his two remaining henchmen.

Mary suddenly appeared from the crowd and rushed over. She wrapped her arms around and hugged him tightly. "Rob. Thank Christ. I thought you were a goner."

He hugged her back, glad of the affection, and took a long breath. He buried his head in her hair. "Me, too."

She pulled slowly back and looked him in the eye.

He smiled back. "I'm fine."

"Shut up." She placed her hands on either side of his head and kissed him.

It lasted several seconds, and Rob was frozen in shock for the duration until she stopped.

He met her eyes again. "Wha...?"

"Don't ruin it," she whispered and kissed him again.

He let her and then kissed her back, enjoying the moment until an image of Matilda flashed in his mind.

He stepped back.

"I'm sorry, I shouldn't."

Mary seemed a little surprised. "There's nothing to be sorry about."

"I know, I just... This is a lot. I'm going to need some time."

She smiled. "I understand."

"Hey." Scarlett hurried over to him. "Are you okay?"

Rob nodded and rubbed the back of his head, wondering if Scarlett had noticed the kiss. "Yeah, I'm fine," he confirmed and reached up to touch his sore cheek. "Nothing an icepack won't cure. What about you? Did you grab the Cardinal?"

"The Cardinal?"

"That's his code name, apparently," Rob explained.

"The Cardinal. Sure, okay." She nodded and smiled. "And yeah, I got him. David and Russ arrived just as he ran outside. He knew them and tried to bribe them, but they weren't having it, so we nabbed him together."

"He tried to bribe them?"

Scarlett grunted and stepped a little closer, keeping her voice low. "I got the feeling this wasn't the first time this Cardinal had worked with them, so we might need to have a chat with those two."

"Noted. Still, not a bad turnout."

"Not bad at all. We got a Mason. A bloody Mason."

"I know. I think Owen said it best just a moment ago. This changes everything."

Scarlett nodded in agreement. "No shit."

59

"The contents of that secret bunker," Scarlett said, "were very disturbing."

Rob sat in the conference room of Retford Police Station, watching a live video feed of the interview that was going on downstairs. Scarlett and Tucker were conducting this initial interview before Owen was moved to a more secure facility.

Because of the family connection, it wasn't appropriate for Rob to be in the room. They needed to remain objective because there was no way they could mess this up.

They had a Mason, finally, although the revelation that his family were involved had come as a total shock. He'd not seen that one coming at all.

"You had torture instruments all around the room," Scarlett continued, "many with obvious stains on them. There were traces of blood and bodily fluids all over the place. Our forensics team are going to have a field day. But that's not all. We found a lot of recordings, both raw and edited, of your victims being tortured, which will take us days to go through. And then, there was the disposal room for butchering the bodies and the furnace for body disposal. This was a slick operation, wasn't it, Owen?"

But Owen said nothing.

"You did this for profit, didn't you, Mr Mason? You set up this organisation to make money from the suffering of others. You monetised it by recording your activities and sold the resulting footage. Isn't that right?"

Again, Owen didn't reply.

"I think it's fairly obvious, Mr Mason, that you kidnapped and killed Roxy Wells to order. You were commissioned by Truman Collins to kidnap and kill her, isn't that right?"

Rob watched the screen. Owen listened to the case against him, his face stoic and calm, while his lawyer, Chance Bentley, took notes beside him.

Rob sat back. It turned out that his guess about the cloned phone was right, too. Rubious, whose real name was Shane Womack, was jealous of Teri and Dan's friendship. He suspected they were breaking the organisation's rules by having a secret relationship, so he'd cloned Dan's phone to find out if he was right. Not only was he right, but he'd also learned of their plot to talk to the press and expose the Red Man's operation to the world. So Shane reported to the Cardinal that Dan was attending this meeting while saying nothing about Teri. He planned to use this knowledge as blackmail to get what he wanted, but it hadn't gone as planned when Teri refused to cooperate.

Out of spite, he'd then relayed the rest of the story to the Cardinal, which had led to Teri being thrown into the cells.

"I have to say," Scarlett said as Owen refused to answer another question. "Your good friend, Mitchell Turnbull, the Cardinal, has been much more helpful than you have. Turns out, this whole Red Man thing was his idea back in twenty twelve. He was working with you, with the Masons, until he had the bright idea of starting up a Red Room, inspired by the urban myth and certain notorious crimes."

"Are you suggesting impropriety by the Mason family?" the lawyer asked.

"Not at all. And you see, that's the interesting part," Scarlett replied. "Because Mitchell won't say what the nature of his work for your family was. Curious, don't you think?"

"Not really," Chase answered. "Continue."

Scarlett sighed. "So anyway, that's when you set this whole thing up, wasn't it? Your quiet little sideline until you took on the Roxy Wells job. I don't think you wanted to take that job on, did you, Owen? Not according to Alec, anyway, better known as Crimson. He mentioned that you and Mitchell seemed to disagree about the Wells job and that you asked Alec to try and cover your team's tracks. You knew it was risky, didn't you? Too easy to track and trace. Too high profile. And you were right, Owen. You should have listened to your instincts and refused, no matter how much he paid you."

On the screen, Owen sneered at her, his top lip twitching.

435

"But that didn't stop you going after Erika, did it? Hmm?"

Owen looked away, refusing to engage.

"You might not have liked Shane taking the Roxy job, but you then went and kidnapped Erika shortly after, didn't you, despite opposition from Shane, who thought it was risky?" Scarlett huffed. "One good turn deserves another, I guess. One thing about that, though, and maybe you can clear this up for me because I'm at something of a loss about it. Why Erika? Why kidnap her? I mean, I suppose you were aware of our investigation into your operation and took her as insurance, but I'm not so sure. You were interrogating her when we arrived. Why?"

Rob leaned in to watch the response, but Owen was giving nothing away. Rob sighed, annoyed, but he had an idea about what Owen wanted to know, after witnessing Nailer and Erika's reunion in the Red Room.

Had Owen spotted that, too?

Scarlett continued. "Little did you know that the rug was about to be pulled out from under you by one of your lovesick, jealous employees. Sad, really." Scarlett shifted forward. "And, with this litany of crimes, the multiple murders and kidnappings we will trace and pin on you, the various financial and other crimes you've committed, combined with the mountain of proof we've gathered, I think

436

it's fair to say that you're going to go away for a very long time, Mr Mason."

"You can think what you like, Miss Stutely," Owen said.

Scarlett looked up. She seemed surprised that he'd suddenly chosen to speak, and so did his lawyer.

"He speaks," Scarlett remarked.

"And as for me spending time in prison, it wouldn't be the first time, if I get sent down, because let's face it, I've got the best defence team in the county."

"Careful, your lawyer might not be able to get out the door if you inflate his head any further."

Owen sneered at her. "Where's Rob? Hmm? Where's my brother? Is he afraid to face me after slapping those cuffs on me?"

"It's precisely because he's family that he's not in here. It would taint the interview."

"Is that right? Well, Rob, wherever you are," Owen said, looking up to the security cameras. "You've fucked up, mate. You've picked your side. Dad will be pissed, I can promise you that."

"I picked my side a long time ago," Rob grunted to himself and muted the feed. He'd heard enough.

60

"You'll be pleased to know that we've arrested Truman Collins, thanks to the records you pulled from the bunker earlier today," Ellen said, speaking over a video call on Rob's laptop. "Those transaction statements allowed us to track down the correct account and tie it directly to Truman." She smiled. "I'd like to see him wriggle out of this one."

"That's great work," Rob replied. "Well done."

"Thank you."

"And that's not all," DI Kristal Powers added from the third window open on the screen, below the two showing him and Ellen. "That info led us to a couple of Truman's less public properties in London, where we picked up several other recordings by your Red Man group. They make for excruciating viewing, as you can imagine, and we will be tracking down the victim from each and giving the families some closure, but there is one interesting point to note from these recordings."

"Which is?" Rob asked.

"In each, the victim is always the spitting image of Roxy Wells."

"Aaah," Rob muttered. He glanced over at Scarlett, sitting nearby, listening in. "So he *was* harbouring a grudge and trying to scratch that itch, but it seems that nothing but the real thing would do."

"Yep," Kristal said. "The lookalikes just weren't working for him, and he had to put up a lot of money to get the Red Man group to agree to this commission."

"He just had to push it that bit further, didn't he." Rob shook his head. "Thank you so much, ladies. I really appreciate your hard work on this. Ellen, when are you planning on coming home?"

"I can probably head back tomorrow," Ellen answered. "They don't need me down here, and I've got plenty to be getting on with up there with you guys."

"Great, see you soon."

61

"So yeah." Scarlett recounted the interview she'd had with Teri. "Turns out that Teri had been interested in computers from a young age, an interest that came from her dad. But when he left her mum, she went off the rails a little, got herself arrested for some petty crime, and did a little hacking, using the skills her dad had given her. Unfortunately for Teri, it was those skills that got her into trouble when she hacked a server belonging to Owen Mason. They were quick to blackmail her into working for them, and that's where she met Daniel."

"So, a productive interview then," Rob said He stretched, working out the kinks in the small of his back.

Scarlett nodded. "She was more forthcoming than some of the others in Owen's employ, that's for sure."

"Good stuff."

Getting up from his desk, Rob ran his hands through his hair and rubbed his face in exasperation. Following the confrontation at the bunker this morning, he'd had a day of endless calls, interviews, and paperwork, which had taken its toll. He felt stressed, annoyed, and frustrated by the whole thing.

It had been a hell of a day, that was for sure, and he still had a whole bunch of questions that he needed to deal with and find answers to.

Approaching the window, he gazed out over the market square as the evening drew in over Retford and sighed.

"You okay?" Scarlett asked.

Rob turned to where Scarlett was sitting, staring at her laptop, typing. Tucker was nearby, too, working hard.

"Yeah, I'm fine. I think I need a minute to myself."

"It's been a day," Scarlett remarked.

"It certainly has," Rob agreed. "A hell of a day." He scanned over the room. An annoying thought occurred to him. What was wrong with this picture?

Nailer wasn't in here, and following his appearance at the bunker, Rob had barely seen him or Erika since. They were in the building somewhere, which made Rob think they were avoiding him, and given the lies he'd told, it wasn't an unreasonable conclusion.

"Go for a walk," Scarlett suggested. "I think we can manage without you for a bit."

"Thanks, I might do that," Rob muttered.

"Go for it. Get some fresh air and clear your head. It always works for me."

Rob smiled. "Cheers. I won't be too long."

Grabbing his jacket and coat, Rob pulled them on and stepped out. Behind him, his colleagues continued to work.

He'd been cooped up in that room for most of the day, so even just stepping outside of that damn room was a relief. He wandered through the station's corridors to the ground floor, twisting his head and arms around to work out the kinks in them. Turning a corner on the ground floor, making for the front entrance, he found Mary sitting in a chair, scrolling on her phone. She looked up. On seeing Rob, she shot to her feet and stuffed her phone in her pocket.

"Hey," she said, nervously.

"Hi. Are you okay?"

"Yeah, I'm fine," she reassured him. "I just… I wanted to talk to you but knew you'd be busy, so I thought I'd just wait."

Rob nodded. "Then you're lucky I came this way. I'd usually use the back door. Just a note for future reference."

She smirked. "Noted."

"What can I do for you?"

She took a breath before answering. "I wanted to apologise."

"Oh?"

"For the kiss. I… I don't know what came over me. I was just overjoyed to have survived. You know?"

He nodded, understanding how she felt. "Yeah, I get it. I know how you felt."

"The kiss... It just felt right, you know? It felt natural and... I quite enjoyed it."

Rob smiled.

"But anyway, I thought I should explain myself and apologise. It wasn't a very professional thing to do. I should have restrained myself a little better."

"Don't be silly. I get it, it's fine. There's no need to apologise. It was a very stressful situation, and honestly, it was a natural reaction. I don't regret it."

Mary smiled and tucked a lock of hair behind her ear. She seemed embarrassed. "Okay, well, if you ever wanted to meet up sometime, go for a drink maybe, I wouldn't say no."

"Aaah," Rob muttered, not entirely surprised by the suggestion. While he considered his answer, thoughts of Matilda bubbled up from the depths, reminding him how much he enjoyed her company and the limbo he'd been left in by her pulling away after finding out about his family.

Should he wait for Matilda to process these feelings about the revelation, or should he write that idea off? It had been a couple of weeks, and Matilda showed no signs of being interested in picking things up from where they'd left off. He probably shouldn't try to rush her, but he honestly didn't know where he stood. Should he refuse Mary's advances and wait or...?

No, he needed to think this through. He needed to decide for himself what he wanted out of life, but after the mistake with Matilda, he needed to be candid about his family with Mary, too.

He waved to the chair she'd been sitting in, urging her to sit, and moved towards the one next to it.

"I mean, if you don't want to, it's fine. I don't mind," she muttered, obviously thinking he was about to say no.

After taking his seat, Rob smiled. "It's not as simple as that. Honestly, I'm flattered, and my immediate reaction is to say yes, but my head is a total mess. I need some time to deal with all this." He waved at the station around him. "But, before all that, I think you need to know something."

"Know what?" She gave him a curious stare.

"I'm a Mason. My original name is Robert Mason. I'm the son of Isaac Mason and brother to Sean, Oliver, and Owen. But I ran away from home at age seventeen and never went back. I changed my surname to Loxley because Nottinghamshire and Robin Hood and all that, and never looked back. I've barely seen my family in twenty years, and they've not shown much interest in me until recently."

"Oh, shit."

"Yeah. I know. I take it you've heard about the rumours that surround my family."

"Of course. But, I had no idea that you were...."

444

"That's okay. I don't advertise it, and outside the officers working in Nottingham, it's not common knowledge. I just thought you should know, although this is off the record, Miss Day."

She smiled. "I promise not to write a story about it in next week's paper."

"Or any paper."

"Sure. Don't worry, I'm not a hack."

"And as for that drink, well, as I said, just gimmie some time. That is, if you still want to be around me, now you know my dirty little secret."

"Take your time. Call me when you're ready."

They got up and strolled to the front door, where he opened it for her and let her out first.

"I'm going for a walk," he said. "I need some fresh air."

"Certainly. See you soon."

"Bye."

She smiled, winked, and strode off. Rob watched her go for a moment before turning away and setting off across the square, enjoying the cool evening air.

62

Wandering across the square to the war memorial in its centre, Rob picked out one of the vacant benches and sat so he faced back towards the police station and the Town Hall beside it.

It somehow felt like he had his own personal storm cloud following him around and casting a shadow over his day. They'd solved the case and brought a murderous organisation crumbling to the ground, so why did he feel so terrible? There was usually a euphoria that accompanied solving a case and catching the bad guys, but today, that feeling was conspicuous by its absence.

Instead, Rob felt annoyed, frustrated, betrayed, and generally angry about the recent revelations. Once again, his family's shadow loomed large over his life and career, and he was left wondering if he'd ever free himself from their influence.

Of course, arresting them would be part of that, but he thought that finally nailing them with a case would be more satisfying than this. He'd thought, perhaps naively, that he'd be thrilled to throw his wayward brothers behind bars, but so far, he felt nothing. Everything was just numb.

Maybe he was worried about what it would mean for the future to arrest just one of them? Perhaps it was the growing threat of Isaac Mason and his firm that was putting a dampener on his mood?

It could be the severe damage to his beloved car, or maybe it was because the one person he trusted above all others had lied to him?

Whatever the case, there was something that had changed for the better, and that was his feelings towards the town. Because somehow, despite everything that had happened, and the knowledge that his family were still around somewhere, he found he quite liked it here.

Maybe it was the feeling of nostalgia he had about his childhood, and the happy times he'd spent with his mother in the park or going to the shops, but whatever it was, it was a most welcome feeling.

Across the square, the station's front door opened, and a man stepped out. Rob immediately recognised Nailer. He stuffed his hands in his pockets and strode across the square. Nailer headed straight towards him, and for a brief moment as his mood darkened, Rob considered getting up and walking away. Part of him didn't want to speak to Nailer right now. The betrayal he felt was almost more than he could take.

And yet, Rob stayed where he was. Despite his frustrations with the man he'd thought of as a friend, a mentor, and as a surrogate father figure, he also wanted to know what the hell was going on.

Rob watched him approach and made a concerted effort to keep his breathing and anger in check until Nailer stopped a couple of metres away.

"May I sit?" Nailer asked.

"It's a free country."

It sounded a little more spiteful than Rob had intended, but Nailer sat beside him anyway.

"Good work today," Nailer said, gazing across the square at the knots of people moving back and forth. "You did well. Really well. And, of course, I'm personally very thankful to you."

"Yeah...?"

Nailer sighed. "Look, I know you're pissed off, but..."

"You lied to me," Rob snapped.

"Well, it wasn't exactly how I'd planned on doing this."

"She called you Dad. I heard her."

Nailer tensed, his lips compressing into a thin line. "Aaah, you heard that."

"Damn right I bloody did." Rob sighed while he tried to get his thoughts in order. "You have a daughter, and you kept it a secret. You hid it from me. What the hell?"

"I'm sorry."

"Sorry? You're sorry? I thought we were close. I thought we were friends? I trusted you, yet you didn't trust me enough to tell me you have a family. Hell, you outright lied to me. You've told me on multiple occasions that you don't have a family. Do you have a partner? Who's her mother?"

"I can only apologise."

"You can do more than that, Nailer. You can tell me what on earth you and Erika were thinking, hiding this from me. Why? Why did you hide this? Am I not good enough for you? For her? Is that it? Are you afraid of me because I'm a Mason? Is that it? Haven't I proven myself enough for you or her?"

"Rob, wait…"

"You two ignored each other when you came to that party at my flat recently. You ran into each other on the landing and didn't even speak to each other. What are you hiding?"

"Stop! Just stop, Rob. I wish it was simple, I really do, but there's a very good reason why we have kept this a secret that I really cannot go into right now. I wish I could, I really do, but I can't. It's… delicate."

"Is it…?" Rob was not impressed. "And I'm not trustworthy?"

"It's not that simple, Rob."

"Then make it simple. Who is she? How did all this happen?"

"All I can say is that she's the product of a relationship from twenty years ago, a relationship that's private and I will not be going into."

"Because you don't trust me."

"I do trust you, Rob. I trust you more than almost anyone else I know, and if I could've told anyone about Erika, you would have been the first to know, but I've not told anyone. No one knows, and I need to keep it that way."

"Why? What's so dangerous? What are you hiding?"

"All you need to know is I have my reasons, and as a friend, that should be good enough for you. And if you trust me at all, you'll leave it there."

"That's easier said than done."

"But you need to. If you value Erika's safety at all, you'll trust me, say no more, and leave this be."

Rob grunted in annoyance. "If her secrecy is so important and so critical, then why is she living next door to me?"

"Because she's young, impulsive, and was curious about you."

"Me?"

"She knows about our friendship, Rob, so as my daughter, naturally, she would be curious. I didn't encourage her to move in to the flat next door, but she's an adult, so there was little I could do."

"Curious? Why would she be curious about me? I'm no one." Pulling a face, Rob took a long breath. "I honestly don't know whether to believe you or not anymore."

"I'm not lying to you, but I also can't tell you everything, and I ask that you respect that."

"Respect? Where was your respect for me?"

"Rob, please."

Rob shook his head. Right now, he didn't know what to believe, but it certainly wasn't Nailer. Was he telling the truth? He had no way to be sure now that Nailer had taken a hammer to the trust that they'd shared. "I wish I could trust you over this, Nailer, but that trust has been shattered into tiny pieces."

"We need to work together, Rob. I'm still your boss."

"I know. I guess we'll have to make do." Annoyed and no wiser, Rob got to his feet.

"I'm sorry about your car, by the way," Nailer said.

"Likewise for Erika. I hope she's okay."

"Thanks."

Rob nodded. "I'll see you around."

63

With the sky darkening as the evening rolled in, Rob wandered into the Old Police Station bar, keen to get a drink. He'd had a hell of a day and needed something to take the edge off.

After his fruitless meeting with Nailer, Rob had returned to the office to get a few more hours of work done, preferring to bury himself in the case and the mountains of paperwork they had to work through while they continued to gather evidence, ready to hand off to the CPS at some future point. He had a feeling that Nailer was either lying to him or being clever with the truth, but either way, the trust between them had been left in tatters by the deception laid bare following the conclusion to this case.

He'd still not seen Erika following the arrest of Owen, but she'd been whisked off to the hospital straight from the crime scene in order to deal with her injuries. As far as Rob knew, she'd survive and ultimately recover, which was a small comfort after a year of lying to him. Apart from her being Nailer's daughter, he suddenly found himself questioning everything he knew about her. Who was she really? Was she Erika Masey, or Erika Nailer, or something else entirely?

He ambled into the building. Rob was brought up short when he saw Sean Mason propping up the bar, apparently waiting for him. Sean smiled and inclined his head, indicating that Rob should follow him. He turned and strode around the back again.

Rolling his eyes, Rob followed his eldest brother around to the former cells. Unsurprisingly, he found his father waiting for him. Rob stopped in the doorway, reluctant to step all the way in.

"Isaac," Rob stated in greeting.

"Call me Dad."

"Piss off."

Isaac grunted and took a moment to gather his thoughts. "You've left me in something of a quandary, son."

"Is that right?"

"Absolutely. On the one hand, you've revealed this side hustle of Owen's. You exposed his idiocy. Something that could have rotted from within, like a tumour, and taken us all down, and for that, I'm grateful. Thank you."

"I don't need your thanks."

"Perhaps. But that leads me to the flip side of this particular coin, Robert. Because as much as I'm grateful, you have arrested one of my sons, and it's likely he will see jail time. You've hurt me, Rob. Me and this organisation.

Normally there are dire consequences for such actions, but as I said, I'm torn."

"I don't give a shit."

Isaac looked a little surprised. "Is that right?"

Exasperated with these games, Rob sighed loudly. "Isaac, I'm really not interested. Just leave me alone, okay?" He turned to go, already fed up with listening to his father's voice and veiled threats.

"It was good to see you, Rob."

Rob ignored him and walked away. He skipped the bar, preferring to go to his room and check out the mini-fridge instead.

Besides, he needed a good night's rest.

64

"It's a bit shit," Guy muttered after Isaac finished relaying recent events to him over the burner phone.

They matched up with most of what Guy already knew of the case following Rob's raid on the Retford property this morning, but that didn't make it any less shocking. When he'd first heard about it, he couldn't quite believe what Owen was doing. Running a Red Room right under his family's nose was audacious and idiotic but also, in some ways, impressive.

However, the brutal nature of the enterprise was less of a shock, given Owen's temperament, so it wasn't a totally brain-melting moment.

Owen was always the most violent of the brothers.

"Well, Owen was certainly enterprising, that's for sure."

"What he did was not just risky, it was bloody moronic. It could have ended everything for us.

"So, you're glad it's been exposed?" Guy asked.

"I suppose I'm somewhat grateful..."

It was a reluctant gratitude, that was for sure.

"What's your next move?" Guy wondered if the firm might take direct action against Rob or the EMSOU as a whole.

"As regards what?"

"Loxley, Owen, any of it?"

The voice on the other end of the line paused before answering. "Right now, I am unsure. Owen and Rob have given me a lot to think about."

"Okay. Let me know if you need me." It was essential to remain relevant and useful, Guy resolved.

"I will. Do you have anything to report?"

"Not much, only that I think Bill might be hiding something."

"Like what?"

Guy sighed. He thought back to the meetings he'd had with Bill and the sudden death of his father in what Guy thought were suspicious circumstances. "I'm not so sure that his dad's death was an accident, at least not in the way that it's been recorded."

"So, what do you think happened?"

"I think Bill killed him, accidentally perhaps, but killed him nonetheless. His mum would have been there and realised what would happen to Bill should he take the blame, so she took it, using Graham Rainault's reputation against him and claiming self-defence."

"Are you sure about this?"

"No. It's speculation at this point."

"So you don't have any proof?"

"No. None," Guy admitted. "But, if I could get him to confide in me, he might be useful."

"Or, if you found proof."

"Or that," Guy agreed, although he was at a loss as to how he'd find such proof. While speaking on the burner phone, his personal phone buzzed, attracting his attention.

Guy grabbed it, checked his notifications, and found a message from Erika. Somewhat surprised, he opened it.

We need to talk.

We do, Guy thought after reading those four words. We absolutely do.

65

Climbing out of the taxi, Rob slammed the door shut on the modern vehicle, lamenting that he wasn't bringing his beloved Belle back home yet. She'd likely be in the garage for weeks, getting fixed up at great expense, while he was forced to use cabs and pool cars.

It was all highly frustrating.

Looking up at his building, Rob was suddenly reluctant to walk inside, knowing that Erika might be in there somewhere, and she still had a key to his apartment. He couldn't believe how friendly he'd got with her, and still, she'd been unable to trust him with the knowledge that Nailer was her father.

Taking a deep breath to steel his nerves, Rob gripped his bag's handles tighter, marched towards the door, and let himself in. He stalked up the stairs, and Erika's door came into view. For a moment, he thought she might actually open it and say hello. Maybe she'd apologise to him and try to smooth things over like her father had.

But he reached the top, her door remained stubbornly shut, and no sounds of movement came from within.

She'd been seriously hurt in the Red Room, of course, so she might be in the hospital, or maybe she was staying with her parents? He had no idea who her mother was, and it seemed like Nailer wasn't going to tell him either. Was she still on the scene, or had she left Nailer a long time ago, leaving him alone?

Or was that a lie, too? Was Nailer's assertion that he was a confirmed bachelor a complete fabrication, too?

At this point, he wouldn't put it past him.

Rob grumbled quietly to himself, annoyed that their friendship had come to this. It was a sad indictment that he constantly thought of the worst possible option when he thought about Nailer and their friendship.

Turning away from Erika's apartment, Rob plodded over to his front door and made his way inside. Reaching the kitchen, he was greeted by a black furball that meowed loudly at his return. Rob bent down and picked up the precocious feline and hugged him close, glad for the show of affection. Still holding the cat, Rob spotted something on the side nearby and walked over. It was a note with a key lying on top.

He read it.

Rob. I'm sorry for the deception. I wish this had played out differently. I wanted to tell you so much. I've returned your key in case you want to use someone else to look after Muffin in future. I'm going to be away for a few days, so you won't see me around for a bit. Again, I'm sorry. Much love, Erika.

"Well, shit." Rob read the note back a second time before he turned away. He felt terribly sorry for her and for everything she'd been put through. No one should have to undergo such torture. It was horrific. And despite his misgivings towards the lies she and her father had told him for twenty years, he did feel genuinely sorry for her.

Still cuddling a purring Muffin for comfort, Rob wandered across his apartment to the nearby window and gazed out at the River Trent.

"What a bloody mess."

THE END

Rob Loxley will return in book 6.

An Ill Wind.

Available here:

www.amazon.co.uk/dp/B0CKJ12HQV

Author Note

Thank you for reading this fifth book in the Rob Loxley series. I really hope you enjoyed it.

This one is perhaps the most personal of the books yet, given its set in my hometown of Retford, where I grew up, and still regularly visit. I know the town well, and I hope that comes across in the book.

It was kind of strange to think about such harrowing and dramatic events happening in my hometown, but it was also fun, and I think the series will most certainly be back at some point in the future.

Rob does have some unfinished business there, after all.

And, after everything that's happened in this book, I think that, despite it all, Rob has found a new affection for this little market town that could.

Rob will be back in book 6, An Ill Wind, and I'm looking forward to writing that very soon.

If you enjoyed the book, please consider leaving a review on Amazon for me.

Thank you.

Andrew

Come and join in the discussion about my books in my Facebook Group:

www.facebook.com/groups/alfraine.readers

Book List

www.alfraineauthor.co.uk/books

Printed in Great Britain
by Amazon